Finding Idyllium
Earth's Stolen Future
N Joseph Glass

Monocle Books, N. Joseph Glass

Copyright © 2024 by N Joseph Glass

All rights reserved.

No part of this publication may be reproduced, distributed, or transmitted in any form or by any means, including photocopying, recording, or other electronic or mechanical methods, without the prior written permission of the publisher, except as permitted by U.S. copyright law. For permission requests, contact the author at www.glassauthor.com.

The story, all names, characters, and incidents portrayed in this production are fictitious. No identification with actual persons (living or deceased), places, buildings, and products is intended or should be inferred.

ePub ISBN: 979-8-9907484-0-8
Paperback ISBN: 979-8-9907484-1-5
Hardcover ISBN: 979-8-9907484-2-2

Part One

Mars was never going to work

1 | Idyllium Mission: Day 1

"He's alert," somebody yelled.

The gurney slammed onto the concrete and he felt his brain explode. Pushed through parted glass doors, a squeaky wheel laid a soundtrack for the rush down the hall where florescent bulbs strobed overhead, pounding his eyes like a migraine. Three or maybe four medics scampered around him, his first glimpse of people on another world. One waving a flashlight confirmed his pupils constricted as they should under the assault of the focused beam. He struggled to twist his torso, but the grip of the strap cinching his forehead to the gurney immobilized him.

An abrupt stop jarred him. He watched people in scrubs stick sensors to his temples, steal his blood, and unbutton his shirt to splay a spider web of diodes to the scaffolding of monitors over his head. As he became more lucid, he robotically answered their questions, which they told him confirmed he had no concussion.

"Where have you taken me?"

No one answered.

His eyes widened as an IV port pierced his cubital above the forearm, and a bag of clear liquid floating above caught a shimmer of the intense overhead lighting and the room spun.

He reached his right hand to his left wrist. *Gone!* Without his bio-pad, Captain Marc Sanders had no way to find his team...

2 | Earth:
5 Days to Crossover

Roberta Hillthorpe kicked off the red stilettos, leaned back as far as her chair allowed, and surrendered to the weight of the world. Two worlds, actually.

She planted her feet on the smooth glass desktop, cleared of all clutter save for the holographic display. Fondling a tumbler, she considered her liquid advocate as the weasel who invited himself into her office stood there waiting for a "Good morning, Walter," which she didn't offer. He must have been acutely aware their roles had flipped and, despite his appointing her as his second, she ran the United Global Alliance in his name.

As the Strategic Counsel Leader of the UGA, she had dedicated the better part of her time to finding humanity a new home. A real estate agent for the entire planet, she mused. While touting it to the public as their salvation, they didn't have the years needed to migrate to Mars—if that were even possible. As the planet choked on its last breaths, Roberta intently worked out her true plan.

Breaking the silence of her thinly veiled annoyance, Chairperson Walter Vescovi asked, "Are we sure we've exhausted all diplomatic options?"

"*We*, Walter?" Roberta dropped her feet to the tile floor with a thud and huffed deliberately. "The *one time* you insisted on being involved, and you blew our chances for that."

"We asked for refuge, migration of over four billion people from Earth to their world. It seemed a fair question."

"And I had an answer that would have kept the option on the table. Why you had to tell their prime minister's office about how our industrialization ruined the environment..." She exhaled forcefully through her nostrils. "And it horrified them when you explained the nuclear incidents that ruined our ecosphere. Anyone should have expected it would."

"They had the right to know."

Weary from a conversation they had replayed too many times, Roberta hoisted her elbows onto the desktop and leaned forward. "And they shut us down. Now, this is all we have."

"But occupation by force? And for goodness sakes, Roberta, sending nuclear warheads over there... They have nothing like that. It's one reason their planet is still pristine."

"Look, when we took office, we pushed *Mars* as our only hope. Even now that it's a bust, we're still selling it to the masses. Finding Idyllium was our chance, it's our future. And it's the only one we've got."

Letting Walter stew for a bit, Roberta mused over how the James Webb telescope searched the cosmos for a habitable planet. When astrophysicists reexamined what they had classified as *echoes* of Earth, their discovery resurrected a hope Roberta had considered dead and buried. "When we found Idyllium, we got our second chance. I intend to take it... I will save the four and a half billion people under our care."

"But to undermine their economic, social, and political systems? To take out their defenses and then invade an entire planet? Do we have the right?"

"We have the right to *live*, Mister Chairperson." Hillthorpe stood and rested the knuckles of her balled fists on the desktop. Towering over the unimposing man, she spoke to his reflection on the desk's glossy surface. "We're not the bad guys here. *They* refused to help, sentencing us to death. Now, their own deputy PM is working with us to remove their prime minister and allow our infiltration and future migration."

"Just don't detonate any nukes over there. If that is to be our new home, let's not ruin it like we did this one."

Roberta sighed. "As I've told you, that is a last resort."

Banishing the anxiety from his squeaky voice, Vescovi asked, "Will the first team be ready?"

"The *advance* team. Why do you think I'm spending so much time in this dreary hellhole of a compound? I'm personally overseeing their final preparations."

"And you're sure about the two civilians joining the mission?"

Roberta cackled. "Sharon is hardly a civilian. She's been on several assignments, and she's the best environmental scientist we've got."

"And the journalist?"

Technically her boss, Roberta allowed Walter's questions to trickle onto her forehead like an unrelenting drip drip drip. She endured the torture, knowing it granted his conscience permission to scribble a signature on whatever executive orders *she* needed to draft.

"Communications specialist. We have plenty of qualified marines, for sure, but Marc asked for her specifically. Besides, Kat's a friend, and I trust her. She'll be ready."

"Perhaps such an unusual make-up of our team will ensure the opposing force on Idyllium is not an exact match of doubles from the team we're sending."

"The brainiacs first told us the world there is a mirror of ours, down to the hemorrhoids on our butt cheeks. Doppelgängers, they called them. But they based that on a multiverse theory, and our best minds now think that doesn't exist, that we have found one single parallel world."

Walter rocked on his feet. "Should Captain Sanders expect to encounter himself, Commander Mullins, and the others when they get there? Exact duplicates of themselves fighting to protect Idyllium from... us?"

"No. They have no *me* running things on Idyllium, luckily. I have someone over there looking into it for me and, going back over a century... not a single doppelgänger."

"Good. Very good. Our future is riding on this, and time is running out. We can't afford to fail."

"Walter, you know me well enough by now. I always have a contingency plan."

3 | Idyllium Mission: Day 1

ONLY THE MONITORS REPORTING his health status broke the silence of the space, the tones' regularity wearing on his last nerve. Questions crowded the unknown hospital room. Had he been brought here to heal in goodwill, or had he been captured? If this was his jail cell, the fate of his people on Earth hung out of reach beyond the bars. He was never grandiose or boastful. A realistic view made him good at his job, which, today, meant saving the world.

A powerful urge to urinate prompted another question: *How long have I been here*?

An answer came in the form of a lively nurse who looked too serious to be the bearer of good news. Marc hoped that was her default, the result of a morbid job he was sure had to level its share of depressing scenes on anyone subjected to it daily. Under that light, his job didn't seem as heavy.

"Hello, dear. Or should I say welcome back?"

"Welcome back? From where? Hope I had a great time."

"You had a decent fall, it seems. Quite a good knock on your noggin you took, a golf ball of a bump it gave ya. But not to worry, the good doctor took a little mallet and tapped it back down, good as new." She chuckled over the cartoon imagery in her words.

"And how? I mean, what got me that knot on the noggin, as you called it? Something I said... to a lady, no doubt."

"Oh dear, I haven't those details for ya. I thought you'd be the one tellin' me. After all, I wasn't there with ya now, was I? Best learn yerself to be more careful, eh?" Her smile filled the room with a softer and more mature stature than her years merited.

"I need to pee."

When he tried to sit up, the woman reached for his chest and pushed him back with an ease Marc found disturbing. He hadn't realized how feeble he'd become and didn't relish the novel sensation it brought.

"What did you give me? I feel like I've been beat by seven men… or had *way too much* whisky."

"Oh, I'd'a joined you fer that whisky there. The initial sedatives should be close to worn off by now. You'll be up and back to yerself soon enough. Right as rain, you'll be. Doc says no long-term issues. Now, for the short-term one…"

She extended a hand with the solution to one of Marc's problems. Although not the most pressing, relieving his bladder into the bedpan made his eyes roll into his forehead.

"I need to go. I'm late for something very important."

"Not just yet. Ya got yerself a nasty bump, and nasty bumps on the outside of yer brain tend to mess with the inside bits."

Marc grimaced but said nothing, and the nurse stepped toward the door. Stopping mid-turn, she retrieved his bio-pad from her pocket and walked her eyes over it. Marc watched helplessly for several breaths and wondered if she knew what it was or had ever seen one.

"Whoever ya are, you must either be a rich one or with the government. Looking at ya… I'm going with government."

"Why'd you say that? I don't strike you as the wealthy playboy type?" He tried a playful chortle.

"See, there's proof ya got a sense of humor there. Rich or poor, my friend, you are *no boy*." The room filled with her laughter. "Here, let me switch this on for ya. Be back to check on ya soon enough." A wall display pumped more illumination into the light-saturated room.

With a hearty wink, the full-figured, flirtatious young nurse laid his wrist-pad on the table by the door and sauntered out. Relief filled him at eying his lucky keychain beside it. Rubber-soled shoes bade the nurse's farewell in squeals pushed off the polished floor. He needed his wrist unit but lacked the strength to stand.

The advert on the television did little to arrest Marc's attention until a reporter named Belinda Mayers ignited the pixels on the screen, and he raised the volume. Before uttering a word, the reporter caught his eye. Blond with a bobbed cut just below the jawline, her straight hair shone like silk under the gleam of the studio lights. Those blue eyes seemed almost electric. They radiated an energy powerful enough to draw him in, trusting her instantly. Marc eagerly absorbed Belinda Mayers's words.

"...and this is the fourth such takeover this week alone. Political and financial analysts agree, this is most peculiar. This morning saw the largest corporate merger in Greater Britannia's history when Massive Kinetics acquired Xeronic Bio-Pharmaceuticals.

"I'm joined live by Philip Belvedere, our chief financial correspondent in New London Town. Philip, please tell us what has the financial world on its head. What should we know about these recent takeovers and amalgamations?"

The man had that financial analyst look about him. Enough professionalism to his suit, a tie slightly off center, and ruffled hair that said he'd had a long, hard day.

"Certainly, Belinda. It is most unusual. There have been no committees to valuate these mergers or impose regulations on recent consolidations, especially given the magnitude we are seeing. In fact, GB legislation has long forbidden such transactions under the fair business opportunities articles of commerce."

"Astonishing. I'm sure the question everyone is asking is: How are we seeing violations of our commercial legal system right under our noses?"

"Someone, or ones, in high governmental positions must be allowing this. Until we hear from the Minister of Commerce or the PM, we know nothing more."

"The larger part of us in Greater Britannia are not financial experts. Would you tell us why this has so many concerned?"

"Of course. Sudden movements such as these cause ripples to flow through the entire economic system. We're seeing massive fluctuations in the stock market and an increase in interest rates. Costs of natural energy and basic goods have skyrocketed. An alarming increase in unemployment proliferates the empire."

"And all this in just two weeks. Alarming, indeed, Philip. But we're under the Global Stability and Equalization Act. Should we worry about fluctuations in the world economy? Isn't this a situation where GB will stabilize the system and keep any from suffering hardships or becoming impoverished?"

"In theory, yes. The global empire has kept that balance for a millennium, and that specific act is a key contributor to the lack of petitions for independence. While global peace and world citizenship are potent factors, the delicate balance of our socialized capitalistic economy is the glue holding the empire together."

"Thank you, Philip. More to come from the capital, so stay tuned. Now, let's check in with Derek on the local weather."

As a weather forecaster touted sunshiny days ahead, Marc contemplated the impact of the financial report, evidence of the first phase of the conquest from Earth. His people had been sending spies here for a decade and they were now ready to move against their parallel sister world. Destabilization of the financial system of Greater Britannia set the stage for invasion. Like a cement pillar crumbling to bits from the rust eating the metal rods within it, the erosion began.

The mission demanded Marc go find his team and get on with its first objective. Gauging his strength, he pulled himself to his feet. The room swirled around him, dropping him to his knees to wait behind eyes sealed tight. The wave passed.

The bio-pad he slapped on his wrist took too long to sync with the uplink. An unwelcome red blip announced its offline status. Buttoning his white long-sleeved shirt, he felt the wrist-tap warning of a low battery. He'd have to worry about that later.

Tensed muscles eased at finding the door unlocked and no one standing guard on the other side. His doped-up body lacked the readiness for any physical altercation. Marc carried that thought out of the building and onto the streets. Desperate to reunite with his team, he needed to regain the mission's lost momentum.

4 | Earth:
5 Days to Crossover

Waiting outside the chairperson's office, Marc's mind replayed events that led him to this point, to his accepting to lead this mission. In a few days, he would step onto another world. The last three decades passed like yesterday, his memory vivid. Fidgeting on the rigid wood seat of his high school classroom desk, he watched the report of the nuclear incidents that scorched the earth and knew his life after graduation would not be what he envisioned.

The former United Nations, impotent against the rise of terroristic nation-states amassing nuclear weapons, nearly disintegrated as its predecessor, the League of Nations, had decades prior. As the UN had risen from the ashes of the League, so the United Global Alliance came to be. An allegory came to Marc from a history lesson. Modern-day Rome sat atop the ruins of its former glory. Layers of forgotten versions of itself formed its foundation. Now, the UGA stood on the legacy of the League and UN.

Meant to be a stronger incarnation, supporting nations had granted it greater authority, relinquishing their power to the UGA. Marc saw hubris in one global government accepted by its members as the only way to move the world forward. Perhaps it did that, but in Marc's experience, *forward* didn't always get people to a better place.

Would Idyllium be that place? The answer rushed to meet him as he made final preparations before crossing over. The chairperson, however, took his time. His assistant had told Marc not to be late for the meeting that should have started fifteen minutes ago. Something reminded Marc of Tim and how they met.

The once proud institution known as "America" faded as a childhood memory, its last president taking the fall for the nuclear disaster. In the aftermath of the incidents, the United States and United Kingdom legalized their common-law marriage. The Anglo-American Union, or AAU, came under the articles of UGA membership. While member nations could operate limited armed forces for domestic matters, all international concerns fell under the jurisdiction of the United Global Alliance and its formidable military branches.

Marc started his career in the AAU Domestic Marine Corps. In the DMC, Marc's natural leadership abilities raised him in the ranks. As the biggest of his accomplishments, he had led the operation to thwart the secession of the Northwest corridor from the Union. A young soldier who preferred to be called Tim served as Marc's second on that mission.

The young man showed tremendous potential as a military strategist. Tim fine-tuned Marc's plans for a two-pronged operation to stop the revolution in its tracks. Using espionage tactics, they sowed discord and disunity among enemy troops. The self-proclaimed Alliance of Free States suffered logistical issues, resulting in smaller forces to engage at each encounter. Marc and Tim had averted a civil war, sparing millions of lives its ravages.

When the Secretary of Defense offered Marc a post as platoon captain for the International Corps of Marines under the flag of the United Global Alliance, he accepted under the condition Tim served as his second. Together, they accumulated an impressive service record. Marc could almost forget how pointless it all was. To keep peace in tiny, inconsequential nation-states on a dying planet robbed his work of its grandeur.

Unrelenting optimism from Tim fueled the drive in Marc to be the best, to make a difference while they looked to Mars for their future. Five years his junior, Tim became his best friend, best man in Marc's wedding, and Uncle Tim to his daughter, Jewel. An unofficial part of the family, he'd spent sleepless nights with Marc and Casey at the hospital when they first learned of Jewel's diagnosis.

What had reminded him of Tim? Sitting in the black leather seat, a bit too low to the ground for his liking, Marc's mind bounced all over the place. He considered the chairperson's assistant at the desk. The young man looked no more than in his mid-twenties and vaguely resembled Tim except for the pockmarks dotting this boy's face.

"Captain Sanders, the chairperson will see you now."

Solid double doors of mahogany overlaid with a chessboard pattern of squares swung open. The Italian-Swiss heir to a microclimate regulator company ran the multitrillion-dollar corporation, and more people knew the Vescovi name from the label on their home climate control panel than from his political office.

Marc pulled himself from the low chair. "Thanks."

5 | Idyllium Mission: Day 1

Sunshine soaking into the skin on Saul's face suspended him in the middle of the crosswalk. Chin up and eyes closed, he pondered the urgency of the mission. He couldn't fail a world of billions looking to *this* sun and to *this* world for their future.

A solar-powered transport stopped to grant him the moment. Its passengers exchanged neighborly smiles, and he completed his crossing of the narrow street. To Saul Mullins, he could have been in a rural town, forgotten by time, like the one where he grew up in the southeast.

After basking under the warm, gentle rays of the benevolent star, Saul summoned his senses and returned to the shadows. He knew the world to be an immense place, yet he couldn't shake the fear of being recognized. Although unlikely anyone would spot him strolling the East Lansing neighborhood, miles outside of New London Town proper, he thought it best to be cautious.

Marc Sanders, you moron. Where'd ya go?

Commander Mullins had little concern for Marc's well-being. His best-case scenario for this side mission would have been to find his lifeless corpse. He'd take command of the operation and do it his way, but not because he didn't think his captain had the mettle to carry out the mission. With his impeccable fieldwork success record, even Saul had to see why they'd chosen Marc to lead this team. But no one required him to like it.

For the fourth or fifth time, Saul checked his military green field jacket's ample pockets. With no idea what to expect, he carried as many tools and blades as the jacket and trousers allowed. He found another use for the vestment in hiding the bio-pad on his wrist, tucking it under the unzipped flap to use its locator ping to pinpoint Marc's position.

Entering his periphery, the tall man approaching turned Saul into a statue, immovable as marble. He wouldn't call it fear because that would mean he'd lost his edge. He saw what had most concerned him about this mission, second to the import of its success, that is. The existence of a parallel world brought floods of questions, most of which had yet to be answered. One mattered now: Would his doppelgänger be on Idyllium's team, fighting his team from Earth, and what would he do if they met?

Theories of the so-called experts speculated everyone's doubles living near-identical lives. Subtle variances came from alternate decisions taken at parallel moments. Saul was Saul and expected himself to be Saul, no matter the universe. He was sure the Saul Mullins from this side would be equally engaged in his mission, an even match and formidable threat to Saul's success. *Would he have the same scar?*

Sunlight glistened off the man's polished bald scalp, same as it did off Saul's. The male-pattern baldness didn't suit him. Not caring for the tight military buzz-cut soldiers wore, he'd been shaving his head for years. The height matched, about six feet three inches. Even the field jacket, dark gray to his green, looked right. Waiting for a clearer view, Saul saw only two options: hide or attack.

Too dangerous to leave his counterpart in play, he opted to take him out. Overcome by a morbid sense of irony, the dread felt more like contemplating suicide than the strategic killing of a wartime adversary. He hesitated. Tucked in the doorway of a closed shoe shop, Saul peered from the shadows. As the man drew closer, he wondered if his other self had spotted him. *Of course he did. He's obviously just as good as me and was coming to kill his opponent, to preserve his world.*

People scampered between them, removing the man from Saul's sight for a moment. The sun's rays flickering between hurried bodies evoked a childhood memory. Saul had a rare few of those. While he did not appreciate the gift of a small notebook, his kid brother had found a use for it. Painstakingly, he had drawn the same stick figure of a boy and his dog, page after page, almost identical one to the next.

Bubba's face brightened with a huge grin as he bent the edge of the book. Flicking the pages with his thumb turned his crude drawings into a moving cartoon. It had been too many years since Saul savored such a warm memory of his little brother, his best friend. The memory faded, leaving only him and the other him. *Where did he go?*

Closer now, the man persisted. Saul's fingers willingly fondled the ribbed carbon fiber handle of the twelve-inch jagged blade. He would use it to make swift work of dispatching his nemesis. *Quickly done. In, twist, retract. Walk away, leaving him, me, under the cover of this doorway,* he thought in those final anxious moments.

To discharge his duty, Saul deflected any sense of remorse for this grizzly act. He had done it for years and on multiple *operations*—the code word he gave to murder to sanitize the killings. He simply became the arrow finding its target loosed from a bow drawn by someone else's hand.

He nearly persuaded himself that this *operation* was no different.

But it was.

For the first time, he would kill a man he respected: himself.

An unexpected gratitude filled him. He came so close to taking the life of an innocent man. Saul's out-of-place hesitance prevented him from murdering a random passerby. Good-looking and strong, Saul noted, a near doppelgänger for himself, but it wasn't him. Cluelessly the man carried on with his day—a date that narrowly escaped a tombstone engraver's chisel.

When he stepped from the secrecy of the doorway, something hit his thigh. Never had Saul been this careless, so full of distraction to the point of not seeing an oncoming ambush. The assault came in the form of a boy, five or six years of age. Hair like a light-brown bird's nest atop his pale freckled face tried to hide eyes as big and round as Bubba's had been at that age.

Saul's smile proved insufficient to paint a reciprocal one on the youngster's lips. With a pale white face, the child looked up at the stranger towering over him. While Saul would never admit he didn't like children, there was no love lost over them. Still, he felt a profound wrongness in frightening the little tyke.

"Hi." With that simple greeting, Saul ran out of words.

"Sorry, sir." After blurting the words drenched in trepidation, the boy scurried off at full speed.

A blinding glare of white sunlight off the steel of the menacing blade hit Saul's eyes. The knife in his hand and the ghastly scar snaking from the corner of his left eye to his jaw must have sent shivers of fear down the youngster's spine. A beep from his wrist-worn bio-pad snapped Saul back to himself.

The wristwatch-sized display at the end of his arm expanded into a holo-view map of the area. Unable to use sat-link as he would on Earth, he ran sonar pings and mass-density scanners to create a map of the area. Mission prep included preloading AI-enabled topographic data with navigational awareness into his bio-pad, but he hadn't foreseen the need to pre-map the East Lansing district.

Personal bias against Marc aside, he had not thought he was incompetent enough to get himself lost on mission startup. The blue dot blipping over the map found his lost commander. Off

Saul went to save the day, to save the operation, even if it meant saving Marc.

6 | Earth:
5 Days to Crossover

Kateryna Vanderslice freed her arms from the thin silk sheet. Darkness had lessened but not departed in her tiny one-room home as she stood to stretch.

George never conceded the point of making the bed as the only ones to see it would be them when they returned to pull the cover off and climb back in. What he had called a waste of time, Kat considered proper etiquette and told him he was being lazy. What she wouldn't trade to leave the sheet crinkled at the foot of the bed to return to it later with George.

Their time together had ended prematurely. For most, he'd merely been one more tragic loss to the depleted environment. To her, the Earth stopped spinning that day. Yet days came and went, and life, even her life, carried on somehow. The world continued without George Vanderslice—but it, too, was dying. Next week would have been their fifth wedding anniversary and the second she'd spend alone.

Per her morning ritual, Kat stood facing the window that filled half of her one exterior wall. She saw nothing but a cloudy white mask hiding shadows of the world outside. A digital readout appeared in response to her presence.

[22 PERCENT TRANSLUCENCE]

"Full transparency." Kat made the request daily, knowing her job forbade her from offering the same to those living in the despondency her window hid.

An all-too-human-sounding artificial female voice replied with a delightfully unexpected consolation. "Eighty percent transparency granted for thirty seconds."

It had been months since her window showed such a morning vista. A distant orange fireball rose over the hangar at the other side of the courtyard as the waking sun brought life to her little part of the world. From a part of herself she thought dead and buried came a reaction so basic, so sensual, it reminded her of her own humanity. A tear crawled down her cheek, the first in ages not shed in grief, not summoned by the unrelenting heartache rotting her bones from the inside.

That same sun took George from me, she mourned.

Thirty seconds flashed as a nanosecond and took an eternity. The photo of her in her beloved's arms found its way into her hand as it did each morning. Her straight jet-black hair hung lower then. The happiness the picture showed her had become a hazy memory, and aches pinched in her intestines at the thought of losing not only her husband but part of herself. Kat wondered if it could live again, if she wished its spark to return to her blue-gray eyes.

Her gaze cradled such an affectionate longing, a desire to remain as they were for all time. She fondled the band on her ring finger with her thumb. Try as she did to put herself in that photo, she could not. Thoughts of George inevitably took Kat's mind to an image stored only there, clearer than the one she clutched.

He had gone on a routine survey mission. His specialty in nutritional science led him around the world to study soil samples. Kat had used all her vacation days and borrowed from her paid time off to join him twice on longer expeditions. As much as both hated the separation and sleeping apart, George went alone to Sri Lanka. A decade earlier, the last of its famous tea plantations became rice and legume farms, and the island saw a significant reduction in harvestable crops.

George had survived the tsunami and the storm that followed, which was more than the farms had done. Kat could still see the human death toll scrolling below the news reports of the catastrophic loss of key staple food production. As damaged as the isle had been, it was slowly recovering, though not enough to offset the losses over a two-year period and even now yielding less than twenty percent of its former produce.

Her beloved husband suffered "irreversible damage by exposure," as the doctor phrased it. Kateryna never cared for that verbiage, as it reduced the man she loved to a broken object. No, not a damaged object, a man of flesh and blood, the love of her life, had expired in her arms.

Now, work kept her going. At least, that's what Kat told herself. It filled her days and kept her mind occupied. Ironically, she'd been pulling so much overtime lately, her PTO amassed to the point she could accompany George on all his trips—trips he no longer took.

Coffee always came after her morning contemplation. The synthetic stuff soured her tongue like dirty water. Kat had been savoring the last of George's reserve of actual beans he'd taken from Hawaii. Only the ultra-elite likely still had the real thing, and thanks to her lover's resourcefulness, so did she. Her routine progressed to watching newsfeeds with biscotti and her fresh-brewed liquid comfort. She never dunked, considering it a waste of the last of the world's pure Kona coffee.

If her security clearance opened the door before seven, Kat would have already been on her way to work. A two-minute tube ride would take her to her office in one of the most restricted complexes on Earth. No need to rush. A standard day had her working from 07:00 to 22:00, when the cleaning crew forced her out of the office. "Home" provided a place to sleep.

Fifty years, the report said as she dressed. It compared it to the human body fighting to kill foreign pathogens, eradicating a disease from its host. Earth had made itself inhospitable to humans. *No, that's not a fair analogy. Earth didn't do this to us, we did it to ourselves*, Kat considered. The report touted the Mars project and fueled desperate hope in the implausible mass migration of the human population to the red planet, better suited to microenvironmental life than the world they squandered—or so they promised.

Kat had the privilege of being among a select number who knew it to be a colossal hoax. The UGA had converted the hangar across the courtyard into a top-secret film studio. The *Mars colony* sat not a five-minute walk from her apartment. Had she not been on the team that pretended to contact the early colonists and broadcast status updates to the despondent world, Kat most likely would have fallen for it as the masses had.

More than providing false hope, Kat worked on the true solution, the one no one knew or could know. Not yet. Called to the team shortly after being widowed, she balked at the role of false prophet hyping a hope that would never see realization. No matter how bleak the situation was, Kat believed people had the right to know. For that reason, she majored in journalism and communications.

On her windowless tube ride, memories battled the bombardment of adverts and news bulletins. Of course, the day's exposure allowance flashed across the screens. While it applied to most of the world's population, Kat's outdoor activity never changed. She stayed outside only a few minutes a day to walk from home to the tube, to the office from the station, and then reverse the process on the way back. Today, bio-pads everyone wore on their wrists would enforce a hard limit of one hour.

Just another day on a dying planet.

7 | Idyllium Mission: Day 1

People often mocked those of faith. Sharon O'Brien had experienced that firsthand. Of course, she also knew some true believers held on to it with tenacity, lived by it, or even died for it. She believed her father fit those first two descriptors, yet she wondered if his faith would go the distance, giving his life for his devotion. He always seemed so in love with life, she found it hard to imagine he could willingly surrender his.

He'd never say it, of course, but Sharon knew her life choices disappointed her father. He often cited renowned persons of science who hadn't abandoned their faith and insisted she could have both. Always asking her when she would get married, he constantly reminded her of his desire for grandchildren. While she cared for him dearly, some wishes were too heavy for even the deepest love to carry.

As an ecological biologist with a doctorate in conservation biology, Sharon considered her job of the utmost importance. Vital even in the pristine world of Idyllium and the reason she joined this mission. The ruling authority had stifled industrialism and regulated its environmental impact for over a hundred years. While not quite a perfect Utopia, Greater Britannia had maintained a peace lost on Earth with the fall of the Roman Empire—if she could consider the *Pax Romana* peace. More importantly to her, they listened to scientists and put their planet's welfare ahead of greed, commercialism, or pride.

Now, invaders from a tainted sister world, her world, had come to Idyllium. Would they bring the ruination killing their planet to a world with a healthy environment? A dread crept up her legs and twisted like a knot in her stomach at the contemplation, almost removing her anxiety for her missing captain.

Concern for the fate of their team leader hung over the three like a storm cloud's gloom. At least Saul had been the one to go find the captain. The women preferred Frank's company. Sharon hadn't met Kateryna before the first mission briefing, but they had already gotten close. She thought it good to be close—not only to Kateryna, to the team—on such an engaging operation. These stakes were much higher than any of them had faced before.

Saul was another story.

Frank's shyness reminded Sharon of Malcom, clouding her focus with musings of what may have been. The young man's interest flattered her, and his absence created an unusual longing, an unfamiliar aching overtaking her. Sharon pondered how she had pushed Mal away without a hint of reciprocation to his introverted feelings and wished to get the moments back, to be given a do-over. Physicists said parallel lives allowed slight divergence and she hoped an unlikely 'mirror' couple on Idyllium fared better than she and Mal.

The civilian received Frank's unambiguous interest. Sharon didn't know how Kateryna saw the man and his intentions. The widow still wore her wedding ring. While Sharon got little of the backstories of her teammates, she knew of George's demise. It left a little place in her heart to ache for the young widow, her mission sister.

Kateryna wrinkled her brow. "You think he's okay?"

"Cap's one tough nut and an outstanding soldier. I'm sure he's fine." Frank's voice exuded confidence.

With wide eyes begging for the same conviction, Kateryna said, "But he just laid there, like... he was dead."

"He wasn't. Those folks came over to help the cap, real neighborly types. One of them said something about him hitting his head and calling medics."

"I'm sure they took him to a hospital." Sharon tried to keep her own worry from falling onto Kateryna.

"Say what you will about Saul Mullins, the commander is the best at what he does. He'll be back in no time flat with the cap." To punctuate his point, Frank raised both hands and joined them in a pop that filled the room like a thunderclap.

Silent hours kept them company as they waited.

"Hey!" Kateryna emoted with a child's excitement—a needed distraction. "The sun's about to set."

Frank leapt from the grandpa's armchair, as he called it, and the women pulled themselves off the sofa.

A student of nature, Sharon stood in awe at the living artwork painting the sky over the suburb of Central Lansing. Glass buildings in New London Town's distant skyline amplified the luminous rays and blazed as if on fire. A philosophical wrongness ignited in Sharon for admiring it while giving no recognition to the artist. Thoughts of her father became too powerful to contain and escaped as tears clouding her eyes. She collected herself back to the moment.

Kateryna's face glowed in the golden rays. "There are no words."

"My father would call it God."

"No. Don't bring religion into this," Frank objected. "You're a scientist, for Pete's sake."

"I said my father would say that. Besides, scientists are persons of faith as much as religious zealots are. We believe in things we cannot prove all the time. All these years, and we still haven't proven Darwin's theories. It takes faith to believe, no matter what you choose to believe."

Kateryna smiled, pensive. "Well said. She's got a point, Frank. My George always said something similar. He marveled at the perfect balance of life. Seeing that sunset—I'm not a religious person myself—you can see where people like Sharon's dad are coming from."

"Look, Sharon, I meant no disrespect to your father. People are free to believe as they like without being criticized. But don't let that stuff cloud your judgment. We must be resolute in *our convictions*, or we'll fail in our actions."

"Frank?" Kateryna softened her tone. "The lives of billions of people on Idyllium are at stake. We know Earth is dying, and our people are beyond desperate. Religious or not, God's will or man's, we must consider our actions, as you said."

After an appreciative look at Kateryna, Sharon turned to say, "Frank. Can we talk?"

8 | Earth:
5 Days to Crossover

It took several seconds for him to cross row after row of white marble tiles to reach the chairperson's desk. A man of such power and wealth sat as a tiny figure in a high-backed chair of cerise leather. Light reflected off a high-gloss black desk as long as Marc's kitchen. The only things on it were the palms of Walter Vescovi's tiny hands and the upper part of the strategic counsel leader's backside as she leaned against it.

She stared, a vision of greater intimidation than the pale, wrinkled face of the old man could ever rally. Marc felt her sharp gaze like a phasic x-ray reaching the marrow in his bones. His only use for Roberta Hillthorpe had been to recruit Kateryna. Of course, he knew the chairperson had placed the operation in the SCL's charge. Since joining the project, Marc learned how much of the UGA came under her watchful eye. The SCL acted as the person behind the curtain, the actual power of the UGA. Contemplating that, the older man seemed to age before Marc's eyes.

"Welcome, Marc." The greeting came from Miss Hillthorpe. That woman never used formalism or military titles, keeping everyone on a one-way first-name basis. Still seated and looking at his own hands over his desk, Vescovi said nothing.

Marc had hoped the meeting with the chairperson would be a meeting with the chairperson but assumed the SCL would be there. He expected her to use her typical intimidation tactics, even when he saw no conceivable reason for it. Perhaps it bolstered her ego, her lust for power, he thought. The world not being enough, did she feel the need to press everyone in it under her thumb?

Always standing with legs seductively extending from under the short skirts, she seemed to want men to stare. She'd bait them, too, to catch their eyes in the purposely missed buttons on the blouse's placket. The only time poor Tim had met the woman, he melted under the fire of her scolding chastisement for the disrespect his ogling showed a person of her position. Marc saw the sparkle in her eye for the power it gave her. He'd give her no such pleasure.

"Mister Chairperson, SCL." He made eye contact with her then back to the man in the chair.

News media reported the chairperson to be fifty-nine, but to Marc, he appeared older. His thinning gray hair aged him, and the style, if he could call it that, didn't help elevate his withdrawn posture. No one knew him to be sickly, but he didn't exactly portray the picture of good health. The idea of Roberta Hillthorpe succeeding him to the office of chairperson made Marc wince.

The SCL spoke while Vescovi glued his eyes on Marc. "Marc, we need a status update on your team. Go time is fast approaching."

"Yes, it is. My team is nearly ready, and we're on track for target launch date. As my reports state, Madam SCL."

"SCL will do, Marc, as I've told you before. Of course we have your reports. But I hate reports. I can read so much more from a man's expression than from his reports." Leaning forward to bring her nose close to his, she lowered her brow. "What I want to know, specifically, my dear Marc, is... Are *you* ready for this mission?"

"As I said, we are on target for—"

"No, Marc." She placated him with a smirk and stood up straight. "I'm not asking about your team. Sharon is the best ecological biologist we've got, and she's solid. I trust Kat. I have no worries about her at all. Saul was my personal pick, and his men are top-notch."

"You're worried about *me*. Why? The chairperson selected me personally. You know my field record."

"Marc, you're here because... you look good on paper. Not bad looking in the flesh either, I must admit. That Casey's a lucky gal. But what I mean is, you have an impressive service record, yes. Decorated numerous times, blah, blah, blah. But it's not like your record doesn't have some stains on it, too. Tell us about those stains, Marc."

"Stains?"

"Tell us about Tim. I met him once. He also had a stellar service record, didn't he? But there aren't any new entries on that record, Marc, are there? His file's been closed."

"His file's been closed?" Marc's voice rose more than he intended. "That's how you mention a hero killed in the line of duty in the service of the UGA?"

Vescovi's eyes widened, but he remained silent.

"Settle down, big fella. I'm just making the point that he was killed in action under your command. I cannot imagine how one deals with that. I know you had the standard psych eval and were cleared for duty. Now you're about to go into the unknown, with a team of the best of the best. We cannot afford any failures here. We have everything riding on these other-world operations. You can see why we must be *absolutely* sure you're ready for this mission."

"Let me address your concern for failure and connecting that to losing a man. As I'm sure you are aware, that mission was a success. We got the job done. Didn't bring everyone home... but accomplished the mission. I always accomplish the mission.

Before this project, I think it's fair to say that was the highest-priority operation since the incidents. We stopped another nuclear event after learning the Republic of Ukraine had secretly become a nuclear power."

Marc calmed himself with a Neo-Hindu breathing technique. To his surprise, Vescovi spoke.

"And you have completed several operations since then. All, again, were successful."

"Thank you, Mister Chairperson. I'm not sure what this is, then. And this is a heck of a time to question me about this mission. I've been here for almost two years, and we're in the final stages, ready to cross over in days, and you bring this up now?"

Hillthorpe lifted her chin and pulled her shoulders back. "Exactly, Marc. We needed to have a final reassurance before we green-light you and your team."

Neck muscles Marc hadn't noticed stiffening during the interrogation released some of their tension. An ease fell over Vescovi's face, smoothing the wrinkles above his brow. The SCL reclaimed her lean on the shiny black desk. Only then did Marc notice there were no chairs in the mostly empty office other than the red one dwarfing the chairperson.

Turning to the puppet in the chair, the SCL went quiet, and Marc couldn't speculate what would come next. He stood as a disciplined soldier at attention.

"Oh," Hillthorpe said, twisting back to face Marc. "Sorry, how rude of me, I forgot to ask. How is your darling daughter?"

If his outrage at this woman hadn't brought him to the boiling point, Marc escalated well past that now. He heard no genuine concern for his family. Yet another tactic by the woman who had piled on every intimidation ploy she could throw at him, including mentioning Tim and her provocative posturing. Did she bring Jewel into this to assess his emotional fortitude?

A rage-filled outburst readied itself. If not for those Hindu breathing techniques, he would have unleashed it on her.

"She's a strong girl," he calmly replied.

Putting a hand on his forearm, the SCL softened. "We hope one of the positive outcomes of your mission is the cure for your sweet little girl. As I said, *everything* is riding on this. It's why we must be sure you and your team are ready."

"I understand."

"Captain." Marc appreciated the chairperson using his rank. "There is one more thing you need to know."

"Walter? We discussed this. It is in everyone's best interest not to tell him."

"You may be running most of the UGA, Roberta, but I am still in *this* office." When he stood, the years fell from his face, and vitality filled his cheeks with a healthier tone. "Marc, the situation is even more dire than we let on. We tell people we'll begin mass migration to Mars, the glorious hope and biggest hoax of all time, in five years. The planet can continue like this, sustaining us if we're careful, for fifty years. More lies. We'll be extremely lucky to get ten or twelve."

"Ten or twelve?"

"You see, Marc..." The SCL sighed. "Everything is riding on this mission. You cannot fail."

Intense thoughts collided in Marc's skull, horrifying images of billions suffocating on the fumes Earth called an atmosphere. A storm's raging gale cleared the mind's eye, leaving a single frail-framed girl in a nightdress. In that moment, but one life mattered to him.

He dug his hand into his pocket to grasp his keychain and said, "I won't."

9 | Idyllium Mission: Day 1

Darkness covered his movements through the small suburban area. Marc had no idea where he found himself after stealthily exiting the hospital. Strength returned to his muscles as they shed the last effects of whatever drugs they'd pumped into him. His still-cloudy mind fumbled over concerns of doppelgängers from the mirror world living almost identical lives. He felt in no way ready to face his counterpart—or Saul's.

Melancholy blended with hope in a cocktail of swirling emotion as he considered whether his Jewel existed on both sides. If he failed, would a version of his little angel live on, having a full and satisfying life on Idyllium? Marc believed there should be comfort in that idea, and perhaps it offered a little. She'd be a close match—clone or double or whatever they called it—but a different person from a different world, not *his* Jewel.

Then there were theories of people's lives on both sides being so parallel despite divergent courses in their lives, they'd have the same basic experiences. Prominent quantum physicists theorized how, while circumstances may differ from one world to the other, the outcome must always be the same. Marc found no comfort in that fatalistic concept, so he desperately grasped hope. He wondered if the drugs had weakened his grip on reality and tightened his grasp on the keychain in his pocket. Jewel had made it for him the last year her health allowed her to attend school. The thought of two of his precious Jewels suffering a similar fate overwhelmed him as he hid behind a trash bin and gave way to tears.

A mist of gentle rainfall lifted his spirits, allowing him to look with closed eyes to the sky above as it caressed his cheeks with the tears of its own somber silvery-gray canopy. He could get back on his feet and carry on with the mission, knowing someone from his team must have been out there looking for him. His bio-pad hadn't enough time or battery reserve to map the unfamiliar area.

I bet it's Saul. He probably hopes to find me dead.

Before being assigned to this operation, it had been months since Marc had any interaction with Commander Saul Mullins, the next in succession to replace him as captain. One thing became evident when they saw each other before their initial mission briefing: the grudge Saul held against him showed no signs of lessening. Marc had expected a fist in the raised hand that offered a salute, sarcastic as it was.

"The mission is everything."

While the motto always drove men like him and Saul, the words held a greater heaviness than times prior. Marc knew this mission was everything because it truly was *everything*, billions of lives and the fate of two worlds. No amount of physical training could have prepared Marc's shoulders for the enormity of that weight. He considered himself of no consequence. Stepping from the memory to the edge of the alley, he stood as an observer to the passersby.

They have no idea what's coming for them.

Men, women, and children strolled. *Let them be*, Marc concluded. *Should this be their end, let them continue in this blissful state, enjoying their last moments.* If the mission succeeded, most people on Idyllium would never know what Marc and his team from Earth had done for them. History would have no record of Marc Sanders, his team not even getting a footnote in the chronicles of a lost archive in a library database. Studying the faces going by, that didn't matter. In slivers of moonlight dancing over their irises, Marc saw the spark of life igniting the shine of optimism and peace.

A face devoid of such a glint slid into focus, nose to nose, inches from Marc's face. Out of nowhere, he appeared with the same sullen grimace he always wore. Saul Mullins.

"Getting rusty, Cap'n. If I was the other me, or you, you'd be a cadaver now."

"Don't get your hopes up, Saul."

"Heck of a way to start a mission, *sir*." Saul hung a bitter sarcasm Marc could almost taste in the last word.

"Anyone else hurt? I mean, besides..."

"Nope. You're the lucky one. They're all back at the hotel. I'd guess Sharon's prayin' for your safe return. A religious scientist—talk about irony. And Kat, she plays it cool as a cat, but man does she want to get herself a little piece of her captain. She's been a nervous wreck since they took you away. They take you to the hospital or something?"

"Yeah. Just a nasty bump on the noggin was all."

"Noggin?"

"Yeah, she... That's what the nurse called it."

"Could you, maybe, *not* flirt with every woman you meet? A bit of focus on the mission would be helpful. Be nice not to lose anyone else on this deployment."

"*Commander*. Personal grievances aside, we're on an urgent operation, and you *will* respect the chain of command."

"Sir, yes sir." Saul punctuated it with a mock salute.

"And Kateryna... you're way off on that. And out of line. Now, where are we? My device hasn't been able to map out the area since I left the hospital."

"Just outside of Central Lansing—where we're *supposed* to be. This lovely slice of hometown livin' is East Lansing." Chain of command or not, Saul had his default tone, full of sarcastic bite and arrogance.

In the modest hotel room, Marc found Kat, Sharon, and Frank waiting impatiently. Their dim, distraught faces brightened as Marc entered, and their voices blended into an indistinct murmur as the three expressed their relief. When Kat leapt from her seat, Marc raised his hand to stop the hug he assumed she'd throw at him.

"Kateryna, my bio-pad may have been damaged in the fall I took. It didn't do so well mapping the area and it could never pinpoint anyone on the team."

"Snuck right up on him."

Marc's glare aimed to remind Saul to show respect for his command, if not for him as a man, especially in front of the team. He knew it wouldn't change a thing; Saul would always be Saul.

Kat worked on the little device, giving it a rapid charge and checking its control AI. When she wrapped it back around Marc's wrist, she instructed him to try it out.

"Good as new. Thanks."

"Sure. Shall we send our first mission report? I waited until we got you back. I have the equipment set up and ready. Frank did the heavy lifting for me to get it on the terrace."

"Heavy lifting? I've picked my teeth with sticks thicker than him."

Kat frowned at Saul's insult. "He's a heck of a lot more helpful than you. Much nicer too."

"Well, maybe to anyone hot as you, he is."

"Saul!" Marc had had enough of him. "Go take a walk. Check we're secure for the night."

As the brooding man stomped out of the room, Kateryna led Marc to the terrace. Not to agree with Saul, he didn't comment on the size and perceived weight of the equipment. He figured Kat could have handled it and connected it to the fire blazing in Frank's glares at her.

It became apparent Kat needed no help on the comms equipment. She asked Marc to confirm the wording before sending the update. It pleased him how she omitted the mention of his injury and disappearance, presenting the mission as started and on schedule—true *enough*.

"Status report sent, Marc."

"Great work Kat...*eryna*." His remembering to call her by her full name raised the edges of her lips into a smirk. Marc had to admit, radiant appeared to be her face's default setting. Absent of improper longing, he couldn't help being taken in by her allure.

"You've never been on camera?"

"Nope. The thought of it brings me near to vomiting, and I'd hate to soil your shirt."

In the corner of his eye, Marc caught Frank watching from the other side of the glass door as Kat flicked Marc's chest. *Smart, gorgeous, and funny. If she returned his obvious interest, Frank would be one lucky guy*, Marc thought.

A yearning pulled on his heart for his own exquisite, beloved Casey. He couldn't stop worrying about her being the only one looking after Jewel. The emotional toll of that on top of the physical demands hung over him constantly. He hoped it hadn't consumed his dear wife, extinguishing the spark of passion for life he loved about her and longed to see reignited.

10 | Earth:
5 Days to Crossover

Spending her days in this dirt-colored windowless building hung a gray cloud over her. It took effort to fight off regret for walking away from the UGA's capitol building in Chicago, where Kateryna had worked for fourteen years, not counting her internship—a glorified title for a servant's post.

All those years in university qualified her to be more than a gopher. Disillusioned when reality failed her dreams, she had almost sacrificed her career by fighting off Mister Higgins's advances. "Sometimes it's who you know," he'd say. "If you want to get ahead in this field, you need to make friends." Little had he realized how true that advice would prove to be for Kateryna.

After an interview Kat had recorded and edited, a rising star in Chicago's political scene befriended her. Kat had aligned herself with the right person in Roberta Hillthorpe, a no-nonsense powerhouse. Her new ally would have jumped her straight to press secretary as quickly as she had sidelined the career of one Maxwell Higgins. Kateryna never could justify taking shortcuts. She also didn't want that job because of her fear of the camera as much as her disdain for that era's administration.

Keeping what her bosses called "her camera-worthy face" off video, Kat climbed the ranks on her research skills and communications expertise. While on location as a field technician for a live shoot, she met George. Not hopelessly romantic enough to have called it love at first sight, she could never forget the first time their eyes met, lingering forever in a glance turned longing stare that flowed organically into deep conversation.

Walking away from her office in Chicago rescued her from compressing under the weight of early widowhood. A fraction of the Kateryna she had forged herself into carried a box of her belongings from that office. Casting a last longing glance over her shoulder at the glass wall behind her desk, she had left everything behind.

Now, she worked in a sealed concrete box. Like all modern buildings, especially government ones, not a single window broke the tedium of its walls. Antiradiation coating over autofrosting glass became mandatory after the nuclear incidents. Most of the resources to produce them went to refitting offices and homes of the wealthy and powerful. Cement had sealed George's windows decades before, so they moved into Kat's townhome when they married.

That cozy seventeen-hundred-square-foot townhome now housed only her memories, replaced by the cube that would be her dwelling until Kat crossed over. How she wished its pane of glass hollowed the wall in her shared office space instead—the place where she spent most of her waking hours. Kat's new workplace—approaching two years and she still thought of it as new—gave her a way to carry on George's work by providing a future for humankind. Only, he had hopelessly tried to revive Earth's decaying flesh, its soil now refusing to nourish crops.

People often said things like, "too little too late." The government tried, in the last days before the nuclear incidents. Any hope to reclaim the planet, to reverse the effects of climate change, died over three decades back in the explosions. (Accident or act of war argued to this day.) They choked out the last breaths Earth's feeble ecosphere could offer its tenants.

Kateryna always arrived first at the office to wait for Herbert Andrews, Herbie to everyone, to unlock the door to her new life, reduced to being caged in tiny, unwelcoming places. Like a poor magician, the large floor space meant to give an appearance of openness failed to stick the illusion.

While Kat liked to say she worked for Herbie, the entire operation came under the purview of the Strategic Counsel Leader. At two years over Kat, Roberta had clawed her way up, positioning herself as one of the most powerful people in the world. How vulnerable Kateryna imagined her potent friend must have felt begging her to join this project.

"Coffee?" Herbie always asked as he made his first cup.

"No thanks, Herbie. You know I never drink that... stuff."

"You never know. What if the one day I don't ask, you could really go for a cup?"

"That's most thoughtful. But don't expect that to happen any time soon. Do you have today's topic yet?"

"Of course, Kateryna. I know you well enough by now. Relax. Your day doesn't even start for another hour."

"It's only starting *this late* because you refuse to give me a keycard. I'd have had so much work done already." Kat smiled with the words, knowing he had no say in who got a keycard.

"Like seven to ten p.m. isn't enough for you. I can barely get you to stop for lunch, too. Kateryna, the first step is admitting you have a problem."

After a shared chuckle, Kat repeated, "The topic?"

Every morning started the same for her. "The topic" presented the lie the daily update on the Mars project would tell that evening. Kat's job involved researching the topic and creating a talking-points sheet for the "on location" reporter believed to be in the distant colony. Sometimes, Kat had lunch with Monica Sullivan in the campus cafeteria to discuss the topic she would spew "live from Mars" that evening. The resulting script grew into something far more polished than Kat's draft, which didn't need to be much more than a factsheet.

Today, she had no break beyond a quick downing of something light Herbie would get them for lunch. If not for Kateryna, he could have been called the office workaholic. Her afternoon agenda called for another meeting. The waste of time most meetings ended up becoming frustrated her drive to get things done. She hoped this would be different, being vital operational planning with Marc and Sharon.

Marc had arrived first and appeared to have made himself at home in the conference room, lounging over a chair. His pose didn't look at all comfortable.

"Hi, Marc, um, *sir*. Sorry... What do I call you?"

"Marc will do. But with a C, not a K, or you and I will have some colossal problems getting along."

Hesitating at first, Kat chuckled when his smirk told her he was joking. "So, *Marss* it is then." A playful grin accented the intentional mispronunciation of his name.

"See, I knew there was something I liked about you, civvy."

She pulled her pursed lips to one side. "*Civvy*?"

"You're a civilian. And I'm no stickler for titles or formalities. We'll get along just fine. Sorry we didn't really talk before this. I mean, we've been in so many of these awful meetings together." He stood to offer his hand, which she shook. He didn't hold back a firm squeeze but offered it gently. "So, if I'm *Marss*, do I call you Kat?"

"I prefer Kateryna, but it takes more than calling me Kat to offend me... if you were worried." She smiled warmly. Marc came across as easy to get along with, and Kat appreciated his chilled demeanor, ridding her stomach of the acid it churned thinking he'd be a stereotypical military guy.

"Smart *and* a sense of humor. Welcome to my team. Have you gotten to know Sharon at all? There's an amazing eco-biologist under those red curls, and she'll be a vital part of this operation."

"I've spoken with her a little. Is she joining us?"

Marc withdrew his broad shoulders and leaned closer. "She's on an errand and will join us soon. But we can get started. I know the SCL..." Raising his eyebrows, he inhaled deeply. "And about your friendship with her, I—"

"Hold on a second. I didn't get where I am by *any way* you're assuming. I've earned everything I've accomplished."

"Settle down. Though I love that fire in you. It's why I chose you for my team—partly."

"*You* chose me? Roberta brought me here almost two years ago, and I never met you before a few weeks ago."

"But I've been watching you. Oh... that sounded creepy. No, I'm a happily married man." He grinned like a teenager using innuendo for the first time. "Don't get me wrong, I'm flattered by your interest. But I've gotta say no. I've been watching *your career* very closely and following your work. Big fan."

"My work is behind the scenes... *My* interest? You're a real piece of work. How do you even know who I am? And *Roberta* begged me to join this crazy Idyllium mission."

"At my request. She gave me some sway over key team members. Except for Saul, but he's another story. The why of it, that's what you're wondering. Why would I select you, a nobody?" Kat winced. "I mean, publicly unknown. So...? How 'bout now?"

"Now what?"

"Did that 'nobody' remark get me closer to offending you?"

"Carry on, *Marss*." The playful banter livened the atmosphere in the vapid compound.

"We actually have met before. I think I'm less memorable out of uniform. I was with my wife, Casey. We met at the gala for the launch of the Mars project. You remember, where we said our farewells to Monica Sullivan before she launched in her great big rocket ship for... across the compound."

"You're right... you're not very memorable out of uniform. But I remember now. You were that tree trunk in a suit standing beside a model. Casey was in a red floor-length gown overlaid with sparkles of gold flecks. She was radiant."

"She was. You said one thing to me that day, well, I overheard you say it to Hillthorpe. That's what got me following your career."

"What did I say?"

"You said you hated the lie. I saw in your eyes you were an honest person. You only joined the Mars project because you wanted to help people."

"And *you* asked Roberta to drag me..." Her eyes glossed over, and she fought to keep them clear. "It was bad enough being here, lying to people, when I... I thought you were going to Idyllium peacefully. Then she begged me to go there with you... Now, I learned she's talking about killing millions and overrunning an entire world. I would not have agreed to join this mission if I knew that. It's like we're playing God to billions of people."

"That's it right there. That's why you're coming to Idyllium."

"I'm lost."

"We all are. Lost. Humanity is, at least on this side. Sharon and I have some options we need to consider with you. But first, I need to know more about your friendship with the SCL."

Wherever Marc was going with that, it halted abruptly as Sharon entered with a charismatic Irish smile showing a mouth full of pure white teeth. Kat found the green eyes red-hair combination most appealing and knew Mal did as well.

Nodding her head to Kat while laser focused on Marc, she said, "She okay, Captain?"

"Think so."

"Good. As you thought, Saul may be a problem. We need to figure this out. We can't afford any mistakes."

Kateryna couldn't be sure what their exchange meant or how she had become "okay" to them. Marc pulled his hand from his pants pocket and crimped a purple-and-white braided keychain, the kind children made for their parents. Subconsciously, Kat fondled her wedding ring with her thumb. The plastic braid shook in Marc's hand—clenched almost into a fist, bending the keychain between his fingers.

Marc held an intensely blank stare. "We must succeed."

11 | Idyllium Mission: Day 1

"I bet they tried many times to get you in front of that camera, didn't they? You don't look like a behind-the-scenes sort of person." Marc didn't have to try to be sweet. Quite talkative for a guy. Kat found comfort in him not being a blockheaded soldier devoid of personality.

"What? A pretty face to flash on the screen to boost ratings? Is that how you see me, Marc?"

"No. I mean, yeah, I'd tune in just to see you. Who wouldn't? I know you're no one's showpiece or trophy; that's crystal clear. But you gotta admit you look the part."

The back of her neck tingled, and the tiny hairs above her collar stood to bask in the fresh, cool air fondling the skin as it greeted them on the terrace.

"If you weren't married and *so old*, I'd think you were hitting on me." With an emphatic wink followed by hearty laughter, Kat hoped to confirm her joke.

"*Old*? I've barely got a few years on you."

"So, you're saying you *are* young enough to be into me?"

"What? No. I was just... Oh. I see. Okay, you got me good."

"You make it too easy..."

"I would never ask. Perfect gentleman, me. But you know I've read your file. You turned forty a few months ago. I got about nine years over you, so you might want to rethink your definition of old before it includes you."

"Numbers. Meaningless. Oh, there's the green blip we've been waiting for on the display: message delivered successfully. Help me get this stuff inside. We won't send another message to Earth until tomorrow, and I don't want to leave it out here. If you can handle it, old man."

"Wait. Before we go back inside. How are you feeling about the mission? Everything depends on us, our little team. This being your first military outing, all this protocol is new to you."

When she stood and leaned over the terrace rail, Marc did the same. "Look at those people down there. Blissfully ignorant. Happy. Peaceful. And we're going to ensure they stay that way, keep this bright future on Idyllium. Yeah, Marc, I'm good with the mission."

"You're not worried about the other side, our people?"

"Of course. But first, we stop the invasion, then we hope. Who knows what will become of the Earth? What I do know is, what they're planning must be stopped. These people are counting on us."

"Look at them down there. These people have no clue who we are or what we're doing. If we're successful, they'll never know."

"Fine by me. Camera-shy, remember?"

"Oh! Camera. Come on. The evening news is about to start, and we gotta see the latest."

"Latest what?"

"Celebrity gossip." Marc's dimples drilled into his cheeks. "We need to see if the first phase is taking root, and if it started to cause any destabilization."

As the two entered the room, with Marc carrying the lightweight equipment, Kat noticed Frank's glare. That expression turned into a grimace when Kateryna sat on the two-person sofa beside Marc and Frank took the grandpa chair. Marc turned on the holographic wall display and asked it to play the evening news on channel GB 17.

"It was on in the hospital; top story was the recent corporate mergers and acquisitions. I figure they'll run with that and do a more in-depth follow-up on the evening program."

Frank sat and appeared to be sulking. When the catchy jingle played over the opening title sequence, a blonde with the brightest blue eyes Kat had ever seen sat behind the news desk. Studio lights exaggerated the irises, but this went beyond that. This lady had no behind-the-scenes face.

"Seventeen, eh? I'm sure that stunning creature had nothing to do with your choice." Her elbow jabbed Marc's arm.

"Shh. She's the one who led with the corporate stuff. We need to hear this."

When Sharon came out of the bathroom, her showered red curls plastered over her scalp reminded Kat of a wet dog. The captain gave up his seat on the sofa for her and plopped on the floor. After the typical "Welcome to Greater Britannia Tonight" spiel and teasers of the evening's top stories, Belinda Mayers turned it over to a live shot of a seasoned male reporter in Kuwait. The big story there showed a celebration in the streets for the fiftieth anniversary of the small country's unification with Greater Britannia.

Back to Belinda Mayers, she introduced a woman of obvious experience whose report centered on the unrest in Australia. One of the last holdouts of unification, the country normally kept to itself, and GB allowed it. Recently loudening, a voice emanating from the island continent stirred up malcontent far beyond its oceanic borders. A diplomatic dispatch flight from GB had gone missing, presumed shot down.

"More of phase one." Marc kept his focus on the screen. "The unrest, destabilization, it's happening."

Frank raised an eyebrow. "We know for sure spies have been here long enough to have this great an impact?"

"I've been told—and it's top secret and highly classified—they started coming almost a decade ago. Of course, the financial stuff likely took a while. Years. But a nut job in Australia starts screaming, and he's instantly a voice for the people, calling for change."

"Captain, that reporter said he's been doing this for over three years and just now got real international traction," Sharon said.

Kat spoke over the TV voice reviewing the flight path. "But they've got weapons too. They shot down that delegation. That's escalation beyond discord."

"True, but that could be the result of those efforts." Marc pulled his eyes from the news program to face the others. "People become radicalized by the call for freedom, change, anarchy. Besides, it's not very hard to take down an air transport."

Kat wrinkled her face. "Yeah, Marc? That's not all that comforting."

"This isn't good. I mean, what Sharon and Kat told me about the mission parameters. Cap, do you think we should go ahead with this?"

"You see what's happening, Corporal. The world is unraveling. We must do what we can to stop this."

"What about Saul?" Kat didn't care for the man. More than that, she didn't trust him. His lust for leading the mission shone as openly as the skin of his bald scalp.

"I've served with him before. He carries out orders, even if he doesn't agree with them."

"I've served with him too. Don't turn your back on him, ever." Sharon wore the most serious face Kat had yet seen. She appeared to share Kat's disdain for the guy on a personal level.

Marc raised his hand. "Quiet. Belinda's coming back."

"Belinda? On a first-name basis with the pretty TV lady?" Kat offered a smile, but Marc's eyes were transfixed on the screen.

"Now, for a financial news update. Earlier, we spoke with Philip Belvedere, our chief financial correspondent. What he said about the takeovers and mergers was alarming. Some have been hostile. Others formed mammoth conglomerations that violate our fair business opportunities and anti-conglomeration articles of commerce. By close of day today, we still have no news of any committees being established to scrutinize these deals."

With a camera change, the reporter turned her head.

"How is the market responding, and what are GB lawmakers saying about this? Let me answer the second part of the question first. They're saying nothing. They deluge journalists with 'no comment' or 'nothing to worry about' replies. This reporter worries most when someone tells me not to worry and the only detail on why we shouldn't worry is 'no comment.' Something is off in this; I can smell it."

A closeup filled the wall screen with the reporter's face.

"Massive trades occurred all day today. Some companies sold at under fifty percent of their lowest value in a decade, while others skyrocketed. In the last seven hours, we've had reports of seventeen public companies becoming worthless. Petitions for government aid have been filed by over forty-seven formerly rock-solid corporations, and others have done as Saxton Dynamic. June, what can you tell us about that?"

A field reporter named June Callahan appeared on a split screen beside Belinda Mayers. On the vacated corporate headquarters of Saxton Dynamic behind her, thick chains wrapped around the door handles as a virtual "Closed for business" sign. The reporter continued to relate how nine companies had done the same today alone.

Belinda Mayers resumed center screen and closed the segment by announcing the lowest closing rates the market had seen in over a century. Marc muted the audio when they went to a commercial before the weather report.

"It's happening fast." Sharon ran her fingers through her hair, lifting it from her head and working it into a fluffier state. "I hope we're not too late."

Kat feared they were.

"Cap?"

"We're a go, Frank. We move tomorrow as planned. Well, with the current plan. Our mission just became even more critical, and I thought that impossible."

"Can we stop this, Marc?"

"That's precisely what we're going to do. Tomorrow, we enter the summit and complete the first phase of our mission."

"But Captain, don't you think we need to change our tactics a wee bit?" Red curls bounced as Sharon's head bobbed. "As we know, these fallouts are a prelude to invasion. Maybe we should skip the first phases of the plan to stop that, or it may be all for nothing."

"No. The PM isn't nothing. We go tomorrow. Frank, you keep your eyes on Saul, especially when I'm vulnerable. He'd love to take command of this team, to lead the operation. There's a reason we've kept some mission details from him. He doesn't trust me. I wonder if that's why they put us on the same detachment. We've got history."

"What history?" Kat hadn't even heard rumors but had no doubt anyone who knew Saul Mullins had 'history' of some sort.

"For another time."

"Captain? We can assume the invasion will come sooner than later now that so much groundwork's been laid. And when they arrive, they hope to come as saviors. I mean, they've messed up

Idyllium so much, the people might welcome the visitors from another world with a 'save us from ourselves' sorta message." Air quotes accented Sharon's point.

"Like a bunch of messiahs in military uniforms?" No one smiled at Frank's poor attempt at a joke, and the Catholic in the room grimaced. Practicing or not, she didn't appear to like the comment.

"We carry out the operation, regroup after the first op, and weigh our options for what to do next. Now, we need to get some sleep. Big day tomorrow."

12 | Earth:
5 Days to Crossover

Unable to say how many minutes he'd drifted before Roberta Hillthorpe called his name; Mal knew he had lost the first part of the meeting. The Strategic Counsel Leader of the UGA led the briefing with Saul Mullins, Frank Jones, and Malcolm Holland. The three men formed the security detail for the mission the SCL called "vital for the salvation of Earth's population." *Only the best of the best, she called us. Then why me?* Mal couldn't help wondering.

"Malcom! Come on, man," Saul barked.

"Sorry. Yes, I'm fully committed to the mission."

"That's delightful." Saul grimaced. "But what our SCL asked you was if you had any field experience with the new high-yield incapacitation device."

Pulling his shoulders from a slouched posture, Mal stood at attention. "Right. Yes, I have training and field experience with th-th... *those!* de, de, devices."

The ashy-gray flesh on Mal's face flushed pink. The powerful woman resting her backside on the desk's edge beside him stressed him enough. Her legs intertwined like a pretzel extending from her pencil skirt. Getting caught in a daydream tipped the scale to full anxiety, summoning the speech impediment he'd worked so hard to bury.

Saul cleared his throat. "And that's the *only reason* he's even on this mission. But ma'am, any of us can work the thing."

Relief came like a cool drink on a hot day—and all days were hot—when the SCL's soul-crushing gaze targeted Saul.

"Thank you for that unsolicited commentary, Mister Mullins. But let's assume when I want your opinion, I'll ask you for it. This will make things much easier going forward. Oh, and you, all of you." Miss Hillthorpe came off her lean to put her face in Saul's. "No one calls me ma'am. I'm not some crusty old lady. True, I've earned my role here, despite what nasty rumors you may have heard. But save the ma'am for when I hit sixty—if any of us are still around. And if you're counting, that'll be in seventeen years."

The men nodded.

"And that's what this mission's about. Operation code-named *Rebar* is well underway. Your team is the next essential element in our planned occupation of Idyllium. Operation *Needle Prick* must find success, no matter the cost."

Saul, Frank, and Malcom surrounded themselves in silence, unsure if the speech had ended or paused. When Roberta Hillthorpe refilled her water glass, her lean over Mal to reach the pitcher filled him with schoolboy jitters and activated his sweat glands. He feared she heard his dry gulp and may have noticed his wandering eyes.

"Frank, you've been quiet. I like that. Saul, you of all people should know the value of 'speak when spoken to.'" Punctuating the point with lowered eyebrows, she tucked her chestnut-brown hair behind her ear. "Now, Frank, tell me about your concerns over this mission. You're the strategist of the bunch, and the sign on my office door says I'm the *bleeding* Strategic Counsel Leader. So talk to me about strategy."

"Yes ma—Madam SCL."

"SCL will do. No need to add a gender-specific designation to it."

"I agree with Malcom being on the team." Frank nodded at Mal. "The Hertzog Five-Fifty takes some getting used to, and no one untrained should use it. Mal not only had training but used it successfully on his last assignment. And taking out the South African army's defensive array saved the operation and everyone on the team."

"And may, may, may I add... they're bio-locked to a certified user. No one else on the team but me can use it." Mal's own words battled his low self-esteem to justify his place on this team.

The hand she placed on Mal's shoulder made it twinge. The SCL responded by patting it. "Good we have you along for the trip then."

Not to push his leeway with the woman of such formidable character or break her imposed "speak when spoken to" rule, Mal raised his hand. A nod permitted his words.

"I have another concern for the mission."

"*Another?* You've yet to express any concerns. Maybe, tell me all your concerns now. A key part of strategic planning is *the planning*. Trust me, we're not having this meeting because I enjoy you gentlemen's company."

"Right. Sorry. We've heard the speculation and th-th-theories of the other side and gotten some reports from the advance teams. But as I understand it, even after almost a decade we have vuh-vuh-very limited knowledge of that world. Idyllium, I mean."

"We know enough to do what we must do," Saul said.

Mal ignored the gruff soldier. "What I mean is the theories of our doubles over there. What do we do if we see them?"

"Sorry, SCL." Saul turned a steely face to Mal. "Idyllium's a massive place with a denser population."

Turning to the SCL, Mal said, "One theory I believe to be sound—in fact, it has the most support from our quantum physicists—is that our doppelgängers are living lives almost identical to ours with only trivial divergencies from our own."

"*And?*" she baited.

"And, if our doubles *are* living the same lives...?" A surge of unfamiliar confidence freed Mal's tongue of its stutter. "They're most likely going to be working for their military and will be the very ones trying to stop us. If that's the case, we *will* cross paths with them when we get there. Then what do we do?"

The SCL went pensive with a hand to her chin.

Frank shook his head. "I heard there aren't—" The SCL cleared her throat and glared at him. "I mean, another opinion is little decisions would cause drastic course changes in our lives. Saul may be a kindergarten teacher for all we know."

Saul sneered at the idea.

"No!" Mal insisted. "A mirror world means our doppelgängers will be the very ones fighting us, tr-tr-tr-trying to stop our mission."

"Fellas, this is *not* what I meant by strategic planning." Mal raised his hand, and she ignored it. "Although, it's a valid point, and I've heard several theories. I trust your judgment. Do what must be done, and understand this... *Nothing* must interfere with this operation. Am I clear?"

"Crystal, ma'am." The salute Saul gave Miss Hillthorpe may have calmed her inner beast enough not to lash out at him for using *ma'am*.

Raising his hand again, Mal waited.

"Malcolm?"

"Thank you. I just, to address another concern... if I may."

"I thought I said to fire them at me all at once."

"Right, you did. Sorry. This isn't about our strategy or the logistics of the operation or anything. It's just, I mean, do we have full agreement about what we're about to do? We're plotting to overthrow a peaceful and prosperous government, to forcibly occupy another world. Have we considered the morality in that? Do we have the right because we've tossed up our own Earth? Don't we need a majority vote?"

"We're talking about our survival." Saul laced his words with a forcefulness matched by his steely glare.

The SCL wore the blank face of certainty. "The chairperson has the approval of the cabinet and joint chiefs. This *is* a matter of survival. From our first contact, it became clear we were *not* welcome over there, no matter how dire our situation. They may wear the mask of a benevolent society, but it restricts their view only to themselves. We have no choice. Besides, we plan to share the world over there."

"Of course. But we must expect some resistance, right? Likely killing on both sides. And I meant a majority *of the people*, who the chairperson and you politicians are supposed to represent. They know nothing of this other world's existence."

"Part of my responsibility as SCL is to make the hard calls on behalf of the people. That they don't know about this parallel universe and other world is to prevent mass hysteria and global panic. People do one of two things in a desperate situation: riot in the streets and fight and kill each other or rush to the last lifeboat, overrunning and swamping it so no one can use it." When Hillthorpe raised an eyebrow, it carved wrinkles into her forehead. "Which do you think people would choose if they knew about this? Knew we've learned how to cross over to a pristine planet? It's what the Mars Project is all about. Give them hope with a boat they can't swamp because it's on *another. Bleeding. Planet.*"

"But a planet not teeming with lives we're about to disrupt, maybe destroy." Mal knew he had said too much and wondered if he'd get himself pulled from the team.

"It will be mutual survival for two worlds. And you're not thinking this through. That's why the *L* in my title stands for

Leader. It's only a matter of time before word gets out about Idyllium. If we don't do this in a controlled manner, like I am, more people on both sides will die. It's as simple as that."

13 | Idyllium Mission: Day 2

Greater Britannia hadn't been a perfect government, as Sharon had learned in mission briefings. They hadn't become completely tyrannical in their world supremacy, either. At the head sat the prime minister, checked and balanced by Parliament at its capital, New London Town, the seat of power for the global empire.

Despite a few grumbles about its politics, restricted freedoms, and pseudo-socialist approach to its global citizenship, GB had been a consistent proponent of a clean, sustainable environment. Strict regulations against deforestation had been in place for over a century. As an ecologist, Sharon inhaled a lung full of clean air and considered it justification for its continued world domination.

GB granted few mass-production licenses, and those they did required clean, natural energy and a zero-pollutant policy. Every invention, product, discovery, and concept passed a detailed scrutinization process for environmental impact. After their invention, internal combustion engines immediately became illegal to produce. In truth, they could not have known the long-term effects of many of these thwarted inventions, but Sharon considered that to be the point.

Some argued these measures stifled productivity and growth. Through a more retrospective viewfinder, others like Sharon saw how they propelled advances in design, engineering, invention, construction, and innovation. Forcing people to create better, higher-quality items brought technological and social advancement without harmful impact on the climate.

The longevity of a world empire—which had evolved into something closer to a republic—had other benefits. No superpowers emerged on the world scene to engage in pointless cold wars. Nuclear weapons didn't exist. Long before the invention of dynamite, legislation controlled not only weapons but anything with a productive purpose that could be weaponized.

Idyllium had no war when Earth found her.

Upset though that made her, Sharon had a job to do here. As an ecology biologist, she needed to study the current state of the environment and check for any changes in the climate. With the history of foresight as a pillar of all scientific fields on Idyllium in mind, she had deep concerns over what opening fissures between universes might do. While they left the heavy theorizing on that point to the quantum physicists, her job had her monitoring and building forecast models.

"Thanks, Captain. Please set it right there."

In the predawn light, Marc helped Sharon set up her field equipment. To his obvious dismay, it had substantial weight compared to Kat's comms gear. Marc left Frank to help Kat take it back onto the terrace before heading out with Saul to plan their route to New London Town.

"We need all this stuff?"

"We? Captain, this is why I'm on this mission. Critical data on the current environmental state and health of the ecosphere are vital. With all that's clearly started with the invasion plan, we must see if there is any environmental impact. It could determine our next move."

"And why, exactly, are we doing this in the park?"

"The open space gets me better readings."

"Got it." Marc's mouth stretched in a wide yawn.

"Hey, that's contagious, you know. Help me with this."

"I can hardly see. Should have brought night vision."

"You're the one who wanted to come before dawn, *Captain*."

"Yeah, yeah. Always my fault. Thought it'd be best if we didn't attract too much attention."

Sharon needed the hefty amplifier array mounted on the receiver. Marc's distraction and morning chattiness were unwelcome visitors, as she demanded proficiency. He stretched his arms and gazed off at the horizon.

"Captain, sir. I'll need you to help me with this." She pointed to an array mounted on an extension pole. "I need that end in here."

To keep Marc focused before coffee proved to be a challenge. She had forgotten how much he needed his morning jolt. Leaving the hotel at half past four meant the breakfast bar hadn't opened, and no one made the coffee. A decaffeinated captain was less suited to Sharon's purposes. With the equipment set up and ready, she switched it on. A soft electric hum laid a background track over their little outing.

Now into a full workout, Marc went belly down, planking. "How long do you think this will take?"

"I started a thirty-minute cycle, not a detailed enviro-scan. We just need to confirm a few things." Sharon joined in the morning exercises. She stretched every day and varied the second part of her routine. Today, she happened to be in a park. After ten minutes of muscle work with only grunts spoken between them, Sharon had an impulsive notion. "Laps?"

"You think it's smart to leave the equipment?"

"It's barely five. I've seen one guy walking a tiny dog. And we won't go far. Unless you're scared you can't keep up." With that, she took off. Her short, muscular legs made her a good sprinter but without impressive stamina unless she paced herself. Since she made the challenge to Marc, Sharon ramped up to full speed.

"*Hey.*"

She heard his voice ahead of his run behind her. His chuckle likely slowed his start. *He won't catch me.* When Marc came alongside her, Sharon looked at his legs. At about six feet tall, he towered over her.

"No fair. Longer legs."

"Hey, you turned this into a race. Where's the turn?"

Before answering, she let him gain a little and overtake her. Sharon made a quick pivot turn and gave her all to the run. By the time her captain realized what had happened, he couldn't catch back up to her. He found her out of breath with her hands on her knees at the equipment station.

"Cheater," he said playfully, less winded.

"I'm fast, but I'd not call myself a cheetah."

"Yeah, I wouldn't either. Chea-*ter.*" She found his smile cute.

As much as Sharon hated to admit it and never would, she'd always been attracted to the guy. Also, she had met Casey, so she considered herself not Marc's type, even after that one time. Sharon's mood switched dizzily from playful daydreaming to shameful guilt for the playful daydreaming to melancholy—wishing Mal was there.

"Permission to speak freely, Captain?"

"Sharon, you know me well. You don't have to ask. I require formality when needed, sure. A salute now and again to soothe the ego. One on one, like this, you always have permission to speak freely."

"I know. But this is personal. And about the mission, I guess." She hesitated, wondering if she should say it, questioning if she had professional concerns or petty jealousy.

"Sharon? You there?"

"Kateryna."

"What about her? She should be sending Saul's update. Done, most likely. Saul and Frank should be off to recon the route to New London Town by now."

"No. I'm trying to say... Look, you and I are friends, right? Not just captain and science officer?"

"I'd like to think so. Otherwise, I think some of my conduct over the years may seem... less than gentlemanly, ma'am." He offered her a foolishly adorable curtsy. She giggled.

"Good. Because I'm speaking as a friend. Are you and Kat...?"

"*Whoa*. How can you ask that?"

"I know you love your wife. I'm not saying... It's just you two are *really* chummy, and last night, you seemed to have a moment out on the terrace."

"Weren't you in the shower?"

"You were on the terrace for like a half hour. I went in the shower just before you came back in."

"Oh. I didn't notice."

Yeah, I know. Who'd notice me in Kateryna's presence?

When she didn't speak, Marc explained, "But no. Of course not. We do get along, hit it off right away. But I can see why you asked. I mean, two wildly attractive folk like us getting along like we do... one might make certain logical assumptions." His smirk always made Sharon smile.

"One might. Think maybe Frank did."

"He's sweet on her, I reckon. Not sure she's going that way, though. Best to leave any romanticizing for after the mission."

"I agree."

"Good talk." He palm-slapped her shoulder. "This thing about ready?"

"A couple minutes, looks like."

"Good. Sun's about to come up, and people like me tend to turn to ash when it hits 'em."

"Indeed. You know, this is what it's all about, isn't it? The environmental studies. My work. This is what the people of Earth need and what Idyllium is desperate to protect."

"Of course." Marc puffed his chest, muscular and toned, as he inhaled deeply through his nostrils. "You can taste it."

"If we fail? I'm afraid this will all be ruined... like our side. Just a matter of time."

"This evening, we'll make our first move against that happening."

"Oh, it's done."

"And?"

"The system will take time processing the data, but it looks as expected. Pristine. No signs of that changing."

"Let's keep it that way."

"Help me pack this up and get it back."

"Yes, ma'am. Now that this science stuff is done, it's time for my daring heroics."

14 | Earth:
5 Days to Crossover

Jewel arrived as the center of the universe. A memory as clear as the sight that created it, Marc's mental picture of that first look was unforgettable. A perfect girl born into an imperfect world. Marc and Casey hadn't planned on calling her Jewel. They had opted not to know if they would have a boy or girl—uncommon when prenatal medical care had become an almost fanatical religion for expectant parents. So many things could have gone wrong. Any of a host of genetic abnormalities might have been passed as an inheritance. A plethora of complex health problems plagued those living in Earth's dying biosphere.

"She's a perfect jewel."

When Casey said those words, staring for the first time into the gray-blue eyes of her baby girl, Marc knew. Twelve years had passed since the overjoyed new parents readily agreed on the name. While no child could be called perfect in any measure outside a parent's tunneled mental vision, applying the word to Jewel became a challenge, even for them.

"Jonathan Park's Disease."

Three words shattered the universe orbiting their Jewel. Official medical jargon boiled the rare disease down to an identifiable genetic marker. Fractions of specific airborne pathogens from the nuclear incidents swam in the air, and for those with the marker, they exacerbated radiation levels of outdoor exposure. The genetic disorder was transmitted from mother to child even when dormant in the parental DNA.

It meant their precious Jewel couldn't breathe under her body's natural process. At nine years and five months, her lungs became too weak to draw breath, and oxygen tubes have pushed air into her nostrils since. The resulting condition was a highly advanced form of acute respiratory distress syndrome. The devastation to her body caused nerve and muscle damage, afflicting her with constant pain and weakness. Her preadolescent years saw more days in the hospital than at home, and days at home rarely got her out of bed. She'd be far on the long end of the curve if she saw her fifteenth birthday.

With the last of her grandparents passing before she entered her tenth year, Jewel had only her parents. Their constant attention provided care and comfort. She never complained, not once. Her courage and strength astonished Marc, dwarfing his own. Casey had been a rock, sturdy and supportive. Minimal amounts of sleep had somehow empowered her with determined energy.

After three months of fortitude, Casey lost the power to care for herself. She stopped eating and bathing. A mother with no practical help to offer her child was no support for her husband. He had to care for their baby's battle with the terminal condition. Learning what Marc had desperately hoped to keep hidden devastated her. Mother to daughter. It brought a weight that crushed her spirit. Its intense flame joined the mallet of massive guilt, forging her into a person Marc didn't recognize. The strength of character Casey had shown departed. She was gone—a shadow of the woman he loved in her place.

Marc almost buckled under the weight. As the sole caregiver for Jewel, he had taken an extended leave from the International Corps of Marines. He hadn't a hint of an idea how to handle Casey. A battle at first, he got her to sit up for a video consultation with a therapist. Sitting in bed in pajamas she hadn't come out of in days, she scarcely spoke. It took Marc weeks to get her onto the next call with a psychiatrist.

Tim provided invaluable support. He'd been there so often the sofa became his de facto guest bed. After weeks of being at home to care for his girls, Marc had to go to work. The live-in nurse the UGA provided for Jewel did an amazing job caring for her. She and Jewel became close. Marc swelled with gratitude as Peggy became his daughter's only companionship outside of her parents and Uncle Tim.

Casey had lost herself in despondency. With no one looking after her, she withdrew into the void of grief and self-pity. She spent most of Jewel's awake time, which had lessened to a few hours each day, at her side. For her daughter's sake, she became an excellent actor but had let herself go, finding solace in her distilled liquid escapes. As much as Marc tried to keep it out of the house, he kept finding empty bottles. A few times each week, he fought her into the bathtub. Losing the battle often, he cleaned her with a damp towel as she slept or lay passed out from her overindulgence.

Without Marc's knowledge, Tim petitioned his superior officer, General William Brady, to permit himself and Marc to work alternating shifts. Tim had proven to be more than capable of leading the platoon in Marc's absence. He had done it for those first months during Marc's extended leave. More than ever—more than Marc would have asked—Tim ingratiated himself as an invaluable member of the family whenever Marc went on a deployment.

Tim had felt the need to come clean about a four-day stint he pulled in the Sanders' home while Marc went on a mission. As good as they had been at keeping the place booze free, he woke from a nap and found Casey passed out and covered in her own vomit. Jewel's nurse did nothing more than cast a judgmental look over the woman. Tim had freed her of the putrescent bedclothes and bathed her. The image squeezed Marc's intestines in a vise grip. Deep breaths helped him realize how awkward it must have been for the guy, almost as much as it was for him. Marc forced himself to be okay with it and reached for gratitude in place of anguish.

Learning about her bath from the nurse—the guys had agreed to spare her the embarrassment—brought an unexpected reaction. After putting a bit of liquid motivation in her, inhibitions lowered, she asked Tim about it. Marc had been away on another prolonged assignment, this one longer than the last. When Casey insisted he drink with her, Tim gave in and experienced unwanted effects of the alcohol.

Blood boiled as rage grew fire-hot inside Marc when Tim sat him down to confess the infidelity. Tears of a deep and morbid pain soaked the young man's face and softened Marc's. He resolved to let it go immediately or he wouldn't have been able to. His pulling Tim in for a tearful hug must have confused the guy. They never spoke of it again. It soon became clear to Marc his beloved and broken wife had no recollection of the alcohol-induced event. He tried his best to hold no resentment of betrayal against her for it.

He didn't feel he had taken the moral high ground on the matter or consider himself a saint for it. Marc was a man, as shattered and imperfect as Casey. Devastation and constant worry for Jewel had made them both into something... *damaged*. With no intoxication to blame, he had almost succumbed to the same primal urges, the need for self-indulgent emotional release.

Sharon O'Brien wasn't the most beautiful woman he'd seen by any means. But with her red curls, green eyes, and tight athletic physique, she looked rather cute. And she was there. They were four men and Sharon on a survey mission. Marc's ICM unit served as her security detail. He couldn't sleep, hardly did, unless he snuggled up beside Jewel. Three nights in, gazing at what he could see of the stars through the observation tent's clear rad-resistant enclosure, he sat sobbing. Sharon found him in that state and, breaking military protocol, laid her arm around him.

Warm comfort surged through his veins like a drug, cutting off the supply of tears and waking dormant carnal inclinations. His arms enveloped her and pulled her in closer. She resisted, looked him in the endless wells of sorrow that were his eyes, and fell into him. They shared consoling friendship. When Marc's lips met hers, they didn't refuse him. Passion's heat filled him as it hadn't in the year since that crushing blow of learning his daughter's fate.

He gave up on the ideal of "*Marc Sanders*," allowing himself the indulgence of being nothing more than a physical man, to think only of *his* needs when, for too long, he had thought only of Jewel and Casey.

Gratitude eventually replaced his initial sentiments when it didn't happen. He suppressed the beast waking inside him, told to hibernate once more when Sharon pulled away. She didn't concede a momentary pleasure at the ruination of her captain and friend and the destruction of a family. As much as his family meant pain, a pain that would only worsen until it climaxed in unbearable grief, it was his to hold. Awkwardness between him and Sharon took its time, but it faded.

He never told Casey.

Preparing for deployment had become increasingly harder since Jewel became ill. Marc wouldn't allow himself to entertain the thought of never coming home. Casey and Jewel did that enough for the three of them. Regular sessions with her psychotherapist and keeping her sobriety had Casey on the road back to herself, able to care for Jewel in Marc's absence. This time, it would be different, the longest deployment since Jewel's diagnosis.

This operation came with a dose of hope beyond the most powerful medicine—one that came in a bitter pill, hard to swallow.

What the mission demanded of him, corrupting and invading Idyllium, plagued his dreams and monopolized his waking thoughts. What would he do to an entire world to save one life? Altered mission plans flashed through his mind. Would he jeopardize her future, or could he save two worlds and his little girl?

New drugs would keep Jewel alive for a few years and help suppress most of the pain. They even gave her some time off the oxygen. But they offered no cure. She was terminal. Advances in medical and ecological studies had found an unobtainable treatment. Doctors hypothesized that sufferers of Jonathan Park's with ARDS could live long and healthy lives in a clean ecosystem. The goal of current studies shifted to helping patients live long enough for that ecosystem to develop on Mars in sealed microenvironments.

Mars was a hoax. That revelation would have been the final nail in a coffin already laid six feet in the ground—with Marc beside Jewel and Casey, waiting for the shovels of dirt. If not for Idyllium, the knowledge would have crushed him. He had learned of the classified other world and the top-secret location of the "Mars colony." Images of its construction came from a film studio in a hangar on a military base in Utah.

"Highly Classified."

A disciplined soldier, Marc had never broken protocol. His most trusted and intimate companion, a woman from whom he kept no secrets—well, two—never knew where he went or what he did on his deployments. When he had booked his transport to sneak home for a few hours, he imagined it being harder to break such a vital code of conduct, to tell Casey of his mission to the other side. As natural as breathing, the words came out as they sat on their bed with the door closed. When she withdrew into herself, Marc wished he hadn't opened with, "I'll be away for longer this time. I'm not sure when I'll be back."

"No, babe. This is different."

"Of course it is. Away for who knows how long." Expectant tears glossed Casey's eyes.

"I think, I think this is our only chance... for Jewel."

"What... I... What do you mean?"

"This project I've been on for two years. Those trips to Utah."

"*Utah?* That's where you've been going? Here we've been worried sick, not knowing what crooked country or seedy part of the world you were in. And you've been *in Utah?*"

"Sorry. You know all the top-secret nonsense. I couldn't tell you. And I've been on other deployments too. But this Utah project... This is our shot to help Jewel."

"All we can do for her... is comfort her. Be here for her. She won't make it long enough under her current treatments for Mars—if they even keep to that timeframe. Accepting it is what helped me over that hurdle. I wish you'd just quit and stay here. We should be together until..."

"I know. And you've been doing so great. I'm so proud of you. I didn't want to get your hopes up, *our* hopes up. And I think we should wait to tell Jewel. But *we found it!* A place with clean air and no radiation. A place where she can live a full life."

"No place like that exists on Earth."

"Not on *this* Earth."

"My head's spinning. Either I've started drinking again, or you have. What do you mean, *this* Earth? There's only one and we've ruined it. That's why our daughter is dy—" She choked on the last word.

"About a decade back, quantum physicists discovered the existence of a parallel world. Then they learned how to send signals through and how to take crude sensor readings. You know Sharon? She's on the team that started studying the environment there, on Idyllium. That's what they call their Earth. They have a healthy ecosphere, like we had over a century ago. We've even sent advanced teams through. People have crossed over to another world."

"I have no idea what you're saying to me right now." Casey stood from the bed and paced the room. Her hands dug into her auburn, shoulder-length hair, and she rubbed her scalp, muttering.

Marc stiffened, recognizing the behavior that preceded an anxiety attack. She hadn't had one in months. He stood to hold her, head lowered and eyes rounded. "I know it's a lot. I was overwhelmed when I learned of it, too. But it's real. Mars is a hoax started to prevent mass hysteria and global panic. I've been to the colony they show us on those daily updates. Kateryna—you've heard me mention her—she works there. The Mars *colony* is in a studio soundstage in Utah. But this, this new world, is real. And I'm going there."

"*What*? You tell me this... *this*. And now you're going there? You're going to some parallel universe?"

After a tight hug, Marc's gentle eyes calmed his dear Casey. "Yes. I must go. If our mission is successful, we'll start migrating people over there. To a clean world. And much sooner than Mars, even if that were real. We can have Jewel there before her next birthday. She'll live a full and healthy life. That's why I'm going."

"Uh... I... just don't..."

"I know, honey. I know. But we can't tell Jewel. I hesitated to tell you. False hopes can be destructive. Blew my mind. When I learned about it, it was... too good to be true. But it is. We have people there. It's real. And I've studied Sharon's data."

"Is she on the team that's going?"

"Yeah. And Kat and some security forces. Why?"

"I've seen how she looks at you, Marc. And you've been on a few extended deployments together before."

Panic traced up Marc's spine, vertebra by vertebra, met by trickles of sweat snaking down his back. *Does she know?*

"I know... how hard it was on you when I was... not myself. Not there for you, in... many ways. If... back then? If you needed anything I couldn't give you, I understand. But now? I'm here for you now, Marc."

Casey was there for him as she hadn't been in months. They came together in a way as intimate and nurturing as it was passionate and physical. The evening didn't come close to what Marc envisioned when he decided to tell her about the operation. The couple slept intertwined in each other's arms until they woke to check on Jewel. Casey went for a shower, and Marc snuggled beside his precious little girl. Kissing his Jewel's forehead as she slept, Marc found the resolve to do whatever needed to be done.

15 | Idyllium Mission: Day 2

Sharon ceased her work and stood up straight. Hunched over with his back toward the scene, Marc hadn't noticed. She had gotten used to not being noticed. Could that have been what made Malcom so special to her? He had been noticing her far longer than she had realized.

"Captain. Stop what you're doing and turn around."

The face he showed her dripped with panic. His motion to rise and twist formed one deliberate action, the caution of years of military experience to defend against enemy combatants. She thought she could have chosen her words more carefully.

"My goodness." She saw only the back of his head.

Sharon's vibrant green eyes widened to absorb the spectacle and went glossy. Her Catholic upbringing had nothing to do with it. She experienced a higher plane of spirituality, lifting her from the elemental components of her biological being, more than the atoms and molecules of a physical creature. Was this faith? She couldn't know. The emotional reaction resurrected in her at seeing the sun lift itself over Idyllium in a new birth to light the way for mankind moved her in a profoundly "religious" epiphany. Her muscles arrested, unwilling to move, not to miss a millisecond of the visual symphony of brilliant colors brushed across the sky from such a glorious sunrise.

As a child, Sharon had followed her parents' prodding with Mass on Sunday and attended the church-sponsored private school that cost her father a small fortune. Expectations of a "good Irish Catholic family" meant she did her duty as the well-behaved daughter. Her saving grace came from learning no Catholic universities offered her field of study, and she attended uni off Ireland.

Not that she disliked her homeland; quite the contrary. Donegal would always be her cherished birthplace, her home, although she hadn't lived there since turning nineteen.

Her six-year academic path hadn't eroded her convictions. As a university student, she had joined a small nondenominational group and attended the Sunday service in the campus chapel, well, religiously. She had felt her parents' pride in how she balanced her faith with science.

Her devotion eroded slowly, or "drifted away," as one of her father's often-quoted passages warned. It wasn't the science. Sharon saw balance there, having studied nature to the level of detail that showed her design. She considered herself a spiritual person, unsure what that meant beyond holding onto an idea that there had to be more, something beyond herself and the insignificant lives people led.

Her mother, born Katheryn Muldoon and christened Marie, never took the role of a typical modern woman. Few were "housewives" as the term classified them. To Sharon, Mum was a homemaker, a gardener, a parent, a sage guide, a community servant, and the strongest person she had known. When the priest at her modest funeral service pontificated on the reason for her death, the tragic fall on the same stairs she'd walked down a million times coming home from church, Sharon knew her faith had died with her dear mum.

People of religious conviction accepted death as the inevitable destination of all living things. Sharon understood that well. To her, what made faith so appealing to the masses, fewer of them in recent decades, lay in the concept of something beyond that end. They'd say they believed it wholeheartedly, even as Sharon may have. Once. That fundamental pillar of faith appeared so solid, strong enough to support the weight of the world—until it needed to. Ravaged by a grief so deep they can't function, unable to lift themselves from its pit of despair, some reached for hope.

When Sharon tried to support herself upon it, it folded like a paper crutch. The last straw that crumbled her pillar of faith wasn't the soul-wrenching mourning. Three words added that weight. That man wore a robe meant to convey piety, presenting a "person of God" humbly doing his will. Hubris, she had thought. He could have been in a suit and tie, cargo shorts and a T-shirt, or standing before the congregation naked. His words had a greater impact, exsanguinating the last drop of hope from Sharon's veins.

"God took her."

Never having stepped foot in the campus chapel again, Sharon graduated top of her class with honors and received two doctorates. Nine years later, Sharon worked for the government and now had level-two clearance. Few in the world had access to the data flowing into her eyes. They raced her through basic to classify her private first class. Before this mission, the secretary of global affairs himself jumped Sharon to sergeant, placing her second in rank only to Marc. Operationally, Saul held that position, but if needed, she outranked him. News of that read like indignation flooding the man's expression and making him even uglier in her sight.

Being a military scientist brought much better people into her life, Marc for one. They had become good friends. And Malcom Holland, Mal, was so shy and sweet. How she yearned to have him with her now. A new friendship budded with Kateryna, and Sharon hoped it would continue after the op.

Many such connections deteriorated once the close quarters of a mission ended.

More memories of her mum rushed over her and filled her heart—this time with no added weight. That vault of emotion floated in its proper place, not retreating to her gut, where thoughts of her mother often sank it. Tears descended the curves of her full cheeks and slalomed around the spatter of freckles, gently joining the dew over the grass blades below. Part of herself uniting with the soil became a perfect metaphor for life and death, as Sharon experienced them at the same time in a cascade of sensations.

Perhaps there was *more.*

"Sharon? Are you okay?"

The world hadn't stopped for Sharon O'Brien. It only gave her a brief pause.

"Yeah, Captain. More than okay."

"Let's get back to camp. Need to get ready to move out."

Outside the hotel, they loaded the equipment into a small transport the concierge provided as a shuttle to the station. They'd be on its first run, so no need to lug the stuff up three flights to their room. While Marc savored a coffee from the breakfast bar, Sharon loaded a plate with fruit and carbs to fill her stomach. It failed to satiate the hunger the rising fireball had awoken in her.

"Just coffee? On an empty stomach?"

"Not hungry. I'll grab something when we come back down with Kat." Looking at his wrist device, Marc added, "We've got forty-seven minutes 'til the shuttle leaves."

"Saul and Frank?"

"Meeting us at the station."

Waiting for her to finish breakfast, Marc snatched and savored Sharon's blueberry muffin. Her bio-pad alerted her to updates from the morning's sensor data. Marc got another coffee while she parsed the report. When he returned, he raised his coffee cup to his lips with the sensuality of a lover's kiss. Sharon wiped the mental image and presented an abridged review of the initial readings.

"The air is pristine, and the ozone layer's healthy. Wee traces of pollutants found, but nothing over normal. Weather patterns are stable, and Idyllium's magnetic field is in balance. Solar radiation's at a perfect level, sustainable for healthy outdoor activities and good for the skin. It's producing healthy photosynthesis."

Marc raised his eyebrows and withdrew his lips. "Wow. All that from a thirty-minute scan. With this ecosphere, would you say it can support humanity indefinitely?"

"Yes. That's what we must protect. They've hit the economy. With zero response to the sudden financial crisis, we must assume infiltration into the government."

"I told Kat to keep her equipment set up so we can send your report off before we head out. We've got only the minutes we need to get that done and get on that shuttle. Let's go."

Marc finished his coffee, an act that appeared satisfying. Yet like a touching goodbye, disposing of the cup overlaid his face in sadness. Sharon never drank coffee and didn't understand the obsession people had with the bitter drink.

She followed Marc up the stairs to get Kat and collect their things to head to New London Town. His pause at their room door stiffened Sharon's shoulders. A finger crossed his lips, and Sharon noted the caution in his hand as he turned the handle.

Marc flung the door open and charged into the hotel room. Kat jumped out of her skin—and skin was all Kateryna was wearing. Sharon's wide-eyed ogling matched the intensity of

Marc's stare. After an open-mouthed couple of seconds, he dropped his head and raised a hand over his eyes. The sudden jump-scare disturbance startled Kat at first, but she looked remarkably unfazed at having people in the room with her unclothed self. It would have mortified Sharon.

"You guys scared the pants off me. Literally." Her chortle came with no discernible shame. Marc continued to hide her from view. Sharon couldn't look away from the tall, toned sculpture of a goddess not even trying to cover herself.

"Sorry. Ka... I... We..." Marc shook his head. "I thought something was wrong."

"Wrong?" Kat reached inside her bag on the suitcase stand.

"The door wasn't locked. And... I knew you were in here alone."

"Yeah. Sorry for barging in on you... naked."

"No worries, Sharon. I'm not prudish. Had a shower and forgot my things out here." Once Kat slipped into her clothes, Sharon gave the all-clear, permitting Marc the use of his eyes once more. "Got a message for me to send?"

With Sharon's environmental report sent, Marc helped Kat pack up her gear. Each snatched their backpacks. Kat and Marc grabbed a quick bite and guzzled a coffee before they rode the shuttle transport to the station. People they passed on the streets went about the business of getting their day started; adults going to work, children heading off to school. A little slice of suburbia, so ordinary and basic, Sharon found it magical. Her musing drifted back to her childhood in Ireland, and she was the little girl she saw skipping along the sidewalk.

"It's weird. All that economic chaos flooding the news channels, everyone in a panic over it. Look at these people, going on with their day without a wee care in the world."

Kat rested a hand on Sharon's shoulder. "Blissful ignorance. That's the primary job of the media. Sure, stories like we saw last night sensationalize things and get some worked up. But for most, they won't react until they feel an impact from it. That could take a few weeks."

"Besides, we're here to carry out this mission so they don't have to worry."

Kat turned to face him. "Spoken like a true jarhead, Marc."

16 | Earth:
4 Days to Crossover

Every field operation required a soldier to be in peak physical condition. Today, the team would have the last examination before mission launch date, and it made Malcom Holland a nervous wreck. To pass this medical checkup, he needed to be clever, more so than last time, as it would be more extensive. All the preparation and training would have been for nothing if he got booted from the project. Operation Needle Prick had been cleared for go, and he desperately wished to be a part of it.

Not that *he* felt inadequate. But would *they* consider him to be so? The ICM medical evaluations team held such power, the ability to decide who got to stay on the team and who didn't. If they said no, he'd sit this one out with nothing to do but wish his team luck before they crossed over to Idyllium without him.

A simple enough plan. He reviewed it in his head as he incautiously hobbled along the corridors of the UGA Utah complex toward the medical offices. Mal crashed into Sharon coming from the opposite direction, having finished her physical. The collision toppled a small tablet from her hand onto the polyvinyl floor, bouncing once off the edge before it landed facedown with a dull pop. Mal reached for it, tapping heads with Sharon, who gave the occurrence a hearty chuckle.

"Sorry, Sharon."

"No worries, Mal. You nervous or something?"

"Nah. Just had my mind on other things."

"Give yourself a wee bit o' time. This one's a long one. Kept me in there near an hour, they did."

"Hey, your Irish accent sounds a little more... *Irish* today. It's cute."

"*You're* cute."

The unexpected compliment made him blush. The lightheadedness of blood rushing away from his brain to fill his cheeks signaled the body: prepare for a brief separation from consciousness. Mal fended off the approaching faint by leaning on the wall and closing his eyes for two lung-filling breaths.

"I ga-ga-ga-gotta go. Don't want points off for being late."

"No, go. And don't forget about dinner."

"I won't."

How could he forget? A dream that taunted his nights and occupied much of his daytime thoughts magically morphed into reality. He and Sharon had enjoyed proper conversations. They were getting to know each other, and Malcom very much enjoyed coming to know Sharon O'Brien. Amazing to him, it was reciprocal. They had been out together a couple times, mostly with project personnel, though no one from the team had joined besides Kat. She came for a quick drink at twenty-three hundred, saying she had come straight from work.

This would be their first dinner alone, with no one to support him. For Mal, the nervousness surpassed the fear of the exam steps away from taking him off the op. Not the most experienced when it came to the opposite sex, Mal had dated before. Nothing reached close to serious with Jenny or Megan. He hadn't been trying for anyone new since his diagnosis. A decrease in muscle mass shriveled his flesh—a skeleton in a loose-fitting gray coverall of skin... His diminished self-view had stifled his pursuit of women.

This thing with Sharon happened without looking for her or anyone. Their first conversation narrowly qualified as that, being a two- or three-minute interchange about the ground transport onto which he had loaded her gear. She feared it wouldn't provide a smooth ride for her sensitive equipment. Like a whirlpool, she drew him into her love of life and zeal for everything she did. He found her copiously cute and loved the red curls.

A crush at first, it grew on their next mission together some months later. Wanting nothing more than to tell her how he felt, he dared not tell her how he felt. So good was he at keeping that secret, she had no clue. That "mission accomplished" left him deflated, flattened under a spent parachute that failed to cushion the fall.

The third time's a charm, people said. Mal didn't know why, but he happily found some truth in it. This project paired them for the third time, and she noticed him. More than that, she liked what she saw. Mal's confidence had found room to rise in the new experimental medicine keeping his body in working order and inflating his muscles. Although they were not back to their former state, it bolstered his self-image. The meds even helped tone down the gray and increased the opacity level of his skin.

Of all the senseless ways to die, beyond the expected ones in the line of duty, he never imagined "death by mosquito" on the coroner's report. The mutation—an adaptation hardly qualifying as malaria—didn't carry a death sentence. In one of a hundred people contracting this modern-world strain, a dormant cancer cell in the bone marrow became metastatic.

Unless holding to a highly restrictive antiexposure routine, most adults had these cells keeping their potentially destructive force at bay for the person's lifespan. Antirad treatments had been distributed globally and without cost since the nuclear "incidents."

In those not lucky enough to be in the ninety-nine, the cancer awakened. It wreaked havoc on the bones, devouring white blood cells like a malevolent Pac-Man on a rampage. A fragile immune system resulted in patients often dying from a communicable disease or acute pneumonia. Malaria-spreading bloodsuckers bit millions of people each year, and one of every hundred of those suffered from radon-induced accelerated leukemia. The UGA's Global Health for All initiative continued to do extensive research on the condition.

Mal had volunteered himself into a pretrial alpha test group. They pumped him full of the latest medications the GHFA created to treat RIAL cancer. As a pretrial, it hung on the cutting edge of medical advancement and the extreme perimeter of legal. Strict orders for him to remain in the program included telling no one. To maintain that confidentiality, the GHFA gifted Mal some tools of deception, without which he'd have not dared take the physical.

When the time to draw blood came, Mal tested the main gizmo for cheating the result. Embedded under his biceps, the organic nanochip-powered autodispenser reached its tentacle to the brachial artery. A cocktail of blood fractions and chemicals that promised to fool the test and produce a passing result flowed into him like venom. It was as uncomfortable as it was effective.

The next gadget, a thumbnail-sized wireless transmitter in his pocket, didn't require insertion into Mal's body. He pressed it once when the bone density scan started and again when done. It fed the computer a density score high enough to keep him in the project. No alarms. No soldiers stomped in to escort him to a holding cell.

Finishing at the same time, he exited with Marc, who said nothing until he pulled Mal into an empty conference room. "Mal. What's wrong with you?"

"Wha-where do I start, Cap?" Said jokingly to calm himself, it failed the mission. As his sweat glands activated, Mal felt the throbbing of his pulse on the side of his neck. He sank into the quicksand of speculative anxiety over Marc digging up the secret of his health condition.

"No time for jokes, Lieutenant. Look. I've seen you injecting yourself in the locker room more than once. And today, I saw you insert something into your arm, like some implant. I ain't messing around here. If there's something I need to know, Mal, you gotta come clean."

No. No. No. This can't be happening. How could I have been so careless as to let anyone see me?

"Mal? Is this a drug thing?"

Malcolm considered what his captain would do if he said yes and promised he would get himself clean. "I've got RIAL, Cap. But I'm being treated. That's what those injections are. With the meds, I'm fine and ff-ff-fit for duty."

"*Whoa*. Sorry about that, man. Truly. But how in the world is that not on your record?"

"Being treated privately, out of the system."

"And that thing in your arm? Part of the treatment?"

"Not exactly. It's to help me pass the blood test."

"*What*? You'd fail the medical exam? Brother, I'm sorry for you and all, but this mission is too important. I can't have anyone not in top shape."

"I am. With the meds. But they'd show in the b-b-bloodwork, and the existence of the RIAL cancer. They'd boot me, Cap. And I want to go. I'm good for it."

"I don't know, Mal. You've put me in this here pickle of a situation. And the day wasn't at all crappy until a minute ago. You have any idea how rare a noncrappy day is in this place?"

"Arm-wrestle me."

"What? You sure you're not on drugs?"

"I wanna prove it. That I'm healthy an, an, and strong. You know a guy with RIAL should be weak, brittle boned even."

"If you're wrong, I what? Snap your forearm like a twig?"

"Let's see."

With panic bleeding into excitement, Mal moved around the conference table and took a seat, right elbow on the flat surface. Hesitating, Marc sat and rested his elbow. A clap popped as he cupped his palm to Malcom's. The two offered a silent, stern-faced half nod that meant they were doing this. On "go," their muscles tensed and puffed, and the grunting started. The push from Marc's tree limb of an arm threw a power Mal couldn't have overcome at his healthiest before becoming ill.

Eyes squinted and teeth clenched on both faces. Marc's biceps looked ready to rip open the skin stretched to its limit to contain the bulging mass. In a desperate summons for reserve strength, Mal's lips stretched, drilling dimples deep into taut cheeks. With a moan that followed his arm to the left, he pushed their white-knuckled hands back to level. After struggling to pass ninety degrees, the intertwined fists slammed down onto the table in victory.

"Told ya."

"You're somehow... *stronger* than before?"

"I'm pr-pr-pr-practically bionic. I'm at about a hundred ten percent—from what they told me. Stronger than ever. You see, Cap, I'm fit for duty."

"We'll see. For now... I repeat, *for now*, I'll not say anything. But I want updates. And to know more about these treatments of yours. Like, should I be taking some myself?"

Hearing Marc joke settled Mal into thinking he had a shot to remain on the team and go on the mission.

17 | Idyllium Mission: Day 2

BEING ALONE WITH SAUL never troubled Frank, but he didn't care for it either. In recent weeks, it only worsened. Chalking it up to premission anticipation and the gravity of the operation, he tried to let it slide. This morning, his superior officer, Commander Mullins, had worn Frank's last nerve, and he'd had enough.

It started in the hotel room with his lewd teasing. Before that, Frank hoped he had appeared to be playing it cool with Kat. Now he knew his interest in the comms operator had transmitted on all channels. He figured his blatant obviousness was what made him such a lousy poker player. If Saul saw it, everyone did. Which meant Kat saw it too. Ample devastation for one day. Frank didn't need Saul in his face about it.

A stickler for detail and timetables, Saul surged way beyond frustrated. When Frank delayed, helping Kat take the comms equipment to the terrace, he saw fiery rage in Saul's eyes. Of course, everyone had learned of the gear's meager weight and that Kat needed no assistance with it. Chivalry seemed worth a shot, so Frank jumped on every opportunity to be helpful, kind, or polite to Kat. He had seen evidence of it working, too, in her being flirty and sweet toward him.

The terrace scene played out like a horror show with a gruesome dream-haunting creature. The devilish beast crushing Frank's desires took the form of his captain. Marc and Kat hitting it off delt a devastating blow to Frank's fantasy. He knew Kat had some baggage but hadn't seen her file or spoken to her much. They had been getting along so well before Marc moved in on his action.

More than all that, Saul's callous words spoken in front of Kat rang in Frank's brain all morning. "Leave your fantasy girl be. She can handle it. I'm sure she'll ask Marc if she needs a *man's* help." Humiliation and fury allied themselves to rush as much blood as the rest of the body could spare to Frank's head. It wouldn't have surprised him if steam visibly escaped through his close crop of near-afro curls.

Silence walked beside them as they made their way to the station, scoping the route. Later, the hotel transport would carry the rest of the team and their equipment. What consumed forty minutes on foot would be a few minutes' ride for Kat... and the others. The station had a simple open-air platform with dual tube junctions—a standard suburban commuter line. Saul sent Frank to get the tickets while he conducted a security sweep of the platforms.

Jolted, Frank's jaw pulled the rest of his face, and his neck twisted his head to follow, angling his shoulders. Something hit him, hard as steel. Throbbing pain ran over the surprise of whatever had happened. The bright morning sunlight darkened. He troubled his eyes to focus on the tube tickets scattered on the ground.

"We're supposed to be the best?"

Clarity chased the voice, Saul's voice. Frank realized he had failed some sort of harassing readiness test. The shame of failure took third place to the anger and ache. His guard had dropped on the most important operation of his life. To accept what came didn't make it easier to endure.

"I was just getting the tickets, sir." Frank bent on one knee to collect the fallen items from the ground. Commuters flurrying in the corner of his eye paused to assess the scene playing out; two men in obvious disagreement escalated to physical altercation. When Frank didn't retaliate and accepted Saul's hand to straighten up, the spectators settled and went on with their lives.

"Sorry, Saul. The place was secure. It's so... tranquil."

"And if I were the other me? You think I would upset this peaceful scene before coming in for the kill? Send you advance warning out of the kindness of my heart?"

"I'd not expect kindness from that heart."

"Likely none to be found in my double's either. Both sides are fighting for our worlds, Corporal. And you're filling your head with daisies and unicorns for *a woman*. One so ridiculously out of your league, she forgot you before you said goodbye."

"Sorry, sir. Won't happen again."

"I know. Because if it does, I'll drop a lot more than a bruised jaw on you, Frank. Are we clear, Corporal?"

"Clear, Commander, sir."

"Forget about that woman. You don't have a shot with her, anyway. Our cap'n isn't what he seems, believe me."

"How do you mean? I've served with Cap before. He's a good guy and an excellent officer."

"And a cheat. Take it from me, Frank. That puddle of scum's not feeling an ounce of guilt for busting up your play. Him and Kat, that's a done deal. He ain't the type to lose sleep over messin' around either. The happy marriage he claims? Not even close."

"What do you know about it?"

"Enough. Trust me, forget about that girl. And don't turn your back on our fearless captain, either."

When the hotel vehicle pulled up, Frank's stomach ran out of the time it needed to finish twisting itself into a knot. He chewed on Saul's words as his heart climbed his esophagus to hold position at the back of his throat. Seeing Kat giggling with

Marc almost made Frank vomit. Immediately forgetting the friendly advice, given in a less-than-friendly way, he raced over to help Kat with her gear.

"Hey, Frank. Give Sharon a hand, would ya?" Marc had one of Kat's boxes while she handled the rest with ease.

Sharon handed him two ribbed silver cases with black carry handles. Frank missed a grip and would have sent one crashing to the ground if not for Sharon's quick reflexes. "*Careful*. My stuff's a little sensitive." Her piercing green irises scolded him.

"Sorry. I was..."

"Yeah, I know. You're an open book, Frank. This is critical equipment. No mistakes."

"Yes, ma'am."

"And, Frank, a little advice. You don't play Kat like a pimply high schooler crushing hard on the prettiest girl in school. You gotta up your game if you're serious. But... that's for after the mission. We can't have any distractions."

"I know. I know."

"Got the tickets?"

At the platform, Tube One filled with the capsule train. This marvel of engineering glided in enclosed tubes connecting suburbs to city centers. Frank appreciated the transparent aluminum composite of the tube complementing the panorama offered by the glass top half of the suspended capsules. Cream colored inside and out, they looked clean and modern.

Frank suffered another devastating blow when Kat took the seat beside Marc. He noticed Sharon give the occurrence a concerned look, supplementing his own regret. It made him see himself as that pimple-faced schoolboy with Kat far out of his league. Saul sat across the aisle from Marc with two strangers facing him. Their good spirits faded with their greeting when Saul returned it with a stern "don't bother me" look.

An announcement said they would depart. The tubes had an impeccable record of keeping their timetables. The magnetic virtual rail system floated them along, smooth as butter. Frank, longing for the taste of real butter impossible to find on Earth, had slathered it on his toast that morning. Wonders of nature painted a backdrop to shops and homes flickering by. The suburban townships pinwheeled around the city of New London Town. In the distance, diffused mountains rose to hold up a clear blue sky.

Marc slept for most of the ride while Sharon and Kat chatted. Frank joined Saul in quietly scanning the people on the train, trying to look as alert as his commander.

New London Town came into view with buildings hundreds of years old that looked newly erected. Entering the hub of a massive spider web, the tube opened to a grand structure, where several commuter lines joined. Larger transit tubes entered the junction, branching all over the continent from there. All marveled at the grandeur and arrangement of the station as they collected their gear.

An impressive transparent dome turned the sky above into a true-life nature show so real, it looked fake. Everyone coming and going moved with precision, and Marc said they should do the same, even if they weren't sure which way they needed to go. More than once, he'd said, "The less we stand out, the better."

The team followed Saul through the streets of New London Town. Roving his eyes, Frank saw a gleaming city, clean, organized, and surprisingly cheery. Shops lined sidewalks teeming with pedestrians. Public transports floated over the roads in a steady but moving flow. The architecture fascinated Frank. An aptitude test in high school showed a talent for architectural design or engineering, but no one built anything on his dying planet, so he enlisted in the corps. The fusion of centuries-old buildings with the modern made the city appear as if someone had designed it that way. It looked harmoniously elegant.

The bio-pads' preloaded map of New London Town made quick work of reaching the hotel that would be their base of operations for this phase of the mission. Hotel New Renaissance offered elegance without being overly posh. They chose it for its proximity to the New London conference center. The accommodation ticked a few notches above their usual.

Room service carted in fresh salads to the ladies' shared room, and the men joined them for lunch. Saul protested at first, but even he conceded his approval. Fresh and full of protein-rich legumes, its flavors melded delightfully. First to finish eating, Saul darted off, but not before ordering Frank to stay behind to review the plan for entering the summit gala. Commander Mullins would survey the area around the evening's event. He seemed more driven than usual to carry out this leg of the mission. Frank had thought nothing could top Saul's standard fervor for an op. Of course, it made sense that only Saul could outdo Saul.

"We'll have our names on the list and passes left for us at the concierge." Marc outlined the plan in exhaustive detail...

Sharon squinted. "So, *I'm* staying here, on comms?"

"Kateryna's with me. She's the distraction when I need to move. So yeah, we need you to monitor us on comms."

"I get that she's the better distraction, *okay*. But she's also the comms expert."

"No worries. I'll set everything up for you and give you a crash course. You won't have much to do." Kat made it sound simple, but Sharon didn't look convinced.

"If you say so."

"And Saul left me here to help plan this, from the security aspect. But he's out doing recon, and he never told me the specifics of the plan for this evening. What's my role, Cap?"

"Saul will secure our exit at the event, so that leaves you here with Sharon."

"All right. But she's got a job. What do I do?"

"Her. *No*, I mean... Sorry." Marc laughed at his own faux pas. "You're her security. We're in an active operation, and she's an officer."

"Sure, of course. It's just... Saul goes his own way sometimes."

Marc looked at Sharon then at Kat. Both gave him firm nods of agreement, though he hadn't said a word to either of them. "Frank, we need to talk about what these lovely ladies hinted at with you yesterday..."

18 | Earth:
3 Days to Crossover

Operation Needle Prick hadn't won over anyone on the team, least of all Marc. Choosing names and total operational oversight fell to Roberta Hillthorpe. Marc had recently learned, or confirmed his suspicions, the SCL was *the* authority of the United Global Alliance, the most powerful person on Earth—a thought that made him wince. While he was not fond of Walter Vescovi by any stretch of the imagination, at least the man showed respect for those serving in the military. He also donned a tremendously less abrasive personality than the SCL. Most people did.

Marc had had little interaction with the formidable woman since joining the project. Most times on campus, he didn't see her. Until recently, Hillthorpe and the chairperson spent most of their time in Chicago. They had been more present the closer it came to launch date. A full team briefing, the last one before mission go time, meant he'd have to deal with *her* today.

In the same too-low-to-the-ground black leather chair outside the chairperson's office, Marc waited. An equally impressive door opposite Vescovi's opened to the lioness's cage. The man inching through it was no lion tamer. The long desk and high-backed leather chair looked small across the white tile floor. Keeping to her pattern, she stood as a statue of intimidation leaning against the desk. Toned stanchions climbed from red high heels, tucked under her black leather skirt.

Focus, Marc.

"Marc. Thank you for coming. Always a pleasure to see you."

His legs carried him anxiously across the obnoxiously oversized office.

"SCL. The pleasure is mine." It wasn't.

"You're not a good liar. I know you don't like me, and this is the last place you wish to be. Few people like me; it comes with the job. But, Marc, let me assure you. I'm very, very... *effective*."

Marc cemented his eyes to hers. Like a NASCAR driver, he had to weave around her innuendo and balance resisting her with not getting himself fired for sexual harassment. He'd heard the stories. Every man in his platoon feared this woman. He'd seen the most hardened of soldiers reduced to pubescent schoolboys, sweaty nervous wrecks in front of the prettiest girl in school, one grade older.

Marc didn't consider Roberta Hillthorpe the most gorgeous creature he'd ever seen. That always would be Casey. Yet to this mere human with functioning eyeballs, she looked as appealing as she obviously saw herself. Seductive. Anyone could see why so many men melted to goo before her, and he'd be no exception. His anxiety expelled itself as sweat on his brow when she asked him to take *her* seat, the only one in the room.

He sat in the crimson leather chair, a comfortable height for an adult human. The SCL scooted onto the desk and swiveled around to dangle her legs over his side, crossed at the knee. Her foot brushed his thigh. She crossed way over the line. Marc needed to bite his tongue and endure this. He considered all her previous provocations traps. Today, he couldn't be sure of anything.

"Marc. I'm worried. This is our most important mission. You know that. Operation Needle Prick must succeed."

"Of course, SCL. We've been over this. I never fail, and my team is the best. We're ready. We won't let you down."

"Let *me* down? Funny you should phrase it that way." Her bend and deliberately missed buttons left little to Marc's imagination. And the reality didn't disappoint it either. A war erupted inside him, the primal clawing its way up, the rest of him struggling to keep it at bay. He wiped away the image his mind showed him of what the animal part of him very much wanted to do. Behind closed eyes he saw Casey's radiant smile.

"Ma'am," he said in a throaty voice. "Could we discuss the briefing for the mission? And, if you wouldn't mind, maybe you could..." He pointed a finger at her chest and looked her in the eye with a wide grin. "Put those away, please." Marc's careful playfulness diffused the situation. He'd not get escorted out of the building by security. Not today, at least.

"You're a funny guy, Marc." Hillthorpe straightened her posture. "I can tell I had you... But I had a feeling about you."

"So... I passed some sorta test?"

"You've heard the rumors, I'm sure. I like that people hear them. But as most rumors go, there's a bit of... hyperbole. I've never advanced or hindered anyone's career by such means. No, Marc, not a test."

"What, then?"

"I love power. You already think that, and you're right. It's not like I try to hide it at all. I've had this power—" Acting as both salesperson and floor model, she waved her hand over her torso. "—far longer than my political influence. And, Marc, I use both as I see fit to get what I want."

"Which is?"

"Usually more power. You're a troubled man. I know your history. The pain of losing your second and the tragic situation at home. And look at you, so strong and together. You're unlike anyone I've ever met. You've resisted me, but I could read you, you know. What a part of you wanted to do to me. And, Marc, that's what this was. If you made a move, if you *make* a move... the offer stands."

"*Oh*. Well, you're full of surprises, gotta give you that."

"I can imagine how difficult this has been on your marriage. If you'd like a proper send-off, I'll keep the offer on the table right up to the launch. I'll be here day *and night* until then."

"Most generous." He knew he shouldn't have gone with a teasing intonation. He didn't want to convey he'd ever consider it. A wash of guilt swept through him because he did. He was. If not for the night with his beloved Casey, he questioned if he'd have been able to rally the resistance.

"I like to take care of my team. Oh, wait. I'm not saying I offer this to everyone. I'm not *that* bad, Marc. This is a 'your eyes only' deal, top-level clearance."

"Understood, Madam SCL." He offered the added formality to restore a measure of professionalism to the room.

"If there was any sort of test in there, you showed me how resistant you are. Loyalty to your wife, to the operation, to the UGA? I don't know. Don't care. But I need that same level of willpower on the mission, Marc."

"I don't follow. You're not planning on coming, are you?" He smirked at her, settling a little more into himself.

"No. But you're taking Kat. You know her history. She still wears her ring, but it's two years now. *You* wanted her on this mission. You've seen her—makes me jealous—so you know my concerns. Two great-looking emotional wrecks on a long assignment in a strange place. And don't think I don't know about you and Sharon. And you've got her on the operation as well. It's like I'm sending you off with your own harem."

An uneasiness stiffened Marc. *How does she know about me and Sharon? What does she think happened?*

"No need to worry, SCL."

"Let's hope not. And Kat? She's already chummy with you. She's a real extravert, you know. Friendly, playful. Marc.... if you break her heart or hurt her, I promise I will end you." She patted his knee, stood, and finally moved away from him, allowing his escape from the chair. Marc didn't hesitate to exit when dismissed. Release came like liberation from a POW camp after being interrogated and tortured. He may have preferred that to whatever he just experienced.

After a cold shower, Marc joined the team as they sat through the last history lesson about Idyllium. The most useful parts came in learning how to dress and act to blend in. Some boring highlights of the social, political, and economic systems came before another crash course on how they put environmental preservation over technological advances and commercialism. It disturbed Marc when they presented sharing some of their own advances—which contributed to ruining their planet—as a positive contribution they'd make to the other side.

Roberta Hillthorpe entered to share key details on Operation Rebar. Its progress in eroding each of the aspects of GB and its society from the inside out drew a smile on her face. On schedule, it should unravel as Operation Needle Prick, Marc's mission, got underway. The crafty woman omitted any mention of the four nukes and the millions they would kill from the report.

Technical training followed lunch. With the team issued upgraded bio-pads, they received instruction on the new features. "Without these, you can't come home." The ominous warning came with notice that they'd take two spares for their team of six. While Kat got some system operator training on the devices,

Sharon showed Marc the basic functions and setup and teardown of the environmental scanners.

Sharon trotted off to another meeting with people who understood her science lingo. The security guys had specific training to complete their day, and Marc got a lesson in comms gear from Kat. As the operation's captain, it fell on him to know how to operate all mission-critical equipment. As a backup to the ones expert in using it, he only needed to reach adequacy.

To get it off his chest—boiling and ready to pop from holding it in—Marc took a risk. The SCL considered Kat a friend, but exactly how close, he wasn't sure. Caution to the wind, he told her of the bizarre meeting he'd had with Hillthorpe that morning. Kat's face showed no surprise at all. Roberta, as Kat called her, had told her of the carnal attraction she had toward Marc.

"So, you think *she's serious* about her offer?"

"If she said it, she meant it. And yeah. With *you*, yeah."

"Huh." Marc's bottom lip pushed the upper into an arch.

"Interested? You're not... Are you?"

"No. Of course not. Don't know how to read that confounding woman, is all. And things are good with Casey now."

"*Now?* Has there been trouble?"

"Sick-kid stuff. But we're good. So, I'd never."

"You're a good man Marc. I think Roberta just wanted to be sure of it. I saw it in your eyes from the first time we met."

"Before this mission, I might have accepted that as true."

19 | Idyllium Mission: Day 2

In the flat glass surface stood an image of a woman unsure of herself for the first time in her life. Not a fan of makeup and unaccustomed to painting her face with it, Sharon had applied it for her. A clown looked back at her, not the glamorous distraction they needed her to be. Puckered lips showed a subtle deepening of their natural pinkness, and black eyeliner electrified the blue hue of her irises. If Kat could be thankful for anything she saw in the mirror, it was how little of the horrid stuff Sharon applied.

She checked the drape and movement of the thin-strapped black dress. Kat needed to be the distraction, not the evening's floor show. Poses in the full-length mirror ensured the plunging neckline teased enough to trap the observer in a state of eager anticipation. The elegant length draped long, with a front slit reaching the top of her upper left thigh. Like a revered Diva stepping from the curtain as High Priestess Norma in Bellini's famous opera, each step exhibited her toned leg.

"You look absolutely amazing." Sharon peered from behind her in the luxurious Hotel New Renaissance room they shared.

"Thanks. Not sure about the makeup. I hate wearing it."

"Your face is gorgeous. But believe me... in that dress you're *almost* wearing... guys won't be looking at your face."

"Stop it." Kat blushed and offered a humble snicker.

"Seriously. It's obvious why *I'm* on comms tonight. I couldn't fill that dress like you."

"*Sharon*. You're embarrassing me."

"*That's* embarrassing? The captain and I walked in on you stark naked, and it didn't daunt you. Now you're covered, mostly, and you're embarrassed? I mean, I'd be beyond uncomfortable in that wee dress, sure, but for a whole other reason. I'd look like a tomboy playing dress-up."

"Sharon, no. You're so beautiful. So toned and fit."

"Brawny, you mean. It's called an *athletic physique*." A posh accent came with a joyous smile.

"To me, you're stunning. I'm jealous of your hair, actually."

"Irish red. What can I say? Runs in the family. But you... not a man on Idyllium could resist you in that dress. I just hope you're not too much of a distraction to the captain."

"Well, as you said... he's seen it all already."

The two shared a laugh that carried some of the tension from Kat's shoulders as it left the room. Kateryna's nerves stretched miles beyond uncomfortable about the evening. She had tried to convince Marc she needed to work comms and how Sharon would be a terrific distraction. No words could convince him. He insisted Kat needed to be the delicious eye candy she hated to be, and she saw his point in her reflection. He needed to move unencumbered. Less subtle ways of causing distractions would attract too much attention.

"*Whoa*." Marc entered to review the plan and be sure Sharon had learned how to use the comms equipment. He couldn't do more than stand frozen with his jaw hung open under saucer eyes.

"Looks like operation distraction is ready for action." Sharon smiled. "Hey, that rhymed."

"You look... wow."

"Thank you. I hope I'm up for this. I'm not the spy type. Not even a field agent. Actually, I'm not even an agent."

Marc's head shook as if someone had pressed a slow-motion button. "You'll be fine. I need you to be charming, and I know you know how. And you gotta be gorgeous. There's no way you cannot be gorgeous in that. You'll do great."

"You clean up nice yourself." Kat reached for the familiarity of the banter. Anything to stave off the anxiety twisting in her intestines.

"What? This old thing?" Marc played along. Or he could have been far less nervous about the evening.

To Kat, Marc looked amazing in a tux. The soldier-turned-secret agent man, a super-spy about to infiltrate the gala on a top-secret mission. It had all the excitement of a spy thriller film, one she wished to be watching rather than starring in herself.

"I guess that makes me your Bond girl?" She offered a sultry giggle and a devilish smile. "Sorry. I'm trying to get into character."

"All right, you two. I'd say get a room, but we're in one. And, Captain, you've got a wife and kid, big guy. And we're on a hugely important mission here, and she's the distraction for everyone. Everyone. But. You." As if calling an elevator, Sharon jabbed her index finger into Marc's chest on each word.

"Yes, ma'am. No funny business, ma'am." Marc offered a silly salute that made Kat giggle. She considered they all needed a little levity to calm the nerves for the mission. When he asked her to remove the ring, an emptiness overtook her. He was correct, of course, and for the first time since her wedding day, she slipped it off her finger and tied it under her wrist corsage, unable to consider leaving it behind.

Muffled sounds bled in through the wall. It was not a cheap, thin-walled hotel, but still, the elevated voices vibrated through. Frank and Saul volleyed back and forth in a heated argument in the next room. The walls did their job too well, only letting the variance in tone tell the ears which man shouted. Greedily, the leaves embossed in the steel-gray wallcovering gobbled up the words.

Kat's made-up face stiffened. "Marc. Since we started this mission, I've been on board with our objectives. I know Sharon is too, and we've brought Frank up to speed on the new... parameters, you called it. I think he's good."

"He'll do whatever you ask, Kateryna. And he's not even seen you in that dress."

"Stop. He's been so sweet. And I think he understands what we're doing here. I mean, it's the prime minister, for goodness' sake. But I'm worried about Saul."

"We all are. I'm keeping an eye on him."

"Sure, Captain. Except you and Kateryna are leaving now, and I got him and Frank here with me."

"Don't worry, Sharon. Saul's a pro if nothing else. He'll be here until we need our secure exit from the summit. Then Corporal Jones will stay here with you. Frank's a good man. Oh, we gotta go."

An extended elbow invited Kat to latch onto Marc and begin her role as the trophy girl of the highly decorated General Martin Wallace. She had to hope their fake credentials justified the price, though she doubted the source's reliability. Not a spy, not even a government agent, Kat didn't expect a crucial military operation to rely on shady characters for such important details. Too late for second guesses, off they went, walking the red carpet through a sea of flashbulbs with forged ident-cards and event passes as their lifejackets.

The time came to test the dress and the alluring woman under it. The young man stood tall, his back straight as a board. A disciplined soldier, he checked the credentials at the main entrance like a doorman. Marc prodded Kat a half step ahead of himself, being sure the warrior playing host would take in the full effect. As hoped, his eyes walked all over her, lingering on her chest like a hungry newborn begging for its next meal. He glanced over their credentials perfunctorily.

"Welcome, ma'am. General Wallace, sir."

They entered the Grand Hall.

"We're in." Marc whispered the words but not to Kat.

Another voice blew like a gentle breeze in her ear, as clear as if she stood beside them. The earpiece sent Sharon's voice as electrical impulses directly into the auditory nerve. She received their audio on open feed and could listen to them speak to her in a low voice and reply so only they could hear. The virtually undetectable device made that ear a little deaf to local sound.

"Copy that. Good work, you two."

Glancing down at the assets that got them through, Marc whispered, "She means *you* two." A light slap on the arm and a gleaming smile were Kat's reply to his boyish smirk. The chuckle in her ear said Sharon got the less-than-tasteful joke as well.

Widened eyes scanned the open reception area with childish wonder, igniting a mental debate. Kat considered whether the décor was overly elaborate or just extravagant enough to fit the occasion while being tasteful. The high cathedral ceiling gave the space an elevation beyond its physical boundaries. Stalwart columns of glossy marble rose from the floor to support the celestial canopy. Silvery gray strands ornamented the cream-colored pillars like streaks of lightning twining their way upward. Pulling her eyes from them, Kat next admired the priceless works of art lining the walls. Spectacular original paintings, marble sculptures, and dazzling crystal glasswork.

"Breathtaking," she said to the grandeur.

"You certainly are." Kat's curious gaze found the voice's lips on the prime minister of Greater Britannia. He stood beside her with a kind smile.

"Oh! Mister Prime Minister. Pleasure."

"The pleasure is mine, I assure you. And who's this with you? Few here are unknown to me." His security fanned out behind him like a macabre peacock with feathers of black.

"This is Mar—um, I mean, General Martin Wallace." Kat's quick catch of her tongue substantiated Marc's rationale for telling her to use Martin as his alter ego. It gave her that split-second to correct her lips and introduce him properly.

"An honor, Mister Prime Minister, sir." Marc extended his hand, but the security gorilla beside the PM flashed his palm to stop him.

They had not imagined getting this close. The distraction made for a powerful attraction too. The PM carried himself as a distinguished man of approximately sixty years. Kat considered this well-kept and proper Alistair Burgess, a widower, to be quite intriguing.

As he reached for Kat's hand, his human shield constricted but allowed it. He raised her hand slowly and bent to lay a gentle kiss over the soft skin then stretched up straight.

"I do hope you'll join me for a private reception after the summit. Both of you, of course, General."

"We'd be honored, sir," Marc replied.

"And *that's* why I'm on comms." Sharon's whisper in their ears drew a smile on Marc's face.

Kat directed hers at the PM.

The *peacock* ushered Prime Minister Burgess away as crowds flocked around him. While Marc and Kat stood where they were, Kat's eyes accompanied the PM. She found him elegant, charming, and much more striking in person than she had imagined.

"Anything on DLD?"

Marc's question puzzled Kat. She had worked with distance listening devices and showed Sharon how they worked. With her bio-pad cleverly hidden under her wrist corsage, she dared not risk using it herself. It was why they kept an open channel to Sharon. Kat thought, *The PM was distracted by me, but it's supposed to be one-way.*

"Normal chatter, sir. I've scanned UHF bands as well. The most threatening conversation I heard was Minister Whitehead being scolded by his wife for how he was looking at a certain woman in a black dress talking to the PM. Here's an interesting side note: that woman in the black dress didn't have red hair." Had their earpieces not had autoadjusting volume, Sharon's laughter would have pained their inner ears.

The waitstaff began their rounds with gold-plated trays of drinks and appetizers. The shrimp crackers took Kat to Okinawa for a brief mental revisit.

"Sounds like you're having a grand time there, hobnobbing and enjoying champagne and hors d'oeuvres. Meanwhile, me and Frank here got pizza from room service and warm beers."

After taking another sip of his champagne, Marc grinned. "Hey, we need to blend in." He stopped at two measly sips, so Kat did the same, figuring they needed to stay alert.

"You and Frank? Where's Saul?"

"Stormed out after he and Frank quit yelling at each other. Said he was going to scope your exit."

"A bit early, but okay. We'll need that secure exit."

"Roger that, Captain. We'll be right here. Shout if you need me. Well, whisper, I guess."

Waiters dealt the dinner plates like cards over the sea of round tables in the Grand Dining Hall. Guests sat six around a gold tablecloth. Marc tried to learn about their tablemates without looking like he was trying to learn about them. *He'd make a pretty good Double-O Seven,* Kat thought. Marc's attention soon fixed on the reporter, Belinda Mayers, whom he had purposely sat beside. *He's no cheater and loves his wife, but he sure knows how to James Bond-schmooze all the pretty ladies.*

While they enjoyed their branzino with potatoes, green beans, and rice, Marc scanned the room. His eyes intensified, as if reading a file beside each of the thousand faces of the unknown, like some high-tech surveillance in a spy thriller. It dawned on Kat how often the evening's escapade brought her mind to spy thrillers.

I really am a Bond girl, she concluded.

20 | Earth:
3 Days to Crossover

His kid brother was all the family Saul had, all he needed. They hadn't shared an ideal childhood. A war hero, their father's platoon had ended a five-month micro-civil war that had waged over seven states amassing a body count topping six million. Their dad became a casualty of the deescalation, remembered as a fallen hero with honors. But memories didn't toss a ball with his sons, teach them to ride a bicycle, or shape them into honorable men.

Bubba never met his father. He almost never met the world. Pregnant with Saul's soon-to-be baby brother, their mother died from the inside out when a soldier and army chaplain stood on the other side of the door that opened to the picture haunting the nightmares of every soldier's wife. To safeguard the fetus she nearly lost, doctors confined her to bed rest. She only left the house once in three months, to attend her husband's gloriously somber military funeral. Her depression kept her in that bed long after Bubba's cesarean delivery.

At four and a half, Saul had received military-sponsored grief counseling from a child psychologist. It ended when he turned six and stopped sitting on the stairs staring at the front door. Gamma Mimi raised Bubba and cared for Saul. Her daughter had withered into a dehydrated version of herself—a fiery orange autumn leaf that accepted the change of season, let go of life, and fell to the ground to disintegrate.

"A war hero's widow, Charlotte Maryjane Mullins, was laid to rest at the tender age of thirty-six. She is survived by her two sons, Saul Mullins, nine years of age, and Timothy (Bubba) Mullins, three years of age."

A summary of a life in two sentences. Data-net search results for "Charlotte Maryjane Mullins" found little more than that. To her boys, the words were inadequate. Saul tortured himself every few months with that search entry. Tears summoned by the words dropped more for Bubba, who had never known her as Saul did. Never had he seen the strong woman, the joyful mother, the loving wife. The woman who watched her darling boys being raised by their grandmother had been none of those. The last strength she mustered raised pills and a water glass to her mouth.

Gamma Mimi did her best—a mess of grieving herself—to give the boys a decent upbringing but could only do so much. From the fragile age of nine, Saul took the weighty job of being the man of the house and father figure to his kid brother. Saul taught Bubba how to fish, to swim, and to tie the laces on his shoes. How he regretted not showing him how to ride a bike. They couldn't afford one, and the Earthwide outdoor time allowance had been reduced.

Throughout adolescence and into adulthood, Saul and Bubba stood side by side against the world. They did everything together. Often, that meant Bubba getting into things at too early an age. To take the blame and punishment for his brother, Saul once confessed to stealing a six-pack of what he called "the good beer" from the store at the junction of Johnson and Bells Ferry. Overall, Saul tried to be an exemplary role model and keep himself out of trouble, except when he took the heat for Bubba.

That had to stop when Saul turned eighteen, old enough to be legally viewed and prosecuted as an adult—and get a record. Letting Bubba take the fall for possession of synthetic THC4, a manufactured tetrahydrocannabinol inhalant, proved good for both. Though it would take Bubba a while to see it that way.

The big brother's protective care continued from a distance when Saul left for basic training. To get his brother enlisted at a younger age—nineteen being the minimum—Saul used quickly made connections with a certain General William Brady. The general had aligned himself with a rising UGA political force with great pull with the then seated SCL. (With her looks and drive, Saul had imagined Roberta Hillthorpe would go far.) Whatever it took, Saul would always be there for his baby brother, even if that meant sucking up to a politician.

He considered it his responsibility as the older brother.

Memories scrolling in a slideshow halted abruptly when "the great Captain Marc Sanders" entered the pub and strolled over. Ever prompt—meaning earlier than expected—Saul had a head start in the empty pint glass being lovingly fondled in his hands. He only accepted the invitation for a drink because of its imagined conclusion, one Saul very much wanted to reach sooner than later. Marc slid onto the bench on the opposite side of the tiny booth for two.

Saul knew the pub well. Always in military mode, he had staked the place out thirty minutes ahead of their appointment. Saul raised two fingers to the barkeep.

"Hey Saul. Thanks for agreeing to meet me."

"Mm hm." The *bad kind* of country music soiling Saul's ears now became as pleasant to them as his favorite Willie Nelson song. Compared to Marc's feigned politeness, a hollering baby would have also.

"Sorry it took so long. Should have done it sooner."

"You're a busy man."

"Yeah. This mission is huge, massively important. And you know about my daughter's condition. I've had to leave her a lot for this operation. But it's possible this is how I save her."

"Bit of a savior complex you got there, Captain. But you know what they say—I guess you say it now too—you can't save'em all."

"Look. This isn't easy for either of us. I get that. I've got no clue why they put us together on this mission. *This* operation, of all things. I've been chewed up and spat out twice in two days by the SCL about the importance of it."

"Let me ask you this, Marc. You mind… if I call you Marc? Good." He didn't wait for a reply. "Knowing what you do about this operation, would you want anyone else leading it in your place?"

"Well… no. It's too important."

"So no one in the entire UGA, no other Marine, is qualified as you to lead the team?"

A waitress delivered two pints to the table. Marc downed a gulp then took another before replying.

"I'm not… Look. Yeah, actually. I think my record says the same. It's why the chairperson asked for me."

"No need to get all defensive, Marc. I'd normally turn down an assignment with you, naturally. Haven't had to yet. Seems someone knew better than to put us together before now. But if you and me got anything in common, it's that I wouldn't let anyone else do my job on this op either."

"See. And when I came in here, I thought we wouldn't agree on anything. And look at us. Hitting it off already." Marc smiled as if he thought himself funny and sipped his beer.

"So let's talk about why we're here. You mentioned your impeccable service record. I should say, *near* impeccable."

"Right. That 'near' part's what I wanted to talk about."

"Outside of the mission, that's all we got together, ain't it?"

"Look, Saul. I tried to talk to you… then. And security had to pull you off me. I tried a few times after, but you shunned me."

"Had nothing to say to you. Didn't want to hear anything you felt the need to say to me. And I'm not here now to offer a way out, to appease your conscience. If you got one."

"I'm not asking forgiveness. I'm just trying to explain so you understand what happened. And we can move on."

"Move on? Think I should tell you to 'move on' when your little girl finally kicks it? Is that what you tell someone?" Saul's raised voice turned some heads.

"Let's leave my family out of this. That's low, even for you. I meant *we* need to move on, to work together on this op."

"Working together ain't a problem for me. But if you got a problem with it, by all means, resign. And we can't exactly leave your family out of it. At least not Casey."

"*Casey?*"

"See, Marc... You got no idea what I know. Bubba and I were close. You knew that much. But you still can't see below the surface."

"What are you on about, Saul?"

"After he saved your career, fixed your piss-poor operation plans, you sucked my baby brother into your family. *Uncle Tim*, your girl called him."

"She loved him. We all did."

"Maybe... *your wife* a little more?" He offered a wink.

"*What?*"

"I see below the surface, Marc. Bubba, Uncle Tim, nailed your wife in your own home." When Marc's jaw dropped, it pulled the flesh of fire-red cheeks taut. "Yeah, I know about that. Told you Bubba and I were close. Can't imagine how having a younger, stronger, virile guy giving it to your wife must have felt. How you must have hated him for it. Tell me, Marc. Does the image of him riding your babe wife still come to mind? You gotta wonder who she preferred, right?"

As he wiped the trickle of blood from the corner of his lips, Saul had done it, achieved the result he imagined, hoped to get. This was the only reason he agreed to drinks. After establishing the off-duty posture, he had gotten Marc to throw the first punch. Saul's *restraints* dissolved.

Marc's head jolted back from the force behind Saul's punch. Before he could bring it back to level, Saul stood over the table, launching a volley of fists. Marc took one to the eye before his forearms became a defensive bulwark for his face.

When he tried to stand with Saul pushing down on him, Marc rolled onto the floor, pulling his teammate and bar brawl opponent with him. A couple at the table beside them leapt off their chairs as their table toppled—their drinks reduced to pieces of shattered glass in overpriced puddles on the floor. Brutally, the men rolled, grunted, and each took blows to the abdomen.

The bouncer, a man equal to the rumbling duo in height and a match for their combined girth, broke up the fight, pulling the two apart by their shirt collars. He kindly took their payment before tossing them onto the pavement outside. The two sat, with Marc leaning against the front wheel of a late-model pickup whose owner had retrofitted it to electric. Saul propped himself to his knees and sat facing him. Both bruised and bloodied, they panted deeply. Saul's lungs rejected the inhaled air like Gamma Mimi's cigarette smoke. Every breath clamped his chest.

"We done?" Marc spoke in a hoarse voice.

"Don't think this'll ever be over."

"Maybe the hitting-each-other-in-the-face part?"

Blood from his lower lip stained the back of Saul's hand. "Yeah. I'm done for today."

"For today? That's promising." Marc's reach for a humorous tone did nothing to settle Saul.

"Was some timing, though."

"What was? What timing?"

"You finding out about Bubba and your wife. Then... on the *very next mission* you're on together, he's killed in action. Only one of your entire platoon."

"What are you implying, Saul?"

"Ain't implying. Pretty sure I just said it plainly."

"*Wait a minute*. Look, if he told you everything, he told you I forgave them both. Both were drunk, and Casey... Well, back then, she wasn't herself. Besides, he died months after."

"On the *first* mission you did together."

"Saul. I don't suppose there's any way I'll ever convince you otherwise, but I loved Tim. After that... incident, we stayed close, him and me. I'm not saying it's the same, but it felt like I lost a brother too."

"But you didn't. I did. He was all I had in the world. And my responsibility."

"He was a grown man. It's a tragic shame what happened. But it was no one's fault."

Under the shadow of the tavern's awning, a crooked sneer adorned Saul's face. He accomplished something he'd been waiting months to do and had nothing left to say. Running on rage-fueled adrenaline, he could have kept going until Marc was dead or close to it. A hint of gratitude sprouted for the bouncer ending the fight. He prevented Saul from being kicked off the operation to rot in a military prison for the rest of his days—the likely outcome had he continued.

Saul's smirk stretched into a smile and his eyes glinted through the swelling as he looked in the rearview mirror. A home med-kit would erase any evidence of the altercation.

There'll be an opening on the mission, he considered on the drive back to town.

21 | Idyllium Mission: Day 2

SEMPER FIDELIS, COMMONLY SAID *Semper Fi* in the corps, was the motto of every marine. Frank believed in it as "an eternal and collective commitment to the success of our battles, the progress of our nation, and the steadfast loyalty to the fellow marines we fight alongside." Every marine from recruit to *poolee* to *boot* had the concept drilled into their brain. It evoked camaraderie, unity, and respect among soldiers. It was supposed to, anyway.

Saul was different. Marc once referred to him as "a special kind of animal." Frank had his issues with the guy, but found him to be an excellent commander, loyal to the mission, and not one to permit failure. Throughout his career, Saul had had an excellent service record. No one questioned his place on the team, leading the security detail for such an important operation. That Saul and Marc had bigger problems caused some concern, but Frank trusted both men's allegiance and loyalty to the mission.

Then the parameters changed.

Mission planning spanned close to two years. Frank had spent two months training with a select few of the best the Corps had to offer—plus a civilian and a part-time science officer. The mission changed on the fly, in the field. A bad omen for a soldier, it signaled things were not going according to plan, and thinking of it made Frank rub his hands together. Especially that the civvy and the scientist were the ones to inform him of the change. Under any mission-typical circumstance that would be most peculiar.

Part of the last-minute "audible" change in game plan had Frank remain with Sharon while Saul secured the exit for Marc and Kat. That part seemed to infuriate Saul, and Frank happened to be in the room with him when he blew. Saul wore the rank of commander, a seasoned soldier put in charge of the security detail. To receive change-of-plans notification from his subordinate surely hit every kind of wrong chord, and Saul left no doubt in Frank's mind how he felt about it.

"There was no reasoning with him. I've seen him upset, even question orders—that he carried out anyway—and talk badly about superior officers. But this was on another level."

"He's a bit of a jerk, Frank." Huddled over the comms unit, Sharon split her attention. "Why do you think the captain put him on guarding the exit door instead of being in the summit with him and Kat?"

"Cap doesn't trust him."

"Neither do I. And I think he'd be... *resistant* to the adjusted parameters. We need this to go right this evening."

"Yeah, but Saul is—"

Sharon's shush gesture stifled Frank's words as she fiddled with the device.

"No, Captain. I'm almost positive she came alone this evening." Sharon lifted the LCD display of the comms unit and began pecking at it like a hungry chicken. "Roger that. I'll check."

"What's up?"

"The captain's real interested in that reporter, Belinda Mayers."

"What? Having Kat at his side's not enough for him?"

"Easy, tiger. Don't get your whiskers in a knot. We need to know as much as we can about her financial news updates. She likely knows a wee bit more than she says on air. The captain's been schmoozing her up and pulling info from her throughout the dinner."

"Like what? What are you hearing?" Frank tried to slay the green monster ravaging his insides. Marc's flirtatious interactions with Kat made it a hard enough battle. Now, it clawed at the reporter Frank hadn't met. And her magnetic pull took Marc's attention off Kat, so why did that bother him? It made no sense Frank's musings could find. Flames stirred by emotion rarely did in his experience.

"There've been more bankruptcies and corporation closures than she reported. And she told him there has been a response by the Ministry of Finance, but it was indifferent at best. Said to wait it out, it would pass. That 'nothing to worry about' nonsense she spoke about, only more worrisome. She's quite talkative."

"And she's spilling that over the table? I'm surprised." Frank would have expected her to be tight-lipped on such an enormous story, especially as she had the scoop and didn't seem like one to share that spotlight. He considered if he had projected a glory-hungry, story-hoarding TV journalist stereotype on a woman he didn't know.

"No, just to Marc. She's speaking softly, but I can hear everything she's saying clearly. This comms kit is amazing."

"But Kat's the comms expert, why she's on the team. So how come *you're* working comms and she's in there? I'd have thought you'd be with the cap." Frank paused, his imagination directing his every thought, every word. "And I'd be here with Kat."

"Oh, right. You didn't see the wee dress. Just as well, stud muffin, or you'd be standing in a cold shower all night. She's proving to be quite the distraction in there. Just what the captain needs."

"Oh." Frank could say nothing more.

"Sounds like dinner's about done. They'll move them to the conference room for the PM's speech. This is do-or-die time for him and Kateryna."

"Yeah. The die part's for the PM."

"Exactly. A lot's at stake, and too much can go wrong if there's any slip-up. Glad to have you on board for this. But what do you know about Saul securing an exit? I'd think getting in was the hard part, not getting out. Of course, entering was a breeze for them, thanks to the magic of the black dress and Kat's décolletage."

"Her deck-ol-*what?*"

"The way that dress introduces the twins." Sharon's laughter lined the room, and Frank felt the warmth of blood rushing into his cheeks.

He shook his head to focus. "Well, when things start going down, the PM's security will lock the place tight. No one in *or out*. The cap and Kat will get caught in there with no way out, no matter how much of her chest she flashes anyone."

"Let's hope Saul's got this then."

"I've never known him to not accomplish the mission. He's a stubborn old coot, but he gets the job done."

"We were on an op together once." Sharon spoke with a distant voice, like telling a story of ancient history rather than something she had experienced. "My longest field assignment, and *he* had to be there. All of us, the entire team, shared one apartment. Me and a bunch of guys. Most were fine, but that was a bit too much Saul Mullins for me."

"Mal was on that one. I remember. That's when he fell for you... if you ask me."

"Please, Frank. I can't talk about it."

"Sorry. That was insensitive."

"No. It's just that I wish... So much wasted time. Like all those weeks together, and I barely spoke to him, didn't even see it. All the other guys did, so it must've been obvious. They teased him about it, too, but I was oblivious."

"He's been crushing on you since before that. But that's when it matured into more. I think... he's got great taste."

"That's sweet."

"How long before they're in position?"

"Hard to say. It sounds like they're still at the dinner table, having dessert and coffee. Marc's still hitting up pretty reporter lady for info. She must be into him, leaking information like a sieve the way she is."

"And he's supposedly there with Kat. I'd think she'd consider him taken and not fall for his... *charm*." Frank used air quotes to question said charm.

"Your little man brain doesn't think like a woman's. See, hot reporter lady knows she's hot, right? Made her career on it along with her journalistic talents. She sees a good-looking guy like the captain with someone gorgeous as Kateryna, and it's war time. Him giving her that attention is like a victory. It's a triumph for her to steal his interest from a looker like Kat—to bolster her already massive ego. I mean... Look. If I stood in the same room as Kateryna, and someone looked at me?"

"Wow, Sharon. I didn't think you were so superficial. Doesn't seem a 'modern woman' thing, caring so much about how men look at you. I'd be yelled at if I had assumed that and been told I was being archaic or something."

"It *is* superficial. But just because you don't let something define you doesn't mean it can't feel good to be admired for it."

"Fair point."

"Kateryna's a perfect example. She's playing the part of the trophy wife, there for one reason. But she hates it, hates the makeup I put on her. That is one seriously accomplished woman who is so much more than a pretty face. But don't think for a second she's not flattered by all the attention. A modern woman can be both, you know."

"Another fair point. She's obviously a great distraction. We gotta hope the cap is up for his next part. My goodness, an *assassination*."

Frank tried to play it cool, but those weren't the steel nerves of a marine twined around his flesh, itching under his skin. He knew Marc was good, the best at what he did. But this mission had taken everyone far from normal and deep into unfamiliar territory. No amount of preparation could have equaled the challenge of fighting a covert war between parallel worlds. Frank couldn't be sure which side played the good guys and sometimes questioned his mission objectives, old and new.

"The captain's the best. He doesn't know how to fail." Sharon touched her ear. "Oh... I think they're moving now."

22 | Earth:
2 Days to Crossover

A PERVERSE IRONY. Marc contemplated how a clean, healthy environment would be unwelcoming to the human form so far removed from such a climate. *How far we have fallen.* While the bodies of those living in the radiation-saturated aftereffects of the so-called nuclear incidents hadn't fully acclimated to Earth's failed environment, they had adapted.

Sharon likened it to a newborn being fed healthy foods its body had not developed the ability to digest and process. The effects of the clean environment ranged from pleuritic chest pain and coughing to dyspnea secondary to tracheobronchitis and absorptive atelectasis. Symptoms could lead to pulmonary edema or oxygen toxicity. While Marc didn't get all the jargon, he understood it would be bad. The good interested him more. He had learned the same pristine ecosystem of Idyllium would have the opposite effect on his Jewel—the only part of the explanation that mattered.

All mission participants would have the booster shot of chemicals injected the day of the crossover. With top physical form a prerequisite, every day included a rigorous workout for the entire team. Kat expressed her frustration as it pulled her away from her office for close to two hours every morning. From Frank's easy-to-read face, those hours having Kat around made his day.

Sharon looked amazingly fit and strong as an ox—a competitor to the men in all categories but heavy lifting. Marc marveled at her stamina almost as much as Mal's performance. Whatever he pumped into his system to control his illness, he had become a beast. Not as bulky as Saul, Marc, or even Frank, yet he pressed the most weight of the team. Mal showed little to no fatigue by the end of the ninety-minute workout.

"Malcom Holland, you impressive stallion you." The SCL observed some of the daily sessions for the last days ahead of launch. Roberta Hillthorpe told Marc she'd be on campus every day and she kept her word. Of course, he didn't think that meant joining their workouts.

"SCL. Th-th-thank you. Gotta be ready for the mission."

"You all look in top shape. Especially you, Marc." Her wink to remind him of her offer didn't try to hide itself from the team. She made no effort to overturn her reputation. *Perhaps she gets off on reinforcing it in front of everyone*, Marc assumed.

"As you can see, the team is ready."

"Yes. And you got some fine specimens of men and women here."

Malcom fixed his attention on Sharon. Seeing them reminded Marc of his own near fall from morality at one of the lowest points of his life. As he observed Mal pining over her, Marc considered the transgression he narrowly avoided wasn't solely because of her happening to be there. He found Sharon to be rather lovely.

"You should join us on the mission, Roberta." Shock covered Marc's face until Kat winked over her own words.

"Having you and Sharon is more than enough temptation for these fine, strapping men to endure."

The fitness routine having run its course, the men and women of the team retired to their locker rooms for showers. When Marc stepped into the row of tall, narrow blue lockers to dress, the presence of the SCL wearing a seductively sinister smile didn't surprise him. He had prepared for it by showering under a flow of cold water. Her skin glistened under drops of perspiration. Once again, Marc found resisting her a more difficult struggle than he cared to admit. In haste, he flung the thin metal door of his locker open. It wobbled and flexed as it groaned in protest at being pushed against its will.

The photo of Casey and Jewel—his daughter in a healthier state in the image than he had seen in too many months—grounded him and deadened the physical drive he had no intention of pursuing. It struggled to be enough to slay the beast but stole its last breath. Perhaps the SCL noticed its passing and mourned the death of the creature she seemed desperate to awaken. Or it may have been the arrival of the guys that leveled her smile into a straight line.

"My, my, my. You men *are* the best of the best."

"That's why we're here." Saul seemed unintimidated by her. He tossed off his towel, opened his locker, and retrieved his clothes with no hurried action or shame. He had been the only one on the team to push back her advances. She did not even try to disguise her enjoyment at watching the fit soldier take his time getting into his clothes. Marc, Mal, and Frank waited for her to leave before freeing themselves of their towels and dressing. It made Marc uneasy to see Saul eyeing up Mal.

"You're even scrawnier than I recall, Mal. And we're supposed to be the fittest we ever been. I got no idea how you got picked for this mission."

"Saul, we're all ready and fit," Marc replied.

"He don't look so. Not to me."

"I'm healthier and st-st-stronger than ever."

"That ain't sayin' much. You've always been weak. I guess the only good thing is that you're likely the same on the other side, so we ain't gotta worry about the you over there."

"If we exist on the other side, we're likely the team we'll go up against. Our doubles over there would be just as invested in the countermission as we are in ours." Marc spewed the logic he didn't quite believe in a failed effort to quell the testosterone-fueled conversation sure to escalate beyond words. The room reeked of its stench.

Saul raised his hands and pushed air to the floor. "Nah. The Malcom over there is most likely a florist or something. Hard to believe how ours ever even got accepted into the Corps."

A blur crossed Marc's vision between Mal and Saul, and the bigger guy's head jerked backward, then reset to level. Mal pulled his fist back and joined a second to it in a defensive posture. The antagonist offered a solitary response: a broad and ominous smile showcasing drips of red over yellowed teeth like a horror film poster.

"Not bad, little man. Harder than I'd've expected. But at least you got some gumption to you. Also more than expected. But hear me. You weren't my choice for this operation or the security detail *I'm* heading. And don't forget that while Marc may have operational control over this mission—for now—I'm the lead on security, and you answer to me."

"Understood, sir." Mal's reply came out shaky. His hands held their cautious position with equal unsteadiness. A slowly exhaled breath allowed Marc's nerves to settle when Saul made it clear he was done.

"Let's just hope you're up for this." Saul swaggered off.

Marc's hand on his shoulder told Mal he could relax his posture. Pale white skin clung to his withdrawn face and the shudder of fear trembled through his fists. Marc worried the poor guy might hyperventilate or faint.

Frank looked puzzled by the altercation. "What was that?"

"Nothing. Just Saul being Saul." Marc saw the need to minimize this or risk having a rift his team couldn't afford as they stepped across the mysterious void between worlds. Too much depended on him, the entire world. His driving force, however, lay in the health and future of his precious Jewel.

"He can be a jerk, sure, Cap. But he's a good soldier."

Mal crossed his arms at Frank's comment, hands still in fists. "Emphasis on the jerk part."

Marc needed to be the leader and settle his men. "Look. He was the SCL's pick, for whatever reason. And yes, Frank, he's a good soldier. We can count on his loyalty to the mission. We just gotta deal with his... um, *personality*."

"Roger, Cap," Frank and Mal said in unison.

As they turned to walk out, Marc grabbed Mal by the arm. Frank's departure gave them privacy. As much as he hated to agree with Saul, he worried about Mal's physical condition. And, as far as Marc could tell, Saul didn't even know about the illness.

"How are you doing?"

"Fine. Saul gets under my skin, but I can handle him."

That's not what Marc had asked, though the answer came as a welcome one. He understood well how dealing with Saul could be a challenging task for anyone.

"Good. We cross over tomorrow, so I'm asking about... you know. How *are* you?"

"I'm fine. As I told you, I'm better than ever on these meds they gave me. I may not last much longer than this op, but I'm at a hundred ten percent for it."

"Well, you did give Saul quite a surprise. He wasn't expecting you to land a solid hit like that. I rather enjoyed the spectacle. But your stamina and endurance are what troubles me, Mal. We've got no idea what these meds are or what they might do. You could grow a second head when we pass the void for all we know."

"Then I'd be twice as useful on Idyllium, Cap."

The shared laugh released the tightness in Marc's neck. He carried too much stress over this operation, but how could he not? The UGA had placed the weight of the world squarely on his shoulders. Marc felt gravity's pull on it increase every minute that drew the mission's relentless approach closer.

"Cap." Mal leaned in to speak to his ears alone. "A buddy of mine's been gone for a few months now. He couldn't say, but I think he may be over there."

"We started sending folks years ago. Not long after we learned how to traverse the void and reach Idyllium in one piece."

"Yeah, but… he said he'd be gone a month. That was near three ago."

"And?"

"Do you know any's gone over…? Any ever come back?"

Part Two

An Assassin's Flame

PART ONE

23 | Idyllium Mission: Day 2

THE PEOPLE OF EARTH needed him to be an assassin. This wouldn't be the first life he had taken, the subtle difference between assassination and combat killing not lost upon him. He needed no mental justification to soothe his moral compass. When ending one life saved millions, he saw no ethical dilemma. Life was simpler when viewed in black and white.

He knew why the SCL had handpicked him to cross over to Idyllium. It was for this moment, unfolding as the prime minister would soon take the stage.

This mission required more than ending the man's life: it had to make an unambiguous statement. The welcome address at the GB World Summit this evening ensured it the world's attention. Falsified credentials and a prototype weapon bio-locked to his DNA would get the job done. His people needed Oliver Nelson, the secretary of state and deputy prime minister, to be in office when it came time to make the tough decisions.

To the focused and determined man, the air tasted uncharacteristically sweet, as if the planet were reminding him of the importance of the op. Occupation of Idyllium, a pristine world with clean air and uncontaminated water. With no radiation and not a single nuclear weapon, it meant a future for the remnant of humanity on Earth.

With careful attention, he watched the seductive woman in the black dress make her moves with the prime minister. As he pulled his gaze from the *distraction,* he had to admit she performed her role well.

While the PM and most of the men and women of any actual power or office enjoyed their dinner in a room of a thousand or so inconsequential people, he made his way.

Stealthily, he moved through the crowd, a waiter to anyone who noticed him. No one of account. Hoisting a gold-plated tray of spent hors d'oeuvres plates and champagne flutes in various degrees of empty, he moved to the kitchen. An unguarded door to the storage area—a service corridor of no importance—would be his access point. A quick check of his wrist pad confirmed a fire evacuation ladder from the multimedia control booth dropped into the utility room at the end of the hall, making it the key to accomplishing his mission.

Eyeing the pâtissier licking his finger in ecstasy over the chocolate cake, he thought, *I might grab me a slice on the way out.* Refocused, he found a woman in a gray military uniform at the door—obstructing passage to his post. *There wasn't supposed to be a guard*, he thought, reviewing the details smuggled to him from the secretary of state's personal assistant.

The cake decorator, a profligately energetic young man, shot the guard a wink and slithered over to her. Like a cobra moving in for the strike, he showed his deadly fangs. Two fingers oozing the succulent muddy sweetness widened her already saucer eyes, drawing a smile across her face. Her button nose received a dab of the luscious goo before his fingertips delivered their chocolatey payload onto her tongue. The budding romance of young love annoyed the assassin to no end.

There wasn't supposed to be a guard, he repeated to himself. But there she stood, googly-eyed and blocking his door. Options for the most discreet way to take her down with no one noticing raced through his mind. As he approached the unlucky soldier—in the wrong place at the wrong time—he reached into the side of his vest.

The soldier abandoned her post to follow her boyfriend like a junior highschooler pining over the varsity football star. Finger straightened, then relaxed, the assassin pulled an empty hand from his waiter's gilet. The door had been cleared with a zero body count.

Time to tick that up to one.

In the fifty-square-foot rectangular multimedia room, he watched with a clear view from three meters above the conference room floor. With a few minutes until his introduction, the PM hadn't taken the stage. In the assassin's mag-lens, the black dress looked as good from behind, too good for that tuxedo-clad imposter standing beside her, masquerading as a general.

As hoped, that famous reporter, Belinda Mayers, sat in the front row. *This will get instant coverage by the most trusted face in news.* As he positioned the weapon, extended the barrel, and slid the setting to laser-targeted holographic projectile mode, he whispered to himself, "Mission accomplished," and squeezed the trigger.

24 | Earth:
2 Days to Crossover

Unlike Kat, Marc didn't have a room on campus. He was happy—well, content—to sleep in a barracks-style room with the men of his security detail. Most nights when Marc remained on the compound, the other guys weren't there, and he'd have the space to himself. Alone in his bunk, like so many other nights, he couldn't sleep for the *noise* of thoughts running through his head.

With a ten-year life expectancy for the planet, for the four and a half billion on it, no one could entertain the notion of failure. The need-to-know secrecy versus what the public knew left Marc in a quandary. As on the inside as they let him in, an awareness persisted that he landed closer to the public knowledge side of the scale. Two years on the project and ready for the launch of the most crucial operation of his career, and he only now learned the five decades he and everyone thought Earth had left in her to be but one. With the migration to Mars perfidiously set to begin in five years, the world's hope hung upon a lie.

What else didn't he know?

Roberta Hillthorpe, the Strategic Counsel Leader and puppet master running the world, was crass about it. The last unhidden truth shared by the chairperson fell on Marc's ears despite her protest. It seemed the old man had some independent will and power after all. Yet Marc couldn't help thinking the SCL may have been the only person alive with unredacted knowledge, most likely possessing data and insights unknown even to Walter Vescovi.

For the first time since enlisting, Marc retraced his previous missions and scrutinized memories of his deployments, wondering if he had carried out any under false pretenses. The irritation of doubt wore on him like a wool sweater without an undershirt, its unbearable itch impossible to scratch away. Did that change things now? If anything, his mission became more important. That had seemed impossible throughout the planning stages of this last-ditch effort for survival.

And Jewel's only hope.

With few places to go at the late hour, Marc wandered into the breakroom that served as the dining hall, recreation area, and lounge. Labeling the two-hundred-square-foot room with tables, a sofa, and a few video displays, any of those stretched each definition. Approaching midnight, he expected the room to be empty when he found Kat eating a bowl of Asian noodles. She handled the chopsticks like a pro, something Marc never bothered to learn. He thought it pointless to try, since the fork had already been invented.

"Hey Kateryna. Late dinner or midnight snack?"

"Good evening, Marc. Didn't know you stayed here."

"When I must. I snuck home this afternoon, and I have an early meeting tomorrow. And my girls are asleep now, anyway, so there's no point staying there only to get up and out at five a.m. You always eat this late?"

"Not normally. And not in here. Join me?"

Marc sat across the table watching Kat eat, reasonably sure their banter stayed strictly platonic.

"You always wander around campus shirtless, or is this for my benefit?"

Only when she said that did the awareness that he hadn't tossed on a shirt sink in. "Oh, no. Glad I kept my shorts on. Didn't expect to run into anybody. Sorry."

"No need to apologize. I mean, if you were some gross fat guy, then sure. But this? Chiseled pecks and toned abs on a sexy, hairless chest. No, I can handle this." Kat tossed on an impish smirk.

"Behave yourself, young lady." He smirked right back.

"Young? Why, thank you. We're not all that far apart."

"I know. So, why the late night?"

"Work. The usual. You?"

"Don't sleep much. Especially when I'm not at home. But you often work this late?"

"No. I work until the cleaners kick me out. Usually around ten p.m. Oh, you don't speak civilian, so you have no idea what that means." She shot him a playful wink. "Ten p.m. means twenty-two hundred hours. All the military jargon here... it's like another language. I think I'll add it to my CV when this job's over. 'Fluent in Jarhead.'"

Kat smiled radiantly. Aside from Casey, hers may have been the most symmetrically exquisite face Marc had ever seen. She had an absolute joy of a personality and was so comfortable to be around.

"Sometimes, I forget how out of place this must be for you."

"A little, yeah. But I've been here every day for two years—feels like forever. Not like you, you slacker, you get to go home. You're away from this prison compound for weeks. This is my home."

Looking around the little mess hall, the comparison fit, yet he hadn't noticed it before that evening.

"I must be losing my touch..."

"Oh no, Marc." Kat's eyes pranced over his chest. "You still got it."

"You know, some might consider this flirting. HR would tear us a new one for it."

"*HR?*" Her smile glowed. "Before accepting this job, Roberta assured me they didn't have an HR department."

"Nice. But what I meant about my touch... I've dropped some pretty obvious hints. I mean straight grade D on the cleverness as to why you worked late and are having dinner at midnight."

"Oh, I picked up on those. One thing you should know about me: I never let anyone off that easy."

"*So...?*"

"Right. I had to get a jump on tomorrow's topic."

When she said nothing further, slurping up more noodles, Marc had to dig. If what he observed could be called flirting, she played hard to get masterfully. A long blink summoned an image of Casey to clear his head. "Right. Topic. Of course, I know what that means. But maybe... I think you want to tell me about it."

"A big part of my job is to build the topic for the daily Mars updates. *I know.* The lies all come from me. Hated that idea and only accepted the job—the one Roberta dragged me into, thank her very much—when I learned what we're really doing here."

"Hundred percent. So tomorrow's topic? The late night?"

"Yeah. This evening's update didn't go swimmingly. Monica slipped, and people are afraid it could raise certain questions. I highly doubt it. People believe what we want them to, like little sheep. But we must make sure we do some course correcting tomorrow, just to be safe."

"Monica's a real pro. What did she say that was so bad?"

"Watch the report. You'll see, um, *hear*, what she said."

After taking her bowl to the bin, Kat sat on the sofa, patting the cushion beside hers. Marc sat, and she turned on the display and told it to play the update from earlier that evening. It began with a standard news-show-styled introduction and construction update. The project footage looked rather convincing. They had built physical sets in the hangar to give it the realism needed to sell it to the audience. Being purported as a solution offered to all the world's population indiscriminately, the news program had a global viewership.

Monica looked as lovely as ever, with an electric enthusiasm that came out from the screen and excited anyone watching—a real natural. She touted the five years to completion, as always, with the on-screen ticker graphic flashing the countdown. "Five years, two months, thirteen days." That's when the migration would begin, but not to Mars. If all went according to operational goals, by that date, most of Earth's population would breathe clean air on a radiation-free new world in a parallel universe. When the program ended, Marc hadn't noticed any errors or gaffs and couldn't guess what might have called for Kat to put in the overtime.

"You didn't catch it, did you?"

"Seemed pretty standard to me."

"It was. As I said, no one would catch it. She went off script a bit toward the middle. When talking about the new Vescovi microclimate systems and how they'll provide our healthy air on that rock, she said, 'when we cross to the other side.'"

"People here are worried about *that*? That means nothing. If someone takes that comment and deduces that we've found a way to travel to a parallel world, they deserve a, a... Well, they deserve something nice."

"Exactly. But I wouldn't say *people* are worried. One person. You should have heard how Roberta chewed me out when it aired. Like any of it was my fault. I provide the data, don't even write the full scripts."

"Well, at least you don't have to deal with her throwing herself at you, trying to bait you with her missing buttons, get you off your guard with her physical features on display."

"Who says I don't?" The small space filled with Kat's joyous laughter. Marc's lips vibrated and sprayed drops of spit before opening to a full and hearty laugh.

They said their goodnights, and each took their leave. Marc remembered only when he climbed into his cot that he never took the water he'd gone into the breakroom to get.

Waking refreshed from a restful sleep long overdue, Marc headed off to meet Sharon. After a workout, shower, and breakfast, they met in the little space they gave him to be an office when on campus. Something about her tilted toward the side of different. Sharon always exuded cheer and zest for life as her default demeanor, but she kicked it up a notch.

"Top of the morning to you, boss."

"You're a bit more *Irish* than I remember."

"Sure thing, my mucker."

"*What* did you call me?"

"Means mate, pal. Just in a good mood, is all."

"Well, that's something, then. Is this a professional mood or a personal mood?"

"Both. I had breakfast with Mal."

"I've had breakfast with Mal lots of times. Good guy. But he never did... *this* to me."

"Maybe you don't know Mal the way I do."

"Better I don't, I think. I know he's been into you forever. At least from that last extended op. I guess his patience paid off. Can't say I blame him."

"Wow. Thanks."

"You were the *only* woman there for months."

Sharon didn't join in his jovial laughter, opting to slap him on the arm instead. "Real nice, Captain Meanie. We'll see what happens."

"But Sharon, not on this operation. With both of you coming, I can't be having distractions. How serious we talking?"

"Nothing yet, really. A drink last night with the gang and breakfast this morning. Don't worry, I know how to keep it off mission. It won't be a problem."

"You and I understand all too well how off the rails these things can go. What almost... between us."

"I thought we agreed never to bring... *that* up."

"I think she knows."

"*Casey*? But nothing happened."

"Still. I need you focused. We all need to be."

"Roger that, Captain, sir."

"We need to review your latest."

They examined Sharon's latest data on the deteriorating environment. She explained her revised projections on how their bodies would adjust to the pristine environment on Idyllium. Her studies helped the medical team create a booster to ramp them up to acclamation. The team would get those injections the day before launch. Marc told her about the ten to twelve years, as if she wouldn't have known. Her research, data, and projection models determined that deadline. She had known for months.

Need to know, again. The thought left a bitter aftertaste.

With the official business concluded, they returned to a more casual posturing.

"Pops is really into this whole Mars thing, watches every update."

"He buys into it?"

"Everyone does."

"Guess so. Casey did too."

"Did? You didn't..."

"Had to. She knows Jewel wouldn't make the Mars launch, even if it were true. And me going over there? I had to."

"Just as well. Maybe it gives her a little hope."

"Did your dad say anything about last night's?"

"Mars update? No. Why?"

"Nothing. Just a slight slip of tongue. Monica will correct it today. Kat had to work late after being reamed out by the SCL."

"Captain... Marc. As a friend. Be careful with Kat. Remember *why* you and me almost... happened. You're still in a vulnerable state."

"Me, vulnerable?" He tried to laugh it off, but Sharon's glare spoke of her seriousness. "Okay. Thanks for having my back."

"Always."

25 | Idyllium Mission: Day 2

KATERYNA FIDGETED IN HER seat, getting antsy. Memory of hiding the ring on her wrist drove away the panic of her thumb not finding the gold band to nervously fondle. After a meal that her taste buds would long remember with all the wonder of a full cultural experience, the chocolate cake took her to previously unknown levels of pure decadence. Topping off such a dessert with a fantastic espresso made the perfect ending to the fairy-tale version of her evening. In the reality, she tired of playing the princess and the attention from too many men wore on her last nerve.

Marc's glances at her with "you're doing great" winks told her he had made good use of her *skills* on this outing. To keep her sanity while not allowing vain and shallow thoughts to dominate her as the showpiece she needed to be for the night, Kat invented a game. A mental exercise, she preferred to consider it. She created a rudimentary scoring system in three categories for every guy that worked up the nerve to talk to her. An honorable mention went to anyone whose eyes lingered on her for over thirty seconds but hadn't mustered the courage to speak.

Aide to the Minister of Transportation Hayden Small took a commanding lead for first place. Sitting beside Kat at the crowded table gave the poor bloke an unfair disadvantage. She thought he could have tried harder to be cool about it and kept the points down. He'd scored high in each of the "lustful glaring" subcategories of Kat's scale. When he first sat, his efforts to look like he wasn't trying to see down her dress were commendable.

His cracked voice amassed sufficient confidence to speak full sentences. Once his newfound boldness told her how lovely she looked, he stopped pretending. Like a child rewarded for good behavior with sugary treats, he indulged the sweet tooth of his dilated pupils with all the eye candy they could get. He earned a hundred points for being scrupulous.

Belinda Mayers spewed information like an inebriated attorney divulging client secrets to the sympathetic ears of a barkeep because she "had to tell someone." *Maybe she should have stopped at two sips of champagne?* Kat supposed. When Mister Stares-a-Lot to her left, who decided they were hitting it off, reached the midway point of a monologue about the importance of his job, the call to relocate to the conference center came. The monotone words fell on her ears as a symphony of relief indicating she and the wide-eyed fellow would part.

Go time came, ready or not.

Marc had concluded—what Kat called assumption he called calculated assessment—the best time and place to take down the prime minister would be mid-speech. The opening address would kick off the days-long summit. The operation's importance lay in the rise to power of the PM's successor, Oliver Nelson, a politician more favorable to the aggressive action needed to win the cold war between worlds. SCL Hillthorpe wanted it to be public, to make a statement.

Now the true value of Marc's false persona would face its ultimate test as he readied himself to disobey direct orders for the first time in his career. A trial by fire, Sharon had called it.

Once again, Kat set her distraction skills to full diversion. She and the phony general needed to be in position. Waves of guests flowed into the auditorium and made their way to their seats.

The clandestine pair of nonspies moved toward the front and drifted purposely toward the steps leading to stage left. A wall of intimidation stood in a gray uniform and raised a palm to their approach.

"Corporal. I'm General Martin Wallace." Pushing Kat ahead of him as they stepped up to the man that looked not at all ready to accept any nonsense, Marc did the talking. "We have reason to believe the PM may be in danger. As the senior-ranking military officer here, I need to check the surroundings. I'll need to be close to the PM as he takes the stage and delivers his address."

If he's as disciplined as he looks, I may not be enough to pull this off. With that growing concern, Kat upped her game. Posing in a deliberate lean, she reached for Marc's bogus ident-card and held it at chest height. The stone-faced soldier considered the credential for a moment longer than needed to read its contents.

"No one gets on stage, General."

Maybe he's a leg man?

"Corporal, please let us through." Marc leaned into a step, but the resolute guard stood his ground. "You do *not* want to be the one that stopped a highly decorated general from ensuring the PM's safety and take responsibility for letting something happen to him. Do you?"

"I have my orders, sir. I must ask you to take your seats."

Kat's face brightened. "Tell him we're here. You have a radio. Tell the PM General Wallace and his... *escort* need to see him. He'll want that message, believe me."

If she couldn't get the guard off his guard by being an object for his stare, she would use the prime minister's interest to her advantage. After carefully studying Kat, he must have conceded the PM would surely want that message.

If Marc's hard gaze of annoyance for her speaking out of plan were cut and polished, it could have sliced glass. At once, that look dissolved into satisfaction when the guard relayed the message, and the PM came out to wave them through. Already two minutes late to kick off the summit, he accepted their concerns. The dignified man allowed Marc, whom he called General, to stand a few feet to his side if Kat, called Cathy for their subterfuge, stood between them.

On stage, his face read perturbed. Marc didn't appear to care for having Kat between himself and the PM. His eye found that reporter in a reserved seat in the front row, onto which he shone a bright smile. Any worry Kat had about his being distracted by Belinda Mayers soon vanished as she noted him studying the room, presumably checking for what he called vantage points.

"Ears open. Give me anything, even if you think it's nothing."

"Copy that, Captain." Until the voice in her ear replied, she almost forgot about Sharon on comms.

Marc whispered through closed lips. "Sharp ear for anything that sounds like a weapon. The click of a hammer, the screwing of a silencer, the tick of a scope being focused. You get anything like that, you shout it immediately."

"Copy that."

As far as speeches went, it bored Kat, but she had heard worse. Nothing of substance was ever said at the welcome address. Tomorrow's keynote would be when the PM discussed the financial crises and other pressing matters. Ministers of all cabinet offices filled the docket to address their specific areas over the next three days. Alistair Burgess spoke as a polished speaker, articulate and animated. The subject may have been dull, but not the man presenting it. Kat found him to be charismatic.

"Can you focus at my ten o'clock, three meters up?"

Marc's voice came from her inner ear, not from the man standing beside her. Kat wondered how he spoke so clearly yet concealed his voice from everyone else.

"On it, Captain. Whatcha see up—Laser scope targeting. *Now. Now. Now.*" Sharon's whisper became a shout, sharp but not deafening in the earpiece.

An enormous weight fell over Kat, as if the ceiling had collapsed above her head. Before she realized it, she fell backside to the hardwood floor with a thump, falling onto her side and paining her shoulder. A corner of her eye saw the black blur the statue of Marc had become. He flew high above the stage, a kite with spread wings moving at the speed of a capsule train.

Folding her neck to see over the strips of smooth wood that filled her peripheral, she found Marc, motionless again, lying over the PM. Or the body of the PM, depending. Like ants to a fallen morsel of food, black guard suits converged on the pile made of the fake general and the prime minister of Greater Britannia, Alistair Burgess. Gray soldier uniforms came from stage left and right, one behind the other in tight military formation, closing like a curtain between the stage and audience as the two sides met.

When Kat raised herself into a seated position, she registered the hands gripping her arms. Someone had her from behind and she froze in anxious dread. Like a wet blanket, the black uniforms peeled Marc off Burgess and had two burly guards holding him still. Kat's eyes desperately searched for life in the PM until his escorts helped him to his feet. He stood—*alive*.

Belinda Mayers's presence on the stage intrigued Kat. The reporter spoke to one gray and one black uniform with words her ears couldn't discern over Sharon's repeated calls of "What's happening?" ringing in her head like a drill into the brainpan. Kat dared not speak. She looked over her shoulder at the guard attached to the hands clutching her arms and motioned up with her chin. After an "okay" nod, he helped her to her feet. His paws didn't return to restraining her, choosing to follow the rest of him closer to the reporter. Kat wormed nearer. Her strained ears caught the last of Belinda Mayers's words.

"...is all. As I said, I saw no one else. Nothing else. Then, out of nowhere, that general attacked the PM. Just lunged at him and tackled him to the floor."

To speak in defense of Marc seemed an imprudent course of action, so Kat remained silent. The black uniform told the gray one he saw no bullet or laser burn. No projectile weapon. They hadn't found a threat of any kind. "He's lying," she thought the gray one said. Whatever Marc told them, it appeared as if no evidence had turned up to support his claim besides the thousand plus who saw Marc leap through the air and pin the PM to the floor. So they did the logical thing—the only thing they could do—took Marc into custody for attacking Prime Minister Burgess.

In an ironic role reversal, all attention being on Marc made him a perfect distraction for Kat to slip away unnoticed.

Saul should have secured their exit, a way out with the place locked down. Marc knew the location of that exit. Kat had no clue which way led to her escape. The only circumstance her mind could muster had her try her luck at the main entrance in the reception hall. As she hoped, the doorman who let them in earlier had not lost his shameless interest in Kat's voluptuous figure.

26 | Earth: THE DAY BEFORE CROSSOVER

TEA HAD ALWAYS BEEN Sharon's beverage of choice. Not one for set afternoon tea times with cream and sugar, never that posh or British, she took hers black as a day starter and whenever she felt like having it. English Breakfast or Earl Grey were her standards. The aroma of steeping leaves in her dainty porcelain cup from her favorite tea set saturated her cozy Chicago apartment from a memory. White with pink flowers, she treasured the only thing she had from her mum.

It broke her heart when the last of the Sri Lankan tea plantations closed, the last on Earth. She'd stockpiled, but her reserves had been exhausted long ago, long before Pops's, so she looked forward to him bringing some as she filled the kettle. She lamented over the two-burner stovetop in her modest kitchen. The kettle barely fit under the faucet in the sink, hardly large enough to wash her hands let alone clean pots and pans. Sharon knew it would be the last time she'd make tea here for a while.

Months of meetings and training had prepared her for the operation, one she still couldn't align with reality. Who would believe an entirely new world, pristine, existed in a parallel universe? And she would soon go there. Mind-blowing.

From her kitchen, she glanced over the sofa and TV to the door that would soon let the condescension in. The low coffee table caught her eye, and she wondered about the name, never having rested a coffee cup on the thing. During a contemplative pause, Sharon gazed up the narrow stairs to a loft platform with a mattress and a small chest of drawers and saw the disappointed look he'd surely cast. *Pops should be here soon. Try to be nice.*

Sharon looked forward to the visit but also didn't. As much as she loved her pops, he got under her skin with his loving reminders of her lost faith. His attempts to mask his disappointment involved telling her how much better her life could be if she had made other choices. He had accepted her studies in science when she attended church. To leave the family religion and working for the military, brought a double dose of disapproval. If he ever tried to hide it, he failed.

The cleaning neared done—she'd waited until the last minute, as always—when the doorbell rang. As expected, Henry O'Brien arrived on time. The high ceiling of the loft made the front wall an ideal place for a panoramic window. The scene outside showed the Emerald Isle with its lush green carpet stretching toward towering cliffs. A turbulent sea slapped its waves into the rock wall with thunderous claps she could hear only from a memory. The video wall could show her any scene she preferred, even a live street view of what she'd see if it were real glass.

"Hey, Pops," she said when the door swung open to his round pink face. His *Cheshire Cat* smile warmed her.

"Shay, my darling girl." He immersed her in his typical embrace like a pea sucked back into its pod. No matter the years or accomplishments, she reverted to his little girl every time.

"Sit. Hungry? Dinner will be ready in about a half hour."

"Why Shay, my girl. You cooked for us, did you?" She knew he was joking, knowing she hadn't.

"Delivery." She glanced at her wrist. "Twenty-two minutes out."

"You know, my dear, perhaps if you had a larger home, one with a proper kitchen..."

"Pops, you know I can't cook worth a lick. Don't care to learn either. I live in Chicago with some of the best restaurants in the world. I'll never be able to compete with that, so why do all that work shopping, cooking, cleaning, to have food that's not as good?" She laughed, hoping to end the topic.

"Right. How could I forget? Professional woman."

"Person, Pops. And I have an important job that I love. That's the sorta thing makes most parents proud, and happy for their kids, you know."

"You know I'm proud of you. Just look at you, what you've accomplished with your life. But... look at you. In jeans and a T-shirt. That doesn't scream 'success' to me."

"I have the afternoon off, my last one for a while. And how pathetic am I? I'm choosing to spend it with some old geezer."

The laughter broke the tension. They moved on to the part of the visit where they each filled the other in on highlights of their lives since the last time. He usually had little to say, as his life never broke from a steady loop of predictability. Updates on the exciting life of Henry O'Brien often contained little more than what fundraiser his church did. Only, he said "our church" as if she still attended. Sharon stopped correcting him years ago.

Sharon's updates always focused on work. Probing led to the inevitable questions about a boyfriend and when she would finally get married. Next came the good old Irish Catholic guilt about her being his only chance to have grandchildren. But Pops's usual playfulness and zest of life hadn't accompanied him on this visit.

"Pops, you're more quiet than normal. You okay?"

"Me? Always, my dear."

"No. I see it in your eyes. You're hiding something from me."

"Nothing. Just some simple tests, is all."

"Tests? What tests? What's wrong, Pops?"

"Nothing. Well, we don't know yet. Losing energy and being tired all the time. Figure it's just part of getting old, nothing to worry about. But you were saying something about someone you met on the job. Malcom?"

Clearly, her father resisted going deeper into the subject of his health. Sharon knew him well enough not to push it. Dinner arrived, and they ate their deep-dish pizzas in silence.

As she placed the dishes in the sink, Sharon felt a watchful eye crawling over her back. She left the plates Pops couldn't see for later and carried on about Mal.

"He's a good guy. Cute, funny, and a wee bit shy. But we don't work together, not exactly."

"On the project? Don't tell me he's a military man."

"He's in the ICM, yeah. We're training for the mission and he's on the team. We've only just started spending time together."

"Will I meet this soldier boy of yours?"

"Not today. He's not in Chicago."

Henry's eyes panned left then right. "He's going... over there... with you."

"Pops, you don't have to whisper, the place isn't bugged. Yes, he's on the team that's going. And Marc's the team lead. You remember him."

"Good man, lovely family."

"That's him. It's a great crew, and we're ready to go."

"But Shay, sweetheart, what you're doing..."

"Don't start, Dad." The change from "Pops" to "Dad" raised a red flag in her mind. If not careful, the alteration in her emotional state meant she could get rude. Sharon never wished to hurt him, but that didn't always prevent it from happening.

"I don't know why you didn't refuse with that remarkable stubbornness of yours. From your mum's side, of course... You know as well as me this is an invasion. An entire world, not ruined like we did ours. And *my* girl, an O'Brien, brought up Catholic, leading the way." Worry wrinkled his forehead. Sharon adored how the waves yielded to the smooth eggshell scalp over the male-pattern baldness she called *the Ring of Henry*.

"Marc's the captain. *He's* leading the way, Pops."

It may have been a mistake to tell him about the mission—and a serious breach of protocol. The need justified it in her mind. When Kat had asked the SCL about him, it shocked Sharon to not be fired. Officially, he shouldn't even have known she served as an officer in the ICM. Sharon maintained her employment in the UGA's Science Directorate—a civilian post with a government agency. Not even her coworkers knew about her officer status or the missions she'd been on. It intensified the excitement for her, and she loved living the dual identities.

"Shay, you're part of an operation that will end up killing people. And what would ya be bringing to those people other than the sting of death? Maybe, if we made contact, sent some missionaries rather than sol—"

"Please don't say we can bring them God or Christianity. Shall we list all the nations the Europeans conquered under that guise? I only have *today* free, you know."

"Shay, my love, you're making me own point now. Should I be arguing yours for you, then?" He joked when she thought he'd be angry. A different Henry O'Brien sat beside her, and she held back her questions about the medical tests he blew off as routine. "No matter the stated intention, the so-called humanitarian aid banner we hide our tanks and bombs under, we send in the tanks and the bombs. And the masses follow like mindless zombies. And we do it again and again, don't we just? Look what we did to our homeland, Shay. The resurgence of the Troubles. And the religious divide's worse than we've ever seen it, and a third of our Emerald Isle's charred black because of it. And now a whole world."

"I'm trying to help. Going to Idyllium with Marc's team is a better way than what we've done here. Plus I'm going for science. If not, someone else may go for genocide."

"But even killing one innocent life to save our dying world is wrong, sweetheart. We do this, and we've lost our very souls. Then you'll not see your dear, sweet mum again."

"Oh please, no. I can't handle this now. Don't bring Mum into this, and not like that. This isn't about my eternal soul. It's about right and wrong. And you're not listening to me. I'm going because I can make a difference."

The topic ended, and Pops lapsed into expressing his disappointment in her for more mundane things. Like climbing the stairs to "see the place"—a place he'd seen many times—when he obviously wanted to check if the bed had been made. Sharon saw no point making up the bed when no one would see it. But at least their sparring got back to the basics.

Pops slept on the sofa.

Breakfast meant proper tea brewed from steeping tea leaves. In his relentless optimism, Pops brought enough for his visit and a little extra for when she came home. With the warm comfort in her belly, she and her father left for the airport. When they landed, he checked into a hotel while she headed off to the compound for the mission of her life. Ready or not, she convinced herself she was ready.

27 | Idyllium Mission: Day 2

Muffled voices had come from Marc's earpiece until the only sound was silence. Perhaps a guard had discovered and removed it. Kat's flirtatious conversation with the doorman hinted at her escape from the building, but she went dark, saying nothing. Only the panting of her breaths crackled over the airwaves, slicing through the static. No matter how much Frank or Sharon called out, Kat didn't answer.

When the hotel door flung open as if a violent windstorm had tried to rip it from its hinge, Frank's mind left him. His captain hadn't been taken prisoner, and the need for surveillance ended. Sharon dissolved, and the mission faded into a distant memory. All that existed, on two worlds, was him and Kat—her in the now-infamous dress he gawked at for the first time. The lustful desire it ignited nearly outshined the relief washing over him for her safe return.

"What happened?" Sharon spoke while words worked their way to Frank's lips.

"They got him. Marc's been arrested."

Frank placed a hand on Kat's arm. "Are you all right?"

"Fine. Just... frazzled. That was messed up."

"And the PM?" Sharon stayed on point.

"Alive."

None of them could contemplate the weight of that word. The prime minister of Greater Britannia hadn't been killed.

How would that affect the operation against Idyllium? What atrocity would the people of Earth try next?

The PM lived, and with him, so did hope.

"We gotta get him back!" Impending tears glossed Kat's irises, a deep blue ocean into which Frank dived with total abandon.

"We will." He dared a reassuring hug but pulled away quickly to give the appearance of a soldier trying to console a civilian in distress. He thought he pulled it off.

"Again, what happened? You had an exit. How'd they get the captain? How'd you get out? Where's Saul?"

"Sharon, let her catch her breast—*breath*."

"Okay. But we need answers. We need a plan."

Frank walked Kat to the chair and sat her down. As a loving caregiver, he helped her sip some water and waved the air between them. His look to Sharon requested her to give the woman the time she needed to settle her nerves. "When you're ready."

Kat exhaled slowly. "So, we ended up on the stage..."

Both listened intently as Kat related the events and how Marc had saved her by pushing her down on his leap toward the PM. "He was more than Double-Oh Seven, he was Batman!" Then she related how the guards and soldiers took him after the eyewitness testimony of the reporter, Belinda Mayers. When Sharon asked about Saul and the egress location, Kat explained how Marc knew the exit but never shared it with her. She reached the end of all the information she had to give from what she saw and experienced.

"...and the same poor drooling sap let me pass. Hopefully, he didn't get in any trouble. Everyone knew I was with the guy that jumped the PM, and this soldier boy just let me walk out."

"Who could blame him? I'd have let you walk up to the PM and shoot him dead if you asked me... in that dress."

"Nice, Frank." Sharon's words bled sarcasm. "Can we focus, please? How are we gonna get the captain back?"

"Any idea where they'd take him?"

Frank shrugged his reply to Kat. Without a word, Sharon fiddled with the comms unit. Her face broadcasted a desperation for a sound, a voice, a blip, anything. The comms expert stepped in and did her own fiddling with the controls. Within a few brief moments, Kat removed the headset from her ears, sending its output to the speaker.

"I've got something."

The muffled sounds of at least two human voices floated in the unit's waves. Marc's wrist device must have been in the room. Kat adjusted the DLD settings. She got it.

"...too late for that. We have a holding cell here. We'll keep him overnight and transfer him in the morning."

"He tried to kill the PM. We need him in a secure facility."

"No. The PM is coming to see him here first thing in the morning. Then we transfer him. We are just as secure here as at the precinct, anyway. The place is locked down, and all guests have been escorted out. They're doing a second full sweep of the building, and there's only one way in here, with a platoon of the best our military has to offer. He stays here tonight."

"Guys..."

Marc's whispered voice came as if he were standing next to them, drawing Frank's eyes to the receiver. A dose of reality at seeing the silver square broadcasting his voice brought him back to the moment. Mental distortions returned and Kat stole his mind again, sitting there as she did, beside the unit, in that dress. Frank could have left everything behind if she strode beside him.

"I hope you can still hear me..."

He paused as the rustling of movement trickled through the tiny speaker. "Wait." One word froze them as a narration from a distant voice. The sound of trailing footfalls filled the otherwise silent void until their clatter dissolved. A deep exhale carried its emotional toll over the airwaves.

"Guys. I'm alone. In some sorta holding cell. They're charging me with attempted assassination of the PM. I can only hope they have nothing that can monitor this channel."

"We're here, Marc."

"Kat? Thank goodness you got out. Did you pick up that chat a minute ago? I couldn't make it out, but I think they're moving me tomorrow."

"Yes. You're there overnight, then the PM is going to talk to you tomorrow before the transfer."

"And we can get you then. Our best shot at it is when they move you."

It surprised Frank to hear Sharon express exactly what he thought. A military officer, sure, but a scientist, he didn't expect strategic planning from her. Then he realized how pitifully obvious going for Marc during the prisoner transfer must have been to anyone who'd seen it done in countless films.

"Where's Saul? You may need him if you're coming for me."

"Not back yet. I didn't get out through the secured exit, didn't know where it was. He may still be waiting for us there."

"My bad, I guess, for not telling you how to escape. How'd you—Oh. *Nice work, you two.*"

The cap muffled his chortle, as if trying to conceal his sounds. Sharon let hers out at full volume. Frank felt a step behind everything happening.

"*Mar-arc*. This is serious." Kat's annoyingly playful protest and how she dragged his name into two syllables fell as acid on Frank's ears. "We need to get you out. They got you for attempting to kill the PM. My goodness, Marc, that's the death penalty."

"Kateryna, Sharon, stay calm. Frank, you need to work with Saul. All of you, if you can get me, great. If not, if it's not safe, don't risk the mission on me. Leave me and carry on with the op."

"Copy that, Cap."

"Well, don't give up on me that easily, Frank. I'd really like *not* to get executed for trying to save the PM's life... If I can get out of dying, I'm good with that."

"Of course, Marc."

Frank read the concern in Kat's eyes like a neon sign. Wild thoughts ran the paces through his mind, gaining support from the recesses of his emotional chaos. It scared Frank to contemplate leaving Marc for the sake of the mission because it would put Saul in charge. He also considered how leaving him would mean he'd be gone, unable to steal Kat's attention.

"We'll get you, Captain." Sharon had it together, while Frank's mind needed to reassemble itself.

"Good to know. Don't go thinking I'm dispensable and all. I'm quite fond of breathing, you know. And I'd very much like to finish this mission."

Frank leaned over the silver box. "Cap, we'll have you back, don't you worry."

"And we'll be monitoring you all night, Marc."

"No. I mean, no to *Kat*... not to Frank. Frank, you keep on that idea of getting me outta here. But Kateryna, guys, cut it off now... the comms unit. Don't risk them discovering it just so you can listen to me snoring. And you all need your rest. That's an order. Sync up with me first thing in the morning. And Frank, make sure your rescue plan's a good one."

"Yes sir. Shut it down, Kat."

"Marc, we'll be here. And we'll see you tomorrow."

"Hold tight, Captain." Sharon got the words out as the unit switched off.

The night's experience had left Kat visibly shaken. She'd played the part of a secret agent, her first time in the field. Their captain got captured, arrested, and no doubt slated for execution. Frank searched his vocabulary for the right words to offer consolation, to be the support she'd lean on, establishing himself as a pillar in her life. If not so resplendent an outcome, he had an in to get her to see him in a new light. The words crawled up his throat, reaching for his tongue.

He almost had them...

Saul barged in with a scowl. Frank could see anger raging in his glare, an inferno ignited by an unknown spark. One thing Frank knew, concern for their captain didn't light those eyes and furl his lips into a grimace, demanding an answer. "*Where is he?*"

"Taken into custody. We'll be able to get him out tomorrow when they move him."

Wild eyes blazed at Frank. "We'll do no such thing. The op comes first. Frank, you know this. Sharon, so do you. Kat, you best learn real quick. This was a disaster, a total failure. The captain screwed the whole thing up. He's nothing. The mission is everything. We won't risk it for one man, not any man."

"He knows that. Marc told us to save him only if we don't risk the mission."

Kat was forceful, on her feet with strength of tongue. The gumption momentarily took Saul aback, but only for the seconds needed for his surprise to be consumed by the flames of his fury.

Over a pointing finger, he spoke in a raised voice. "You mind your place, girl. You're here as a comms officer, and that's all the communication I want from you. You don't open that pretty mouth of yours unless I tell you to. From now on, I'm in charge here, and I say we can't risk such a fool-hearted rescue mission.

The captain knew the risks, and he knows plenty about losing people, believe me. We carry on without him."

"*No.*" Frank's voice came in haste, ahead of weighing the pros and cons.

"You listen to me, Corporal. We do as I say, for the sake of the mission." Turning his locked gaze from Frank to pan the three staring blankly back at him, Saul puffed his chest. "There's a chain of command, you see, and anyone doesn't respect that chain's gonna get beat over the head with it."

Frantically, he pecked his finger on his bio-pad. Beeps from the wrist device cut the silence that had fallen like a curtain over Saul's last words, threats as Frank perceived them. He felt a pulse tap his wrist under his device and the women glanced at theirs as well.

"I've set a tracer on your bio-pads. No one moves without my order. And you remember one thing: I'll get the op done; mission accomplished no matter what. And anyone is expendable for the sake of the mission. That means every one of you. We leave New London Town tomorrow, as planned. Now, get some sleep. And put that equipment away."

Saul stormed out of the room, leaving a welcome silence in his wake.

Kat dropped her face into her hands, and the tears found their way around them. Sharon looked on in shock, eyes as wide as golf balls. When he traced a droplet rolling down her forearm, Frank moved over to Kat and put an arm around her to offer comfort—a comfort he knew the civilian desperately needed. In response, she wrapped him in a hug and sobbed upon his shoulder. The wetness of her tears soaked through the fabric, moistening his skin. To return the gesture, he gently squeezed. He became the man he wished to be for her, overflowing with a warmth that ran through his bones. She pulled away, facing him.

When his lips met hers, he floated in a dream.

The slap to his cheek woke him abruptly.

Kat said nothing and pushed away. Frank reached for the word "sorry," but it fled from his lips, leaving him with an open mouth beside her hand's red imprint. Watching from a distant place, he found the sense in it as she leveled her hand from the wrist, palm down, fingers splayed. Her wedding ring caught a glare from the white overhead light and sparkled like a beacon in the night. A reminder she'd been caught in the storm of memories, swept away by the rush of emotion that led to a slap in the face of a new love's interest. At least, that's how Frank interpreted it.

Kat spun and plodded until the bathroom took her from him.

"Frank. That was..."

"Stupid. I know."

"She's not ready. And now she's worried for the captain. She's had a long and arduous evening. And she's a civilian."

"I know, I know. I was just trying to comfort her."

"You're a sweet guy, Frank. But boy, is your timing off."

"What about the cap? I mean, we need to get him. We need him to finish the op."

"I can't even think of Saul being in charge. My goodness."

Frank stopped his hand rubbing his cheek. "But he's right. About the chain of command. He's next in line after the cap."

"Actually... he's not. Secretary Michaels promoted me right before we left Earth. I think for just this reason."

"What do you mean? You outrank him?"

"I do. And I think we'll need to exploit that if we're gonna get the captain back."

28 | Earth: THE DAY BEFORE CROSSOVER

WHEN THE WEATHER UPDATE declared the earlier threat of light rain a false alarm, Saul went for a jog. It wasn't safe to chance the rain, as it often contained acids or pollutants that wreaked havoc on human skin and were a healthy respiratory system's worst nightmare. Evenings when he could, Saul absorbed the peace of a twilight run through the little neighborhood on the outskirts of West Hayesville. He'd made a home there once, but it diminished to the place where he happened to live.

It could have been anywhere on Earth.

It would be the last night Saul slept in his own bed, the one in the duplex he occupied. He rented it from a Yugoslavian family that lived in the adjoining unit, a kind older couple that often offered him home-cooked food. The open meat pies looked pretty good and teased his nostrils with the promise of amazing new flavors for his palate to enjoy later. He accepted their offer and left the food on the counter for after his after-jog shower.

A light tap on his wrist signaled the autocounter for his exposure tracker had engaged. His bio-pad would trace his movements and alert him when to head back. He had twenty-seven minutes this evening. Not bad. As always, he started down Bennington Street, then went left onto Jefferson Avenue. He delayed heading down Main Street—a name Saul gave it, though the sign called it The Anglo-American Way—as the traffic hadn't dissipated. Commuters returning from their city jobs in mundane routine crowded the road.

He came to the smaller of the two remaining parks in town. The municipality pulled funding for such outdoor recreation spots for the little use anyone could make of them. Most of them had devolved into whatever nature made them. Neighborhood groups maintained the two but not well. To Saul, people should have used the exposure time to the full. He called the overuse of virtual reality the ruination of the last few generations. True, he and Bubba couldn't afford it growing up, but they wouldn't have used it even if they had the money. At least, that's what he told himself. He and Timmy had made the most of the outdoor time they had each day.

As he slowed his pace the way he always did in the park, Saul took in the scent of fresh air from the trees. Or the closest thing to fresh air anyone's nose could intake, as polluted as what he inhaled everywhere. At least the scent of pine needles tickled the hairs in his nostrils like nothing else. Saul paused in contemplation of the role the SCL envisioned for him.

Not every time, but more than he considered healthy—one time being too often—he passed his old house. He had built a life there, where he once reached for an impossible chance with someone who loved him. For one fleeting moment, he had thought he could be happy. It fell apart as he feared, only worse than he ever imagined.

Looking in that window again, he stood motionless. The house didn't turn heads, nothing fancy and in no way elaborate. Alyssa described it as homey and comfortable. The only woman Saul Mullins had ever loved filled that home with a warmth he never thought possible. And then it budded into a joyous contentment beyond his wildest expectations.

Bubba had been making a name for himself as an ICM officer with an outstanding record. With his future set, Saul had done his job, raised his brother and made him into a man. A man he looked upon with all the pride a *father* could have. Then that house promised Saul something beyond belief. He had felt he'd been rebooted, given a life to live as any man might, to be a real father to his child.

They had painted the nursery a neutral shade of yellow because Alyssa couldn't accept the infallibility of the prenatal scans. She'd always wanted a girl, and Saul told himself he'd be happy so long as their baby was healthy. Not being good with the roller, Saul and his adoring wife speckled themselves in yellow drops of paint. When he laughed as she tried in vain to wipe her blouse with a tissue, Alyssa dipped a finger in the can and smeared a thick yellow blob over his nose. His kissing her smeared the color over her cheek and the two laughed with a deep elation he'd never again feel swelling in his heart.

Two days later, she woke to blood on the sheets. Saul had been deployed on a comms-dark mission. When he saw his beloved next, she lay in a hospital bed, drowning in her tears. Powerlessness overtook him. The strong man, the soldier, could do nothing but weep with his wife. And he couldn't even do that. He needed to fix it, refusing to accept the impossibility of the task. In his unrelenting pursuit of an ability out of anyone's reach, he distanced himself emotionally and buried himself in his work.

Unable to console and support each other, they drifted apart until she could no longer handle the loneliness that filled the house, more so when he came home. After relentless begging for him to take a position that wouldn't send him away days to weeks on end, Alyssa filed for divorce. He thought his world had ended that day and apathetically signed away the house and took the rental in the tiny duplex across town.

Saul stood by the curb at the lawn's edge, watching. His wife sat there, lovely as ever, in the dining room that used to be his. Now, another man shared it with her. She married less than a year after their divorce. Holding a plate of rice and some or other saucy topping with vegetables, her new husband entered. The plate set before her painted a smile on her face, as radiant as ever. Her head tilted, and her slender neck stretched to receive another man's tender lips to hers. Of course, Saul couldn't see through the cement rectangle where a glass window long ago opened the wall.

If Saul found gratitude for anything, he hadn't been holding a gun at that moment. He couldn't be sure which of Alyssa's husbands would have taken the bullet from it if he had.

The audible alert from his bio-pad got the attention earlier gentle taps had failed to capture. It signaled the time to head back home before reaching a dangerous level of exposure. After another few minutes passed him as a blind spectator to his wife's dinner, the alerts became more insistent. If he ignored it much longer, they would dispatch a team of exposure prevention officers.

Saul tore himself from the window's imagined view.

The hurried pace on the return made up for the alerts he had ignored. Desperately, he tried to remove thoughts of his beloved and her new husband, the child they never met, and the gut-wrenching losses swirling around in his head. As expected, and morbidly welcomed in a way Saul could never understand and had never tried to fight, thoughts shifted to the next loss, one that cut him more deeply. No amount of soul-searching brought him any clarity, only a constant haunting. The death of his baby brother left a more profound hole in his psyche than losing his wife and unborn child—his whole life.

Bubba was his responsibility.

The blame for that found a place. Saul could fault dumb luck and untimely misfortune for Baby Yellow, as Saul referred to the unnamed child who died in Alyssa's womb. While he could blame himself for letting go of his cherished wife, not giving her the attention and support she needed, he made plenty of excuses for it. He had been hurting too. This was different. He could place the blame for Bubba's death squarely on one man's shoulders.

Marc Sanders.

To Saul, it couldn't have been more obvious. Marc had neglected his wife and daughter. Unlike his Alyssa, Marc's wife sought comfort and release in another man, Saul's brother. On the very next mission they were on together, Timmy "happened" to get killed in action. UGA bigwigs advised him not to testify to the affair or his suspicions that Marc arranged for his brother to die.

That direction came from the infamous Strategic Counsel Leader, Roberta Hillthorpe. Reluctantly, he dismissed initial impressions of the woman when she didn't consent to be a sensual release for his pent-up misery. He had misread her flagrant come-ons and flirtation. She was all business.

Parallel universe. The concept came from science fiction, and Saul hated those types of stories. He preferred films grounded in reality. War stories and vigilante films were more his style. A second "Earth" existed, a world exactly like his own but with a thriving biosphere. "It's our future, and I want you to be a part of making it happen," the woman had said.

Saul had no interest in the specifics beyond the clichéd "fate of humanity hanging in the balance," blah, blah, blah. He saw an opportunity. A seed planted by Miss Hillthorpe, though she fertilized it through innuendo heavier than the sexual ones she'd been tossing his way. And in this, he saw a way to find fulfillment.

Marc Sanders would be the team lead on the operation.

29 | Idyllium Mission: Day 3

THE STRIP-SEARCH DIDN'T HUMILIATE him. He had been through this a time or two and faced it like a soldier. They found Marc's tiny earpiece tucked deep inside his ear canal. Moving to the security chief's sublevel office, he worried about his wrist device, and anxiety for his squad, his responsibility, filled him. They had heard nothing since a guard had taken him from the holding cell shortly after they closed comms last night.

He was on his own.

Shoved forward down a narrow hallway, Marc saw that drooly young entrance guard pass. A somber countenance, he likely came from a chewing out for allowing him and Kat into the event. Worse, he had let a suspected accomplice to the PM's assassination plot walk right out the same door. Not an enemy but a misfortunate casualty of the mission. Marc felt bad for the guy. He wondered which remote part of Idyllium he'd be reassigned to in disciplinary action.

His turn came as he entered the small office with one almost square desk. The push on his shoulder felled him into the chair, and the stern look shooting across the empty gray surface came from a face full of warm blood. While someone tied Marc's hands behind him, the man with the crop-cut brown hair and thick eyebrows scowled in silence. Puckered lips under a steely squint implied he'd already found Marc guilty. A few minutes into the grilling session, sleep deprived and hungry, the hammer's relentless pounding in his brain made Marc long for the silence to return.

Try as he did, the action figure of a wannabe soldier didn't buy his defense of saving the PM's life. Even Marc had to admit it looked like an attack, with him tackling the leader of the world to the ground. Lack of evidence of an assassin besides Marc, lessened the man's likelihood of considering a version of the story where Marc didn't attempt to kill the prime minister. Like a slap to the face, Marc remembered a key detail.

"At my ten o'clock, three meters up."

The chief's grimace morphed into a puzzled look. "Is that supposed to mean something?"

"On the stage, I thought I saw something three meters from the floor, at about ten o'clock. That's where the assassin was. Has anyone checked there? You need to check there."

"No one was in the control room for last night's event."

"I think you mean no one *was supposed* to be. I'm tellin' you, someone *was* there... tried to shoot the PM. And I tackled him to save his life. You should be thanking me."

The interrogator pushed a sarcastic breath of disbelief through his lips. Before he could respond, the door behind Marc squeaked open to allow a woman in a gray uniform to slip in between the volley of words.

"Sir, we ran his prints and ident-card as you asked, and the results just came back."

"And?"

"The ident-card's a fake. A good one, but there's no General Martin Wallace in our system."

"I could have told you that." The man's eyes left the guard to glare at Marc some more. "He's an obvious imposter. The entrance and stage guards will be reprimanded for letting him pass. What I don't need you to tell me, Officer Graves, is who he isn't. Tell me who he is." His ferocity for Marc landed unequivocally on the woman and shook her in her boots where she stood, now unsteadily.

"Sorry, sir. We ran all his biometrics and... no match in the system. He doesn't exist. Sir."

"Then who'm I looking at, Graves? Get me something useful on this guy. Dismissed."

No squeaky hinge followed her footfalls.

When the security chief stood, his belly appeared larger than expected. He seemed so fit, with his broad shoulders and square jaw. Marc speculated about how many beers the guy guzzled in a day. The barrel chest tilted forward, knuckles on the table and elbows bent, the harsh lines of a scowl now in Marc's face.

"You don't exist. That's impossible in our system."

"Yet here I am. Maybe there's things about your system above your pay grade."

"And what sort of things do you know that I don't?"

Marc held his initial thoughts from becoming words. "You mean besides the fact that someone, not me, tried to kill the PM? I know the assassin was in that control room you won't even check. I also know that I saved the prime minister's life. And I know how someone could be sitting here in front of you and not be in your system."

"Start with that last one, then. This might even be entertaining."

Marc decided not to go with, "I'm from another world. Take me to your leader." As he spoke of special forces and clandestine government agencies he knew of on Idyllium, Marc read the inquisitor's face and knew he hadn't sold it. Either the guy had no knowledge of such or simply didn't believe Marc to be part of it.

"There's a serious threat against your PM. But not only on his life. There's an operation to undermine the government and threaten the lives of millions."

"I think I was wrong about you, Mister Nobody. You're not lying to save yourself, are you?" Marc released the grip the tension of the situation had on every one of his muscles. "No... You're delusional."

"Look... Would you at least check the control room? Maybe find some evidence there's someone plotting to kill the PM? You don't have to believe me. Believe the evidence."

"We've checked. It's clean. The only evidence we have is the hundreds of people who saw you attack the PM, recorded on video as well. I'm not your judge here, but the outcome is obvious. You tried to kill the PM. You failed. He is alive and well, and soon you'll be dead."

Widened eyes filled the face inches from Marc's before they climbed over his head.

"Mister Prime Minister, sir. I didn't notice you there."

"Chief. I'd like to speak with the suspect."

The chief left the room to the PM, who took the seat facing Marc.

Reading the PM's expression proved exponentially more difficult than the chief's. Marc could not guess why he felt the need to speak to him but welcomed the opportunity. The initial stage of the question-and-answer session regurgitated the same pointless result as the previous one, and Marc knew he needed to make some headway with the man whose life he had saved. He would not get another shot at it.

"Sir, the threat is beyond your life, as I told the other guy. I'm not in your system because I'm on a clandestine mission. I'm sure you know why. The other side is advancing their operation against Idyllium. We have our people in play, working to thwart their efforts. *They* tried to kill you last night, a team from Earth, but I was there to prevent it. And, well, I did, sir. Or we'd not be having this chat."

The gently aged man pushed the chair back and crossed his legs. After a couple of breaths, he leaned forward. "The thing I hate about having clandestine agencies and ghost protocols... anyone can claim to be involved, and guess what? We have no records on you. Sure, we have them in some vault somewhere or on some isolated computer few can access, and that takes time. Let me tell you what I think." He leaned back with folded arms. "You know we'll move fast, and you're playing a gamble that we don't have time to check your claims. You mentioned top-secret intelligence in a matter-of-fact manner, so you know what few people do. This alone doesn't substantiate your story. The intel could have leaked. You could be from the other side for all we know. In fact, you could be the threat against me. I'm not sure you have the words or the time to make me think differently."

"Yet we're talking. You could have let your people handle me. I'm thinking, why are *you* here? As soon as they locked me up last night, they said you were coming to talk to me."

"And do you have a hypothesis?"

"Doubt." Marc leaned into a slouch.

The PM raised an eyebrow. "About?"

"You must have considered if I were an assassin coming for you *and* managed to get on stage beside you... I'd have had a better plan than to jump on you and let the guards subdue me. Look, you're obviously an intelligent man. You must be wondering why I had no weapon or didn't snap your neck. I laid over you like a blanket when you were down and did nothing. You doubt I came to kill you."

"Tell me about the agents from Earth and this plot you mentioned."

30 | Earth:
14 Hours to Crossover

The Sanders' home boasted the same modesty most soldier's homes did. No matter the rank, service record, or number of commendations, ICM marines received a living expense stipend and basic housing. Marc's family moved into one of the two-bedroom units when Jewel arrived. He never opted for the salaried housing alternative, as he and Casey cared little about buying a home. Home meant family, and they were together much of the time.

His last time at home, he hoped that meant *in this house*.

A mental battle ensued over whether the difference may have been real or imagined. Jewel had more energy than usual. Some days, she'd sit at the table for dinner with the family, but those came in rarer frequency of late. Marc wondered if she pushed herself for her dad's send-off meal. While her nurse had become almost part of the family, playing the role of a cousin who visited often, she gave them the evening.

The three sat in light conversation over the meal Casey wanted to cook but didn't. Marc had insisted they spend the afternoon together playing games, sharing memories, and telling stories. He even offered to pay for a catered meal, at-home delivery from a slightly upscale restaurant he used to take Casey to before Jewel got sick. Husband and father, he basked in the warm smiles as they savored the moment.

Doubts had troubled him. This mission would have a massive impact on two entire worlds. He watched his Earth and his child slipping toward the same inevitability. Before accepting the position as team leader, he had mentally argued the immorality of corrupting a thriving society on a pristine world. What some called the sacrifice of millions to save billions he deemed another term for murder. His emotional strata had no way of dealing with the enormity of his daughter's fate.

He had been offered a way to save her.

Idyllium.

The only way.

Justifications precipitously filled his conscious thought when he saw it that way. The corruption from Operation Rebar prepared that world to welcome his people. Their own second in command proposed the plot to take out their PM and replace him, conspiring with Roberta Hillthorpe on this side. An accord to bring the destruction of four cities, leading to a full occupation, was enacted across the void. It lessened the pain when Marc saw things in such an augmented light. Yet after almost two years, he still fought that moral dilemma daily. The closer that day came, the tighter the noose squeezed.

Looking at her wide-eyed smile under the sconce's gentle light, his baby girl almost looked healthy. As she laid her hand on his arm and laughed at her own joke, which Marc had missed for his musings, his fortitude solidified. A little slack, the hangman paused his work. Marc would do whatever it took to save his Jewel.

He'd get her to Idyllium—by way of Avernus if needed. *What father wouldn't traipse through hell to get his child to heaven?* he justified.

Casey gave Marc a better send-off than what that conniving creature at the compound offered. Ripping himself from their bed the next morning proved the second hardest thing he had to do. The first came soon after.

Swirling the sounds of her shuffling feet through the family room, Jewel came into her dad of her own strength and melted into his brawny arms. She shed no tears as she gazed into his glossy eyes and placed her soft lips gingerly on his cheek.

"Good luck, Daddy. I know you'll do great, as always."

"I have my lucky keychain to make sure I do."

That made her smile. "I love you, Daddy."

He choked on the words, "Love you too, Pumpkin."

At the compound on the day of the crossover, Marc paused in shock at seeing Henry O'Brien with several armed soldiers eyeing him. No family members had security clearance to know anything about the project, let alone to be there as they launched it. When Sharon suggested the idea to him and Kat, Marc thought it somewhere between a longshot and a hard fail—closer to failure by far. He couldn't imagine the SCL agreeing to that, yet there he stood, on the top-secret compound.

"Mister O'Brien, pleased to see you."

"You as well, Marc. Big day, eh?"

"That's the understatement of the century." Turning to Sharon, Marc looked dumbfounded. "How? I mean... The SCL okayed this?"

"Kateryna. She said she'd take care of it. I guess she did. Must have a wee bit more pull with the SCL than we thought. I hardly believed me eyes when Kat gave me the visitor pass."

"I can tell you've been hanging with the old man." That got Marc a playful slap on the arm. "At least we have our contingency plan now. More than I hoped for. Has he been briefed?"

"I have." Mister O'Brien reached an arm around Sharon's shoulder. "My Shay's counting on me and I won't let her down."

"Or me, I hope."

"I have the plan, Marc. We'll all be here."

After depositing Henry in the guarded waiting room Marc hadn't known existed, he and Sharon entered the situation room, where the SCL and Kat awaited. The entire team gathered to listen to one final pep talk from the seductive-as-ever Roberta Hillthorpe. Walter Vescovi made an unexpected appearance, his first before the team, to wish them luck and remind them of the stakes they knew so well. The SCL added how nothing could allow this mission to fail. They needed to secure a future on Idyllium no matter the cost.

The time had come. The team slipped into their spy costumes, as Mal called them. The clothes would help them blend in on Idyllium. A final reminder from the operations team, the tech geeks warned them to prepare for a mild fall. They would materialize slightly above ground level to ensure they didn't become a mush of flesh jammed into a solid mass. That visual caused a dry gulp Marc hoped no one else heard.

Stepping into the jump room, Marc noticed the chairperson, the SCL, and Henry O'Brien, with two soldiers closing the door behind them. The audience watched through the observation chamber's two feet of reenforced glass like lobsters at a seafood restaurant happy to stay in the tank. Two blankly serious faces and one pink-skinned look of sheer worry stared at the team. Sharon's dad offered a semiconfident nod.

As team lead, Marc went first. He lifted one leg toward his seat in the cylindrical gray metal capsule and took his place. Saul sat to Marc's left, and Kat took the seat to his right, then Sharon, with Mal beating Frank to the seat beside her. Frank sat at the end next to Saul. Marc thought they should have had seat belts or safety harnesses of some type and flashed back to his first rollercoaster ride when he was eight. This sweat came in greater abundance.

Nothing closed over them and their piles of gear. Marc had expected a blast shield or something. They sat in an open chamber as smoke filled the room. Through its haze, Marc saw the sign of the cross pass over Henry and thought he heard Sharon say, "Amen." It may have been a burst of steam.

The tech's briefing had warned of the shaking, but Marc hadn't imagined its violence. He checked his team. Saul was steel, Frank holding it together. Behind closed eyes, Sharon blanketed herself in a surreal calmness. Pale as a sheet, Kat had sucked her bottom lip in and pinched her eyes tight. Mal didn't look right.

An acrid sulfur odor wrinkled Marc's nose, chased away by a blend of fragrances calling images of cut grass and wet dogs to mind.

The steam bellowing around them squinted Marc's eyes to see the one he knew he should have dismissed from the mission. His grip on the armrest tightened as the shaking intensified, screaming with a deafening, whiney rattle. The sound of warping metal overlaid with a high-pitched and constant hum saturated the air.

Is that blood? Marc thought he saw crimson dripping from Mal's ear. A gruesome image of a melting face from that first Indiana Jones film flashed before him.

The jerking movement of their seats shifted from up and down to front to back. As reality faded away and physical forms blurred into a gray void, Marc saw Mal tilt forward.

31 | Idyllium Mission: Day 3

Frank woke to find Kat fiddling with the comms unit, still in the black dress. A look of desperate frustration soured her face but couldn't rob it if its splendor. In the groggy moments shaking off slumber's grip, the memory of falling asleep on the sofa in the women's hotel room played in Frank's mind. As he rubbed sleep's crusty deposits from the corner of his eye, he noticed Sharon's absence. Alone with Kat, he found himself in the situation he greedily yearned for since the mission began.

He hadn't imagined it like this—she a mess of nerves, the mission in jeopardy. And harder than Saul's right hook to the jaw, his blunder hit him. He needed to apologize, broach the subject immediately and set things right. Hoping his attempted kiss hadn't blown his one shot with the woman, he searched for the right move to smooth things over.

"Morning." It wasn't the opener he had mentally rehearsed.

"Hey, Frank. Nothing on comms since six. I think they found his earpiece, and I can't locate the wristband. We have no idea what's happening."

"Don't worry. The cap will be fine."

The words blanked her face. They were empty words, offering no comfort. As Sharon told him, he needed to up his game, and he'd failed every attempt.

"What I mean is..." He lifted himself from the sofa and plopped in the chair across the table from Kat. "We know they'll move him this morning. We'll get him back. I promise."

"Promise? How can you? No one can guarantee what will happen. What if they already moved him? He could be anywhere on Idyllium by now. What if they—" The communications operator's words ended in mid-sentence as if her comms unit's battery died. She ran the back of her hand under her nose.

"Sorry. I mean, we're gonna do our best. We'll find out when they'll move him. It's our best shot at getting him back. It'll be okay." He pulled back his hand, reprimanded it for thoughtlessly reaching for hers, and prayed to no one she didn't notice.

"I hope you're right." Kat returned to fiddling with the unit.

Frank considered it a futile act of desperation. His mind followed a trajectory toward wondering if she'd be as concerned if he were the one missing.

When the door slammed open, Saul stepped in with no morning greeting, eyed the two, and turned to see the open bathroom door with the light switched off.

"Where's the scientist?"

"No idea." Frank didn't like the look that brought him. He should have known the whereabouts of all team members to report to his commander.

"Gone for a walk to clear her head."

"And what are you doing?" Saul moved toward Kat and rested a palm on the comms unit, leaning over her.

"Trying to reach Marc. Or get something from his device. Nothing."

"I told you to put that equipment away. Do I need to pull out that chain? We go on with the mission. Marc's on his own."

To lure Saul from Kat, Frank stood to speak. "Sir, what mission? You said yourself, last night was a disaster. How do we go on to phase two after that?"

"Taking out the PM was one piece of a much larger mission that must continue, all other objectives reached. We meet at nine at the station. I'm going now to secure the way and get us tickets. Frank, you think you can manage to get these ladies to the station all by yourself?"

Fighting the scathing sarcasm's dejection, Frank saluted. "Sir, yes sir."

"Good." His attention turned back to Kat. "Listen, pussycat, this is our only choice. Marc's a big boy. He can handle himself. Don't worry."

Lewd nickname aside, Frank had never seen Saul so gentle and concerned for the feelings of anyone. Then he shot Frank a "yeah, right" grin as he turned and reset himself to the Saul Mullins Frank knew. An easiness filled the room when he departed.

Kat's eyes went glossy, and she fiddled some more.

Frank laid a hand on her shoulder. "We'll get him."

The brush of the door sliding over the plush carpet retracted his shoulders until Sharon's voice lifted the tension.

"Morning Frank. 'Bout time you woke. Had to get out to free myself of your snoring."

"Where'd you go? How could you go for a walk at a time like this?"

"I told Kat to say that so Saul wouldn't know. I went to the conference center when we couldn't get Marc or his bio-pad."

"Like they'd let you in."

"Aye, they did. Told'em I dropped my purse when rushed out last night and needed my ident-card to travel. I didn't get beyond the entrance hall but sweet-talked a distressed young guard into revealing some detail. Turned up me Irish charm, I did. Poor guy blabbed on about getting reamed out for letting Kat and the general through." Air quotes bracketed *general*. "I played the compassionate barkeep and let him go on until he told me the captain was being moved at eight. A van will collect him with a driver and two guards."

Frank closed his eyes and gave her a raised-chin nod.

"Wow. Way to go, Sharon. I told you you'd make a great distraction."

"*And I* didn't even have to pop the girls out."

As Sharon's jovial laugh faded, Frank grasped the timetable she had mentioned. "Eight?" He raised his wrist. "We've got just over an hour."

"And Saul? Saw him storming out as I came up the stairs. Said he told you to take us to the station."

"Yeah, but you outrank him. What are your orders, sir?"

"Oh, I can get used to this. But never call me sir again, or my next order will be your castration."

The van arrived at eight, as expected. When the split rear doors flung open, two guards hopped out and marched into the building, leaving the driver in his seat. Frank nodded for Kat to begin, and she hurried off in a white sports bra and athletic shorts. Timing would be critical; too soon, and the guards would be at the ready. From a distance, Frank watched as the cap, with hands tied behind, trudged between the guards toward the van and climbed in the back. A thunderclap popped as the door pulled shut. Touching his ear, Frank said, "Kat, go."

The vehicle hummed as it rolled to the corner. Kat jogged across the street in front of it and tripped on her own feet in a believable fall. Her knee bled, and her palms looked raw in Frank's viewfinder. She played the part well, lingering on the pavement. With pain scrunching her face, she cradled her damaged joint and rocked.

The van waited.

Slowly, Kat scooped herself from the cobblestone and collapsed when her injured leg gave out. The driver offered her his full attention. Up again, weight pivoted on one leg, she took one small hop. Her pause moved the driver's hand to the door handle. Another hop. Another fall.

The door swung open, and the chivalrous gentleman rushed to aid the beautiful damsel in distress. Frank couldn't believe how a scene he'd watched play out in so many bad cop shows worked so well. Sharon's turn.

Popped out from behind a tree, Sharon tossed a gas canister in the van's open door and disappeared. The man leaning over Kat looked like he could have shot his eyes out at the smoke-filled vehicle. A very different face he showed Kat wiped the color from hers.

The red face froze, eyes bulged. He vibrated violently before folding at the waist and hitting the ground. From an extended hand, Frank hoisted Kat to her feet, not remotely as hurt as her acting led the now-tased soldier to believe. Frank told her to hurry.

If Sharon had done the second part of her job, the rear doors would be unlocked. Frank opened them to find the two guards and the captain slumped over each other and pulled Marc from the bottom of the human pile. He had to act fast, as the effect of the gas wouldn't last long. With Marc laid on his back, one shoulder dangling off the van's bumper, Frank snapped a small silver capsule and waved it under his nose. His captain's head rose, and his eyes popped open wide, rolled, then hid behind thin slits in his eyelids.

"C'mon, Cap. You gotta work with me here."

Frank hunched and pulled Marc's arm over his shoulder to yank him to his feet. Wobbly legs offered little assistance in supporting the thick fellow's weight. With a hand under his chin, Frank lifted the cap's head. When the tuxedo jacket caught the door handle, Marc's body jerked, and his head dropped. He hit the ground when Frank lost his hold, his own arm having become dead weight.

He felt heat.

No, pain.

Frank sat on his backside, his captain flinching on the ground beside him. What happened eluded him for a few cloudy seconds. The torn fabric on Frank's vest wasn't there before. Strands of black thread twisted out of the hole from which crimson lava flowed. It burned. That he had been shot came to him like a sucker punch. A bullet meant for his captain had blown through his shoulder and out the other side.

Return fire flashed.

It didn't come from Frank's gun, locked in his firm grip and aimed at the ground. One of the guards, belly down and hanging out of the van, took three shots at a building at the end of the street. In the viewfinder, Frank caught the turn of the sniper as he retreated from the rooftop.

After locking eyes with the guard, the two found clarity in sync. The man attempting to free the prisoner and the officer guarding him drew assault rifles on each other. With hurried force, the van door met the guard's head with a thud, robbing him of consciousness. Sharon's red-cheeked face looked at Frank from around the side of the vehicle. In unison, they turned to see a swarm of guards running from the conference center down the street. Sharon assisted Frank's one good arm in dragging their captain around the vehicle.

"C'mon, Kat. Where are you?" Sharon asked the street ahead.

The screech of rubber trying to hold the road came ahead of the sight. The hotel shuttle cart leaned around the curve as it took the corner at near-tipping speed. A confident-looking Kat held the wheel, laser-intense focus shooting from her eyes.

With a little more help from his muscles, Marc got onto the cart with Frank's aid. Sharon climbed in beside Kat, who took off in haste, dropping Sharon into her seat.

Neck limp, Marc's eyes rolled over the scene. "Vat smeened to go werl."

Kat pushed air out in an exhaled laugh, and Frank shook his head. Sharon turned to see Marc then considered Frank's abused shoulder.

"Hospital?"

"Can't risk it. We've got a medical kit. Kat, carry on to the safe house."

"Someone shot you?" With surprise in his eyes, Marc slurred the words like a drunk.

"At you. Hit me. Yeah. And…"

"And what?"

"Guys… It was Saul."

32 | Earth:
The Day of Crossover

Henry O'Brien tried to hide his fear and appear strong for his darling daughter. Inside, he trembled over the unknown, the mysterious other world and the "hocus-pocus" means of getting her there. Fundamentally, he disagreed with the mission to Idyllium but trusted his daughter—more than he feared she knew. He had no trust in the machine that shook her violently and filled the room with smoke like some overhyped magician's stage prop.

Given Shay's recent outburst when he mentioned religion, the sign of the cross may have been too much. He needed to express his faith, even if she no longer shared it. Wordlessly, he prayed for her safe arrival and noted how that pushed his former petitions for her to see the light and do the righteous thing to second place. For the first time in his life, even after losing his dear wife and the spiritual ruination of his daughter, he questioned if anyone heard his silent requests. So many seemed to have gone unanswered, and he desperately needed this one to be granted.

Get her there safely, Lord. Please look after my Shay, he repeated in his head as that *diabhal* contraption jerked her about. He kept the Gaelic quasi-swearword from his prayers but would have to face the confessional for letting God find it musing in his mind.

Something happened that couldn't have been right. Its relevance didn't present itself until the smoke had cleared. Henry gasped when the blue-gray gases funneled like little tornadoes into the return ducts. Although expected, the sight of his little girl and her teammates having vanished with the cloud sent his heart racing. Had it worked or gone horribly wrong?

Who was that on the floor?

The sultry creature beside him jumped to her feet. The old man clasped the armrests so hard Henry thought he'd rip them from the chair.

"What's happened?" Henry asked, afraid of the answer he desperately needed to hear. "Who's down? What's happened?"

"It's Malcolm," the woman said. Her name escaped him.

"Well... go help him. Check he's alive or something."

The woman stood as a mannequin in the window, only she spectated the scene on the other side of the glass. "I'm the bleeding SCL, not the janitor. And you're lucky to even be in this complex, Mister O'Brien. If I hadn't owed Kat—"

"Is he...?" the old man asked. Henry hadn't heard him speak before. The weakness of his voice didn't surprise him.

"Looks pretty dead to me, Walter. His skin's practically melted off his face."

Henry picked himself up and squinted at the glass. "Dear God."

"Oh, I'm sure your god had nothing to do with this. Walter, I'll handle this on paper."

"On paper? What about that poor boy in there?"

"Mister O'Brien. Implication is obviously lost on you, so allow me to translate my earlier words. When I said you were lucky to be here, I meant keep your mouth shut."

Henry sat and watched as people in white coats lifted what remained of Malcolm's body onto the gurney. He all but lost his breakfast as fluids dripped from the young man's cuffs and hems. Only then did he remember the name Sharon had mentioned, the team member who had caught her eye and captivated her heart. The glint in Shay's eye shone as the spark of life Henry missed terribly in her mother. He imagined it going out when Sharon learned what had happened. If she even made it over there.

The SCL tapped on the tablet in her hand. "Looks like they made it."

"Can we bring them back?"

The look Henry received for breaking the *keep your mouth shut* directive hit him like a good Catholic school nun's scolding.

"The whole point of this was to get them there. They're there. Besides, it's a one-way trip. We don't have these transfer chambers over there."

"*What?*" Henry pointed at the empty chamber. "Did *they* know that?"

The glare lingered before the callus woman stormed out. The chairperson said nothing, shaking his head as he stepped around Henry to follow his second in command out of the observation room. A youthful figure filled the doorway of the small space and led Henry back to the waiting room under armed guard accompaniment.

"Do you know what's happened to my daughter?" Henry asked his escort.

The man paused then closed the door. "They crossed safely is all we know. We need to wait for their first update transmission. They have a comms system, but it can only send across the void, not receive."

"You mean we can't talk to them?"

"Afraid not, sir. We'll get regular updates. As far as we know, the rest of the team is fine and starting their mission."

"They're down one man."

"Yes. But if anyone, the loss was acceptable."

"Acceptable?"

"Sorry. I know you're a civilian. I'm not being cold about it. We had three security personnel on the trip but one captain, one scientist, and one comms expert. I mean... the mission can continue as planned. Our future is in their hands."

"Son, I need you to do something for me. I'm not permitted to stay, but I need to know as soon as you hear from them that my Sharon is okay."

"I'm not sure—"

"She's my only child. I lost her ma years ago. Please. Just to know she's okay."

The man's subtle nod gave Henry hope. In exchange, Henry gave the man his number.

"And... they really can never come back?"

"That's what I understand, sir. But we'll all be headed over there soon enough, so don't worry."

"The most useless words in the English language. *Don't worry*. You must not have children."

"No sir. Please, I must escort you out."

"Before we go, I need one more *wee* favor."

PART THREE

Through the Void

33 | Idyllium Mission

When the team from Earth landed on Idyllium five days ago, their landing vectors had scattered them and their gear across a small park. Marc had slammed headfirst onto the paved sidewalk and didn't get up. Kind citizens rushed to his aid, and the ambulance arrived in minutes and took him away.

Exiting the hospital later that day, the air tasted crisp and clean, fresher than anything ever to fill his lungs. One breath reaffirmed his decision not to sacrifice this pristine world on the altar of self-preservation. An uncrossable line to save an Earth they had ruined pushed the bounds of his moral compasses. Kat had told him she wanted to pull out when she learned about the planned nuclear attacks only a week ago. With the hope of a more peaceful solution offered by Marc and Sharon, she had agreed to remain part of the mission. Friends with the SCL, she expressed confidence Hillthorpe would welcome a less devastating option once they had succeeded. Marc had formidable doubts.

When Saul found Marc, the gruff soldier related how he had been vigilantly on the lookout for doppelgängers and, thinking he had seen his Idyllium counterpart, almost killed an innocent man. He also confirmed Marc's fears about Mal not landing with the team, presumed dead.

Reunited, the team began phase one of their mission. Hillthorpe's plan outlined a crucial first goal, the assassination of Prime Minister Burgess with Marc pulling the trigger to ignite the cold war into a fury of flames. Fueled by multiverse-based theories circulated around the Utah compound, the team assumed their Idyllium doppelgängers were working against the incursion from Earth. Expecting a contingency team, Marc transformed from would-be assassin to defender to protect the PM from whomever his SCL had sent to ensure the job got done.

When Frank identified the sniper who missed Marc's head by a hair as Saul Mullins, Marc couldn't know if the Saul from Earth or from Idyllium had taken the shot. Did Roberta Hillthorpe have a second team in play, or was Saul the chess piece she used at a critical moment in the game?

34 | Earth:
1 Day After Crossover

For Jewel, life meant being alive and with her family. The crushing loss of Uncle Tim had crept into the home, under the darkness of night, to rob her of the will to continue. It seemed pointless, prolonging the inevitable. When someone so healthy and full of life ran out of it, she couldn't imagine a future with her in the world. The dream of Mars now taunted her. She'd not last long enough to get there, no matter how much her parents tried to reassure her.

Peggy helped lift Jewel from her melancholy by becoming more than a nurse. With the young woman's life reduced to the few people in it, having a friend when previously she had only her parents lifted her spirits. In the house every day except Sunday, Peggy listened sympathetically, read the stories Mom didn't like to read, and created fun little games playable under the constraints of Jewel's physical limitations. She filled the role of the only friend the dying girl had.

A comfort cradled Jewel like an infant in a swaddling blanket when Daddy was home. A rock to her and Mom, he had been relentlessly by her side for those first months. His deployments were shorter than in earlier years, yet he always seemed to take longer to come home. To be the strong young lady he told her she was, Jewel mustered every bit of energy to stand, walk, and sit at the table for dinner when Daddy sat there. Those precious minutes hung on the precipice like a teetering boulder, its inescapable plunge looming in the next weeks, days, or hours. Every fleeting moment with Daddy could have been their last.

Mom's recovery still had a way to go, but she had found the strength lost to the bottle. Everyone had pulled out their best tricks and employed subterfuge masterfully to shield Jewel from unpleasant truths. She knew. To give credit where due, her mom had put up an amazing front. Under a mask of confidence and character, the once-vivacious woman she had known as her mother had washed away. And Uncle Tim had been so kind and helpful. Suspicions ran high in the young mind of a girl not too short of years to understand. Things were different after, and he had stopped coming around when Dad went on a mission.

As her mother climbed back into herself—months of progress getting her closer to the summit—Mom did her best to counter the loss of Uncle Tim. Jewel's mother also worked tirelessly to fill the chasm carved into her daughter's heart by the absence of Dad. The idea of wanting to be a perfect blend of Mom and Dad when she grew up faded from Jewel's thoughts when she faced the reality of her situation. She'd not be like anyone when she grew up. At best, Jewel would only see a couple more birthdays. She made herself okay with that by worrying more about the devastation her parents would endure. Would they endure it? Would her mother collapse again, lost forever this time in a void of emptiness? With Dad but despairingly alone?

A middle-of-the-night coughing fit roused Mom from her bed and hurried her into Jewel's room. By the time her mom had reached her bedside, Jewel had the oxygen tube ripped away from her nostrils and a handkerchief over her mouth. Dad's; it smelled like him. Mom rubbed her back, as always. Although it didn't help, Jewel never said so. A technique learned from Peggy, Mom pushed the straw of Jewel's water bottle under the cloth and between her lips during a lull in the coughing's violence. Short sips helped.

The handkerchief held little phlegm, and Jewel tried to remember if that was a good sign or if she needed to release it and this meant something else.

Jewel watched unfamiliar eyes cautiously bounce side to side in her mother's eye sockets. Under the faint light, Mom's black-hole pupils sucked the room in. She leaned in close to Jewel's ear as if a precious secret meant only for it would fall from her lips.

"Sweetheart, I know you wore yourself out for Dad before he left. Do you feel strong enough to walk?"

"Now? Where?"

"No, my precious Jewel. Maybe soon. We need to get you rested these couple of days."

"But my next appointment isn't for three weeks, I think. Is something wrong?"

"No. Maybe... for the first time in a while, something is right."

When Jewel tried to sit up, her mother's hand forbade it.

"We may need to take a little trip, is all. I want you to be as strong as possible for that."

"It's been, I don't know, maybe a year since I've been anywhere besides the hospital. I didn't even get to go to Uncle Tim's funeral."

"I'm sorry for that, sweetheart." Casey cradled Jewel's cheek in her warm hand. "Now, I'll gather a few things for the trip and keep them in my room. One small bag is all we'll need, plus your oxygen."

Mom rose and moved toward the door, switched off the light, and stood as a silhouette in the doorway.

"And not a word to Peggy."

35 | Idyllium Mission: Day 3

The motel room they called a safe house reminded Sharon of the one she had shared on her first field assignment. Small, dingy, and poorly lit, it left her wondering if they had hourly rates. The security escorts assigned to that mission stayed unknown to her. She never saw the two men again and had little conversation with them during the three-day operation.

Her action-film-inspired expectations had deflated like an out-of-gas hot-air balloon. Those days filled themselves with mindless scans on the poisoned soil in Kenya. The men did little more than play cards or look at what her dad called *girly websites* but meant pornography. Sharon shutting them down on their first comparison of her to what their tablet showed them stifled all conversation.

Every deployment since had been miles better in purpose and in teammates. Except, perhaps, the longest of them, the one shared with Saul where she had missed Mal's less-than-subtle interest. Saul's detaching from them made the current team much more comfortable.

Mal didn't make it. Had the oblivion between worlds swallowed him, or was his lifeless body back on Earth? The image of him lying dead on the transfer room floor became a haunting behind Sharon's eyelids.

It didn't break her heart, an expression Sharon understood but didn't care for, as she hadn't been swept off her feet or fallen head over heels for the guy. She liked him, and that *like* showed signs of blossoming into something she very much wanted at this point in her life. She dared not call it love, unsure she knew what that meant. Did it matter? He didn't make it. Not since her Mum had she ached so entirely.

Tending to Frank's shoulder, she watched from the corner of her eye as Marc walked about the cramped room with a shower towel around his waist. Sharon almost had him once, when desire had overtaken the carnal parts of her mind and body until she slew the beast. She didn't want him now, not in that way. Yet a part of her longed to find comfort, like he had sought in her on that night under the scantly visible stars.

Kat had been unpacking her gear and assembling the comms unit. Sharon had no clue what they would report back to the other side. What should they tell the SCL, and what should be carefully omitted? By now, they must have expected the report of the PM's assassination, the first phase of Operation Needle Prick. Miss Hillthorpe had repeatedly stressed how vital that would be to the rest of their mission and for the success of Oncoming Storm to follow.

Fuller clarity settled her mind when a properly dressed Marc exited the bathroom. Sharon finished the patch-up job on Frank's shoulder with what he called *skin glue* and injected him with an anti-infection gel. "Good as new."

Facing Sharon and Frank on the other double bed, Marc sat beside Kat. The bed frame squeaked in protest of the added weight. "We need to talk."

"And send a report. I've got the equipment ready. Marc, what do we tell them?"

"Yeah, what was the plan, Cap? When Kat and Sharon told me about switching the objectives, why we needed to *save* the PM instead of taking him out of play as ordered, I assumed you had the whole thing planned out."

"I do. Well, did. I knew Saul was a problem but hadn't quite worked out how to handle him. I hoped he'd see the assassination failure as an unfortunate miss of our first goal and move on with us to the next. Then, I'd have to tell him what we were doing and deal with him somehow."

"Not the best plan. A wee bit too much riding on luck and what-if scenarios."

Frank snickered. "Aren't you Irish all about luck?"

"Oh, we have the luck of the Irish, we do. From the blight and famine to the Troubles to the half-charred rock the Emerald Isle is now... And have ya heard of a wee boat called the Titanic?"

"All right. We need to get serious." The face Marc wore showed full agreement with his words. "Kateryna, I'll word a message for you to send. We'll report that the team from this side stopped us. Then we—"

"Sorry, Marc." Kat set the LCD display on the thin, lumpy pillow beside her. "I'll send that, of course... Last night? We were the team that was supposed to assassinate the PM. We decided not to, in violation of our orders. But... did you stop an assassination attempt, or was that some kind of act? And for what purpose?"

"Contingency. The SCL isn't a military strategist per se, but she thinks, plans, and connives like one. And she's been sending people over here for a decade. When she questioned my ability and loyalty to lead this mission, it confirmed my suspicion. She must have a second team to ensure each mission objective gets done. Team two took a shot at the PM, and I stopped it."

Sharon brushed a red curl away from her eye. "So... when Kateryna sends *our* message, won't that team also send one reporting what really happened? The SCL will know you didn't only not follow orders; you stopped her second team."

"It's why I had Mal play up the talk of our doubles over here most likely being the ones on the mission against us. We'll say *they* stopped us. The Marc Sanders from Idyllium saved the PM."

"Um, Cap? There aren't..." Frank paused. Sharon noticed the crow's feet deepen as his eyes drifted toward the ceiling. "Let's hope they buy that."

"Don't worry about the update for now. We need to discuss the second objective... and Saul. Where is he, and what's he doing?"

"He tried to kill you, Cap. The hole in my shoulder would be in your head if you hadn't fallen. He must want to stop us."

"Maybe it was his doppelgänger," Sharon suggested.

"No," Frank quickly rebutted. "I got a good look. He had the same scar; it was our Saul."

"Marc, would he do that?"

Sharon looked at the only civvy in the room, imagining how strange the situation must have been for her. Her first mission, on a parallel world, was bizarre enough for anyone. "He would," Sharon confirmed. "He's a jerk, stubborn, insensitive, and mean. But he follows orders."

"He does," Frank agreed. "Always. And he gets the job done. He tried to kill the cap because he stopped the assassination, went off mission. He must have gone to the station to head to step two."

Marc raised his palms. "Everyone... let's stop the speculation. Yes, Saul will continue the mission, but that would have us meet with the new PM tomorrow, so that's changed. Step three was to take out their defensive sensor grid. That's where Saul's going. We don't know any more about the SCL's secondary team, so we don't worry about them for now."

"But, Cap, taking out the grid requires the Hertzog... and Mal."

"He's right, Captain. Mal..." Sharon paused to keep herself together. "He was on this mission for that purpose."

Frank hurriedly opened and checked every equipment case and bag. "It's not here. Cap, the Hertzog, it's gone."

"We weren't gonna use it, anyway. We're not taking down that array and leaving this world without an early warning defense system. Besides, it's coded to Mal's DNA."

"So, Marc? Then why's it missing?"

36 | Earth: 2 Days After Crossover

Roberta Hillthorpe sat in her plush leather chair, leaned back, and hoisted her bare feet onto the smooth, hard desktop as she routinely did when drifting into contemplation. A familiar sourness crinkled her nose. As she connected the buttons to her white chiffon blouse's placket, she watched the chairperson's assistant stagger clumsily like a boy who'd had his first beer. He'd surely want more; she had no doubt. The possibility didn't seem likely for the kid, but neither did the first.

The SCL got what she wanted when she wanted it.

Already five minutes past the meeting's start time, she had no qualms about making anyone wait, not even the chairperson and secretary. Knowing they'd ponder over the youthful assistant with the disheveled hair exiting her office didn't concern her. Roberta didn't care to note the young man's name so had called him John.

The two men entered when *John* motioned them in, and the door closed behind them. Roberta stood and pulled and straightened her pencil skirt. Secretary Michaels had more grays yet less hair than the last time she had seen him, and the chairperson stood with his usual pallid and charmless character. It had been years since she and Walter *had a beer* together. Solomon Michaels never played Roberta's games, so she kept a suspicious eye on him.

The meeting would be a mere formality to keep up appearances, as neither of the men feigning masculinity in her office held any genuine power as far as she was concerned. Soon after advancing to the office of Strategic Counsel Leader, Roberta began redefining roles, expanding the reach of her authority. The only one who could veto her actions wouldn't dare. Walter Vescovi never used his power as she did and furnished her with his, uncontested. He filled his days playing augmented-reality golf and dutifully sat in meetings as needed. Michaels had expressed his disapproval of the power structure Roberta had built. Any ability to do something about it had been stripped from his office before he occupied it.

After a firm handshake with each of her guests, the SCL took her typical position, leaning against the back of her desk. She had had all the chairs removed from her and Walter's offices to keep meetings brief. More than that, it maintained a level of discomfort, giving her command of the room. Leaving her seat empty was a power play and let her showcase her legs and use other intimidation tactics as needed. She hadn't ever used recreational drugs but considered they would pale compared to the euphoria of watching men sweat and squirm in her presence.

"Gentlemen. Solomon, thank you for coming." Solomon Michaels had scheduled the meeting, but Roberta never attended a meeting she didn't run. She also insisted on remaining in Utah for the duration of the mission, so the secretary came just for this. "We have some updates on Operation Needle Prick. Our first report said they arrived safe and sound and immediately got underway."

"Excuse me, Roberta." Solomon using her first name made Roberta scowl. "I have some questions about the operation, starting with the marine who *didn't* make it. You said the team arrived safely, but Lieutenant Malcolm Holland died during transit."

"Well, Sol, I have no idea where you could have heard that." Roberta flashed a hard look at Walter and continued, "We pulled him from the team at the last minute. Turns out he had faked his health exams and was unfit for the mission. He died during stress tests he insisted on taking in a desperate attempt to qualify."

Vescovi looked at her the way he always did when she spontaneously invented a story to cover a questionable decision or action after being discovered. "Why haven't I heard about this?"

"I saw no need to mention it until we get the autopsy results." She had the postmortem report detailing Mal's illness and why he died in the turbulent second stage of transit. "Once I have it, I'll send a follow-up report. Sol, the team *as we sent it* did arrive intact and is actively working the mission."

"And where are they in their objectives? Walter's timetable had Objective One done last night, and they should be on their way to Two."

A snorted half-chuckle escaped Roberta's nose. Her initiatives and project plans often circulated among the joint chiefs under the chairperson's letterhead. With the secrecy of this phase of the operation restricted to the three in the room, she hadn't bothered to work under the guise of Vescovi's authority.

"We haven't received the team's status update on that, but I expect it soon. I have no reason to doubt they have handled the prime minister as directed."

"Handled? Look, Roberta, when you and Walter presented this plan, I was in favor of it. In fact, all the cabinet members approved the initial investigation of the other side and the espionage. Later, when initial negotiations failed, you convinced them to support Operation Rebar to prepare for our introduction to their world, to present ourselves as helpful neighbors to bail them out of financial and political crises. I've been on board. But as we've gone on with the overarching operation, you've reduced those in the know and only I am apprised of the details."

"Sol, I haven't got all day. Do you think you could get to a point, or shall I put in our breakfast order?"

"The point is, you've been more and more secretive because you knew the UGA joint chiefs would never support the assassination, let alone nuclear detonation over four of their cities. You didn't even convene the cabinet, knowing they would never condone this."

"And my skirt is black. You really want to waste my time exchanging obvious facts? We know UGA leadership is a joke. The chiefs do as they're told, and cabinet members hardly do a thing for the chairperson besides letting him win at AR golf. *Even I* can beat him. So, yes, I take matters into my own hands and get things done. It's why I'm here. Most of the time, the chiefs prefer not to know *how* I get things done as long as they get done."

"You do *not* have *carte blanche*, Roberta."

After giving the secretary a steely glare, Roberta raised her wrist to speak to the device on it. "John. Come in here and show Secretary Michaels my credentials."

When the door swung open, a more put-together version of the young assistant entered.

"Now, John."

"Actually, it's Peter, ma'am."

"Do I look like I care? And if you call me ma'am again, especially after our earlier... *collaboration*, you'll be cleaning toilets in our Siberia facility by the end of day."

"Yes, ma—SCL."

"*So...* Show him, John. I apologize, Sol. It's getting harder and harder to find good help."

When *John* raised his hand, it held a gold small-caliber handgun with an ivory handle. He pointed it at the secretary, whose eyes widened in a desperate attempt to refute what they saw.

"You see, Secretary Michaels, Sol... things run smoothly under my watch. Don't you agree?"

"*Enough!*" Walter's voice hit a level she hadn't heard in years. It stimulated her as an unexpected turn-on. That he had tried to exercise *political* authority over her squashed it in haste.

Michaels kept his eyes on the slender barrel tip pointed at his head. "You're crazy. And Walter's a fool for giving you such power. Having one soldier with a handgun will not buy your position forever or keep you from answering for this."

"Oh, but you're missing the point... as you most often do. This pimple-faced boy is no soldier. He answers the phone. He's never even held a gun before this moment, but he *will* pull that trigger if I tell him to. You see, your little mind can't even understand what power is, so how could you ever wield it or control it?" Roberta paused to show the secretary a sinister smirk. "He and I made a little agreement just before you got here. I own him now. And I own this operation, the whole thing, from those first scans of that world to the climax of Oncoming Storm. And I'll do my job the same over there to ensure our people's future."

Solomon Michaels stood with stiff shoulders and darkened fabric on the underarms of his suit jacket. "*Please*. Don't try to mask your lust for power with righteous intent." His voice reached for strength but cracked like a pubescent boy's. Roberta knew she had him.

"That will be all, John. And put that back in my bag."

"Yes, SCL. Thank you." The boy with her purse gun exited, but the tension in the air remained. The sensual high elevated Roberta more than her morning's physical activities.

"Where were we? Oh yes..." The SCL walked around her desk and took her seat, leaving her two seniors to stand. "We expect the PM has been handled. That puts Oliver Nelson in charge of Idyllium. We have him and his assistant, Susan, in our pocket—and they willingly assumed that place. The assassination was Oliver's idea. Maybe he just wanted power. I don't trust him, so of course, I have a contingency plan with Susan to ensure no interference with the detonations."

"The nuclear option is only to be used if they don't accept our help for the financial and political collapse. That's what I agreed to. We want to go over as saviors, not conquerors." Solomon got his normal voice back, but the fleshy tones took their time returning to his paper-white face.

"We proceed as planned, and if we get what we want without the nukes, so be it. But nothing stops us from getting onto that pristine planet. If Oliver turns, as I suspect he will, Susan will back us on the contingency plan."

"We put all these words on it to avoid saying what we're really doing."

Roberta sat up straighter. "Blowing them to kingdom come. Killing millions. The words don't scare me, Sol. It's why we're here, to make the *big-boy* decisions. We do what we must to survive. We've run out of future here."

"I'm not saying I'm not on board. Just that we need to fully explore options and do what will ensure the *best* future... for both worlds."

Vescovi and Hillthorpe remained silent as the balding politician confidently swaggered out. Roberta allowed him the moment to feel he'd made his point, gotten the last word. Nestled in the confidentiality offered by the closed door, she rose and slinked around the desk to take the chairperson's arm.

"Don't worry, Walter. I'll take care of him."

37 | Idyllium Mission: Day 3

THE SHOWER'S STEAM ESCAPED the open door like a child fleeing elementary school at the end of the day. When Kateryna stepped back into the room, she couldn't believe she had to spend the night here—not only for sharing it with the guys. Mental images of the clientele the motel likely hosted abseiled down from the ceiling like a thousand spiders and crawled over her skin. With a clean body in fresh bedclothes and assuming the bedspread hadn't been properly washed in ages, she stripped the bed down to the bottom sheet. Only then did she notice the room's emptiness. A silent Marc sat glossy-eyed at the table in the unwelcoming space, isolated by his tablet's spell.

"Frank and Sharon?"

"Getting some things at the store. Oh, I didn't arrange this, so don't get any ideas."

"How can you be so jovial? What are we going to do?"

"Send your message. Look, besides Saul being on his own, this is all going according to plan."

"I'd hate to see what *not* going according to plan looks like." She pushed a smile, taking some of Marc's lightheartedness into herself.

"Yeah, Tim always helped with strategizing things." Kat didn't recognize the name but didn't interrupt. "I have two messages for you to send. I didn't want to say earlier in front of everyone. Let's prepare the standard update report, then I have an address for another."

With Marc's words polished a bit and corrected for grammatical errors, Kat sent the update. It reported the failure of the assassination attempt and how the team of their doubles thwarted it, putting Marc behind a rifle and placing his doppelgänger on the stage. Kat couldn't help thinking about all those phony stories she helped Monica report about the Mars colony. The irony of how much "doing the right thing" involved lying stung like waiting for Herbie to open the office on a high-rad day. Marc had her include an optimistic view for the rest of the mission carrying on as planned, despite the setback.

"Sent. Now, what's this second message about, and to whom?"

"You know how Hillthorpe is. Well, she's not the only one."

"Tell me about it. When you pranced around here in your towel, I thought you learned a thing or two from her about intimidation tactics."

"*Kateryna*." Marc smirked when Kat couldn't hold her giggle. "I mean her contingency plans. I've got some of my own."

"Sharon's dad?"

"That's one, but for another thing. You're not the only one with friends in high places. Well, yours is as high as it gets. But mine aren't too shabby. Few people know of the details of our mission. Only the chairperson, the SCL, and the secretary know about the assassination attempt. I got a channel to send messages to the cabinet members' group address. They'll all get this next message."

"Who'd you have to seduce to get that?" Kat said with a wink and a smirk.

"Called himself Blacklight. Wait… no seduction, I assure you." His face lit with a wide smile. "He's a good man, I think. Said he's the personal assistant to one of the higher-ups directly involved. I assumed Secretary Michaels, as most of the joint chiefs are excluded from the details of our operation here. A quick search said Marshal Johnson filled that role."

"And this informant, maybe Johnson, called himself *Blacklight?*"

"A black light exposes the filth and fluids, residue left by... *unsavory* activities. Anyway, he said not everyone is happy about the assassination or the nukes, but Vescovi goes along with anything the SCL does. While he fully supports the rest of the operation, this Blacklight told me the secretary pushes to do everything possible to avoid obliterating four cities. But he knows he can't stop the SCL."

"I like this Secretary Michaels. And I think my trust in you was well placed. But how is sending the chairperson's cabinet a message going to change anything? Roberta holds all the cards, and they cannot overrule her."

"Yeah, I know. She's the evil empress about to conquer an entire planet."

"*Evil?* I'd not say that. Ambitious, sure. Aggressive. While she loves power, that's clear, I've spent time with her. I've seen her use her powers, personal and political, to help. The Global Health Initiative was her idea, and she got the funding for it. You can guess how. Roberta *does* want to save the people on our world."

"And thirty years ago, that extremist group wanted to save our world by exterminating a third of its population."

"Let me guess: *you* stopped them."

"I was in high school. Ironically, the incidents did that anyway shortly after, wiping out about half the people on Earth."

"True. But that sealed our fate rather than free us of it. Now, what am I sending the cabinet members?"

"We need it to look like a routing mistake. We can't make anyone think we have this address or meant to send the message to it. Think you can work some comms magic to make that happen? Make it look like a follow-up to the one you just sent to the chairperson's office."

"You mean to Roberta." Kat traced the cracks in the ceiling as she thought. "Okay, I think I can route it like that. So, what do we say?"

Sitting beside her to read her screen, Marc had Kateryna type a message explaining Saul went missing. His exact words were "going off book," and he refused her suggested edits. He had her clearly mention the assassination attempt in a way that sounded like natural follow-up, not like they were reporting it to the cabinet address.

"All right... Let me think about this." While Kat loved doing research and could compile facts to be turned into Monica-worthy news reports, she never wrote the full scripts. "What if we say that Saul may have thought you were the other you, from Idyllium, who stopped you from assassinating the PM? He likely thought he was shooting at the enemy."

"Or maybe that he was the other Saul, from this side?"

"But that doesn't line up. You were arrested for attempting to kill the PM. The other Saul would have assumed you to be his Marc, so he'd have saved you, not tried to kill you. Sheesh, my head hurts trying to keep it all straight."

"I know. Mine feels like when Saul bashed my face in a week back."

"He *what?*"

"Another time."

Marc leaned his head to the side and rubbed his neck. Instinctively, Kat reached out and began massaging it with one hand, then pivoted and placed two on his shoulders. His rigid muscles pushed back on her fingers with tension a professional masseuse would struggle to remove.

The situation's reality came to her like an abrupt scene change in a film. They were alone in a motel room—likely used more for sexual encounters than sleeping—sitting on the same bed and she had her hands on him. His rock-hard shoulders turned to lava and her hands withdrew. Marc's leap from the mattress meant a similar clarity found him.

"Um... Sorry, Marc. I just..."

"No, it's fine. And thanks, that actually helped. But I appreciate the caution. You know, two *wildly attractive* people... in a high-emotion situation."

"*Two?* Got a pretty high opinion of yourself there, old man." Kat's laughter turned Marc's face red, and he joined her in a chuckle.

Marc sat on the bed across from her and listened as Kat retold the story of the assassination attempt in a way that made a believable addition to the first report while exposing the hidden details to the chairperson's cabinet. He approved the final edit and gave her the address. Kat didn't know what, if any, good that would do, but Marc's confidence settled some of her insecurities.

"Marc? I'm feeling a little better about our chances now and what we're doing. But I hate surprises. I'd feel much better if I knew the whole plan. Is there anything you can tell me?"

"You have most of it. The only other secret I have is a list of our covert operatives working on this side."

"Really? That's been kept super top secret. Wait, I thought only Roberta would have that. How'd you get it? Not a favor exchange, I hope."

"I hadn't thought of that. Might have been the easier way to get it... more enjoyable too."

Kat reached to slap his knee but missed. "*Marss.* You're so bad."

"No, you're right. Not about me being bad. I mean the list. She's the only one *on Earth* who has all the names. The SCL has been conspiring with the deputy PM here on Idyllium, and he was set to replace the PM when we killed him. He has the complete list, and we're do to meet with him tomorrow."

"But you said we'd skip that since the deputy hasn't succeeded the PM."

"Saul will skip that part. We'll go as planned and get that list."

38 | Earth: 2 Days After Crossover

It had been a turbulent couple of years since Jewel's diagnosis. Casey marveled at her strength of character and bravery. She tried to have the same and believed she did, at first. Those first few months she cared for her little girl, poured all the positivity she could onto her, desperate to give the girl the hope she didn't have herself. Then it all fell apart.

With pity-filled eyes she watched her precious daughter sleeping, slowly dying. Casey shed tears for failing her. Those months when she drowned in her own despair kept her from being there for her family. Peggy the nurse took over the role of caregiver for Jewel, and Marc had to pile the burden of his alcoholic and depressed wife onto his already sagging shoulders barely supporting the weight of him slowly losing his little girl. Haunting memories of that would likely outlive Jewel.

A twinge shuddered down her spine when Casey's mind filled with images of Tim. He'd been so good to their family, and she'd treated him so poorly. Embarrassment flushed her cheeks thinking of that loving friend having to awkwardly bathe her. Then a very different feeling chased the shame away and filled her with remorse. She had craved having him want her. Not that she would have ever given in to that longing, never considered being disloyal to Marc.

Just to be noticed... To feel desired.

Jewel's snort snapped her back, and Casey checked the oxygen flow, straightening a bend in the tube. Her efforts to spend that last evening with her dad and wish him well on his assignment the next morning had taken their toll. She hadn't gotten out of bed since, and Casey pushed away thoughts of what the color that avoided her daughter's cheeks meant for her next few days.

Peggy's arrival called Casey from the bedside.

"Time for me to administer Jewel's weekly treatment." Peggy no doubt wished to shield her from watching whatever that treatment involved.

Casey had to wrestle herself away from Jewel's side with all her newly regained strength of will. "I'll go prepare her breakfast." It had been months since *the bottle* entered the house, and she had determined to keep it that way. Busying herself with her little girl's care fortified her resolve.

While Casey prepared Jewel's breakfast—a nutrient-rich drink—Peggy stepped out from the bedroom to say she'd finished the treatment and Jewel sat up, awake and hungry. Since she sobered up, Casey developed a rapport with Peggy, though nowhere as close as the nurse had with her patient. Trust hadn't yet matured to where Peggy left Jewel in Casey's sole care during a shift, so she stayed close. Now a permanent fixture like the brown cement rectangle occupying the space where a glass pane should invite warm sunlight into the home, Peggy was unwelcome for the reason for her presence and sorely needed for the same. Casey had gotten used to ignoring the nurse to speak openly with Jewel.

With eyes permanently set in a worried state, Casey observed the frail young lady's cheeks withdraw in a feeble effort to suck in her liquid nourishment. "You're doing so well, sweetheart." Jewel pulled her lips into a half smile as the first signs of life on her face in over a day.

"Thanks, Mom. Any word from Daddy?"

"No sweetie. It's one of *those* missions."

"Radio silence. He told me. I must've forgotten. He's a real hero, isn't he? Keeps us all safe."

"He is. You should be very proud of him. And he's a good man. Not many of those left in this world."

"Mom... are things... *good* with you and Dad now?"

Casey tried to pull the shock from her face. Jewel's alertness came with unexpected maturity for her twelve years. Realization that her innocent little girl likely understood her actions over the course of the last two years, her depression-induced alcohol dependence, and perhaps even her wrestling with feelings for *Uncle Tim*, opened her eyes wide.

"It's okay, Mom. I'm not a baby. I could tell things got rough and can't imagine how hard caring for me is on you both. I wish I wasn't such a burden to you."

"No, no, sweetheart. Don't ever think that. You are and always will be the best thing that's ever happened to us. Your dad and I love you so much. You're never a burden. Never." A tearful embrace followed the words.

"I love you too, Mommy. And I'm glad to see you and Dad looking... *happy* again."

"We hit a rough patch, you're right. But we're good now. Very good."

"I miss him when he's gone."

"Me too. I asked him to stop, to stay with us. But, my sweet Jewel, this mission... well, it's different." Jewel's eyes almost found their luster, and with a light grunt, she sat up a little more. "He didn't want to say... but he's working on something for you."

"For me?"

Casey got up and slid the door to Jewel's room closed as she gave Peggy an "I need some privacy with my daughter" look. When she returned to the bed, she spoke in a quiet voice.

"For your... condition. We don't know yet, so he didn't want to get your hopes up."

"Mom, we know I'll never make it long enough for Mars. I don't think I'd survive the trip even if I did."

Casey closed her eyes to the thoughts of her Jewel speaking so rationally and calmly about her impending death. She had told Marc she accepted their daughter's fate, but she considered no parent ever could, not fully.

"Not Mars, honey. Dad's gone somewhere. Somewhere with a clean ecosphere the doctors said could stall your sickness and let you live a healthy life."

"There's no place like that, Mom. What are you talking about?"

Taking her hand in a gentle squeeze, Casey said, "He's gone to another world. I know, it sounds crazy. I couldn't believe it either. About ten years ago, the UGA found a parallel Earth, clean and healthy, and then learned how to cross over."

"And you're saying Daddy went there? To another planet?"

"He's not gone to another planet on a spaceship. He said it was more like stepping over to a mirror world. And he's planning to take us there, to Idyllium. You'll be able to live a full life there."

Conversation continued as Casey tried to convince Jewel of what she couldn't fully believe herself. She saw the wonder fill her dear girl's eyes, and the spark of hope gave them a glimmer Casey hadn't seen in months.

"But how does it work? How'd Daddy get there?"

"I have no idea about the science or how any of this works."

"But... it worked, right? Dad's okay? He made it there?"

"Yes. His team is there, safe and sound."

"If he can't communicate, how do you know that?" Casey watched the glint in Jewel's eyes darken in worry for her father.

"Sharon O'Brien's father got word from someone at the base."

"They told *him*, but not you?"

"No one is supposed to know about this mission, or that the other world exists. Jewel, you can't tell anyone, not even Peggy."

"I'm confused. I mean, the whole thing, it's just... But if he can't talk to us and we're not even supposed to know anything about that other Earth, how are we supposed to go there?"

"I need to call Mister O'Brien."

39 | Idyllium Mission: Day 4

As the sun contemplated its rise, Marc helped Sharon run some more environmental scans in the courtyard behind the motel. He thought it pointless. They knew Idyllium to be pristine, and nothing of the events of the last few days would have changed that. It gave him something to do. Waiting for the results afforded Sharon an opening to talk, robbing Marc of the silence he had been savoring.

"Captain, you really believe we're on track, or was that just a team morale thing?"

"We are. Saul was always going to be a variable. We stopped team two. The PM is alive. We're meeting with his deputy later today to get critical intel and then we move on to stop whoever Hillthorpe sent to take out that defensive sensor array."

"Yeah, but we have no idea who that is, how many, how well armed. And you said Saul is going to try as well. But first, we'll meet with the guy who planned to assassinate his own PM and convince him to help us even though he thinks we failed."

"Easy-peasy." Marc knew the odds were against them.

"Can't you be a wee bit serious for once?"

Kat appeared behind Sharon. "Serious about what?"

"Oh, hey. She's got the mission jitters. I was just leveling the tension."

"Jitters, really, Captain? What do we need from the deputy PM, anyway?"

"Besides the SCL on Earth, he and his assistant are the only ones with a complete list of our operatives. We expose that, we might have a shot at stopping the economic chaos over here. And we'll flush out Deputy PM Nelson and whoever else is working with him."

"I always knew one of these days, your cowboy ways of running a mission would end in disaster. I'm starting to think this is the one."

Kat turned to Marc with a raised eyebrow. "Cowboy ways?"

"Trained in Texas." He smiled at her and turned to Sharon. "Look, every lucky streak's gotta end sometime. Let's not let it be this time. We need to get that list."

"Um, Marc? Even if we get that list, how are you going to get it out there? No one would trust you. You're wanted for attempted murder of the PM. And now, you're an escaped fugitive."

"That's where you come in. I'll need your comms voodoo... um... *expertise* to get Belinda on the air to tell the people here what's going on and to read the list."

"Belinda Mayers? That's your plan? She's the one who ID'd you at the conference. I saw her telling the guards on stage. Why would she trust you?"

"Because the PM will tell her to."

"Captain... I think you've gone cuckoo for Cocoa Puffs. Sir."

Marc let out a short-burst giggle. "Aren't you supposed to say, 'me Lucky Charms'?"

"What was that about being serious? Marc, why would the PM tell Belinda Mayers to trust you and report what you tell her to say?"

"He was curious about me and why I didn't kill him. Even *he* saw it was a piss-poor attempt at an assassination... if I was an assassin, I mean. It's why he came to talk to me before you so kindly broke me out of jail. Excellent work on that, by the way."

"Hold up there, Captain. How'd you go from him doubting you wanted to kill him to him working with us and getting that reporter lady to do as you ask?"

Marc smirked, and Kat's words came ahead of his. "Don't say your charm. Oh, and please don't say you seduced him."

That brought Marc to a full and hearty chuckle. "Nah. Told him I'd get you to go on a date with him. He said to wear the black dress."

"Nice, Captain. Real nice."

"But you didn't see how Kateryna looked at the guy."

A pop rang in Marc's ear from the slap on his arm.

That woman standing in the alley clearly wasn't Oliver Nelson. He must have changed the plan when the *deputy* part hadn't been removed from his title. A black suit stood at each of her sides, and Marc knew that meant more unseen security nearby, maybe snipers. He didn't have the team to handle that, so he faced a possible ambush alone. Frank had gone to scout their next journey, and Kat stayed in the motel to modify the comms gear. Around the corner, Sharon waited in the transport they "borrowed" from the Hotel New Renaissance, told to keep her foot over the accelerator.

Head straight and eyes checking vantage points, Marc paced his steps in an unthreatening approach to the mystery woman. The alley narrowed to about twelve feet wide, and the buildings walling him in had three floors casting heavy shadows over his view. Not seeing other security didn't convince Marc they weren't there, considering how well-trained they must have been. He'd have to deal with what he saw. This time, he didn't have Frank's shoulder to take the sniper's bullet for him.

"Who are you?"

The woman folded her neck to look him in the face. "Why'd you fail?"

"Another team. Your side. Who were they? Did you send our doppelgängers?"

"There *are no* doppelgängers. We went back a century, and not a single match from your world was found here. We sent an update to your SCL before you came to Idyllium. It seems our parallel worlds are not exact mirror images, but that changes nothing."

What the woman said pricked his mind, but he stored that for later. Marc eyed the bodybuilder of a man on one side and the slightly less huge one on the other. "Please remove the muscle so we can talk."

The face under the black bobbed hair turned to the bigger guy, pulling his eyes off Marc.

A taser slipped out from the sleeve of Marc's jacket and a flick of the wrist sent an electrical jolt through coiled wires into the lesser hulk's neck. Slipping between the woman and the distracted bodyguard, Marc spun and slammed an elbow into the giant's windpipe.

The first guy dropped to the ground, convulsing like a hyperactive chihuahua, while Marc wrapped his other arm around the petite woman's neck. Marc backed against a steel fire exit door behind a human shield. Still gasping his breaths, standing but hunched forward, the thick man in the obvious government-security-black suit raised his fists and attempted a few steps. Marc introduced the boot at the end of his leg to the guy's lowered face and removed his consciousness from the moment.

"How many more?"

In futility, the woman clutched her tiny hands onto Marc's brawny forearm under her chin. He contracted his muscles into a tighter choke. A raggedy gray cat screeched out what no one could describe as a meow and scurried off from behind a trash bin.

"Call them off."

In response, she waved her hand in a half-circle.

"Now, tell me why you're not Oliver Nelson." Marc held the pose, pushing his words out behind the squirming lady's ear.

"The deputy PM sent me. I'm his assistant and he's fuming you blew it. We figured the mission's off and didn't think you'd even show."

"We'll get the next phase done. I'm moving my men to the power grid to take down the alert system now. I need the list."

"What list? Let go of me."

"I know you brought the list of our operatives in case the mission wasn't over. It's not. I need to contact my people to coordinate the next move, make sure everyone's in place when the defense system goes down."

The stunned goon moaned, working his body toward a *ready for action* state.

"That's my job. And it's not like I have the names written on a piece of paper in my pocket."

Marc reached down the V-neck blouse under the woman's blazer, felt around, and pulled a small data chip from her bra. "We're on the same side, remember?" Marc spoke to his wrist, "A getaway car at the end of the alley wouldn't go amiss."

Scratching sounds of cement deconstructing the faux leather jacket harassed his ears as Marc slid his back along the wall with his shield in tow. Sharon pulled up in the transport. Marc released his prisoner and jumped in, shouting, "Go, go, go!"

As the silent electric vehicle rolled forward, Sharon smirked. "All go according to plan, Captain?"

"When does it ever? But I got the file."

"Push the deputy for any other intel? Do we know who their team is on this side? Does he know who our SCL's second team is?"

"Wasn't him. He sent his assistant."

"That woman? When I saw her run from you, I thought it was a response to your usual charming nature."

"Nice. Just drive."

"Kinda wanted to confirm if the team has any of our doubles on it. Can you imagine if we've got to deal with two Sauls?"

"No. She told me there aren't any. No doppelgängers of anyone from our side here, I mean."

"Um, Captain? If the deputy PM's assistant knows that... our SCL must know it as well."

"Yeah, she told Hillthorpe just before we crossed over."

"We told the SCL *our doubles* stopped us killing the PM."

40 | Earth: 3 Days After Crossover

THE BROKEN TABLET TAUNTED her from the trash bin—a webwork etched in the glass like a barrage of lightning over the supposedly unbreakable screen. Granted, it had taken Roberta several tries to shatter the base display. Its halo-projection protested with flashes of color reflected off the high-gloss desktop. Roberta imagined it resembled a psychedelic trip. With repeated bangs, she wondered which would give first. In the end, the desk won.

The source of what summoned the unbridled assault on the device could only be speculated. The result stood on the other side of her massive, thick mahogany doors. Roberta couldn't delay any longer. She'd take control of the room then the situation. So why did it unnerve her to let the powerless cabinet members into her office?

Get it together. You're Roberta bleeding *Hillthorpe. They have no authority over you. The SCL holds all the power, and they know it.*

Sufficiently reassured by her mental pep talk, Roberta tapped her bio-pad and told John to let them in and bring the tea. She had him prepare a tray ahead of their arrival. The warm, spicy-sweet aroma of Masala Chai saturated the room as its steam escaped the ceramic pot he carried in.

Of the four women and two men, only three accepted a cup of tea. The smile illuminating Roberta's face came not from the chai. It sprang from watching their curious expressions as her first-time visitors noted the lack of chairs. Most of them had never been in her Chicago office, either, which had the same "everyone else stands" furnishings as this one on the Utah compound.

"Where's Solomon?" Amanda Blackshaw asked. A friend of Kat's and about the only one Roberta respected of the group. She thought the blue business suit looked good on her with her wavy blond hair.

"You didn't hear?" Nicholson. Roberta considered him the know-it-all of the bunch, which meant he knew nothing of import. "A bizarre story. An aircar lost control and crashed into his condo. Since it has a glass window, the thing flew right through it and crushed the guy while he sipped a scotch on his sofa. Died instantly."

"Not a bad way. For Sol, I mean. To go out quickly, sipping his scotch." Mike Bradly always spoke his mind. While Roberta normally respected that about someone, she often thought his mind would be better off keeping its mouth shut.

"Yes, I think he'd have chosen to go exactly like that. And he was just here, in my office, yesterday."

"Sorry, Roberta. I know you were close." Where Amanda got that idea, the SCL would never know. "I guess he came for the same reason we're all here."

"Yes. You all know Operation Needle Prick is underway. And it seems, by some *mistake* in our message routing, you recently learned some details about it. So, what can I do for you?"

No one hurried to speak first.

Cindy Peterson set her teacup on the desk. "Let's start with the assassination attempt on the GB prime minister's life. What were you thinking? Did Vescovi sanction that?"

"Like he could ever tell *her* what to do. Or not do." Josephine Garret always looked with disdain upon Roberta. The oldest of the group, she had once held the office of the SCL. Roberta thought it a consolation prize when Walter offered Josephine a cabinet position. Perhaps she did as well.

"Let's at least pretend a little harder to be nice." The SCL puckered her lips over her chai and inhaled to slurp the hot liquid into her mouth. She had read somewhere it enhanced the flavor. True or not, she did it to watch how the rippling noise bothered people. "Walter and Sol have been involved in all the details of Needle Prick. I do nothing on my own without their support."

"Yeah, right." It may have been the first time Roberta heard Lindsey McLaughlin's voice. The group's junior, she rarely had anything to say.

Bradly's eyes circled the room. "Walter's not here and Sol's, well... So, we just have to take your word for it?"

"No, you don't, Mike. None of you do. You are *advisors* to the chairperson. If you thought that gave you any control over his office or mine, let me correct you here and now. I don't yet know how that message about the PM got sent to your group, but you better believe none of you want to be the person responsible. And I *will* get to the bottom of that. I will do as I see fit to ensure our future. Anyone has a problem with that, you can join the *bleeding* Mars project. It's just across the compound."

The room settled, and Roberta did her duty as the chairperson had requested. She outlined the details of the operation, including the defensive grid, the delivery of the nuclear payload, and the subsequent invasion forces. The enormous funding of the project became clear to all when the SCL spoke of the twenty-four-by-seven work she had commissioned in two hundred complexes around the world to meet the deadline to construct the colossal transfer machines needed to send garrisons of soldiers and tanks.

To Roberta's surprise, Josephine lent her support. She had been one of the few involved in the initial efforts of the chairperson's office to present the UGA petition for peaceful migration to the new world. An eyewitness, she watched it crumble into oblivion.

"To refuse a dying world, over four billion." The gray-headed woman stepped beside Roberta and spoke with more power than she expected from the elder's voice. "They've not been good neighbors. We can offer an exchange: our people merge with theirs and we help them rebound from their political and economic collapse. If they don't accept this, we will likely need to go to Roberta's Plan B. I hate to say it, but if they won't be reasonable, we have no choice."

Amanda and Lindsey protested, both speaking of the need to take the moral high ground. The SCL tossed scolding words at them in a raised voice when they spoke of what was right in the eyes of God until she remembered something about the history of such believers.

"You people have an amazingly selective memory. An insignificant part of your holy writings is about peace and nonviolence. You forget that most of your religious history wreaks with so-called righteous wars, slaughtering people by the thousands. When the blessed ones needed a home, the occupants of that land were massacred so they could take it." Roberta squinted to dramatize her retrospective. "And what have you people learned since then? Almost every single war in our history has had religious motivations."

Silence gave the SCL the room to continue, as she expected. This charade of formality gave her the opportunity to assert herself and continue with her mission to save her world.

"Even if we must use the nukes, which is likely, we're talking about a very small percentage of that population. Then we'll be sharing the promised land with them. If you ask me, I'm being a heck of a lot more benevolent than any of your deities ever were. And..." She looked at the ceiling then back to her audience. "I cannot believe I have to remind you, but it seems I do. In ten years, we'll *all be dead*. Four billion of us. You, your children. Everyone. I promise you; I will do *whatever* it takes not to let that happen."

By the time she dismissed her *guests*, Roberta had Mike joining Josephine in offering full support. Amanda and Lindsey remained adamant and *know-it-all* Nicholson joined their team. Roberta thought Cindy leaned in their direction, nodding to Amanda's pontification, but she wouldn't commit.

The emptiness of the oversized office became a cozy comfort, and Roberta closed her eyes to the acoustic void. She couldn't decide if she wanted to sit, eat, or take a walk. She poured herself two fingers of whiskey. When she called John into the office, she wondered what he may have expected. The mind game consumed her focus for the seconds it took him to traverse the tiles from the door to her desk. Looking through the flexed toes of her bare feet over the high-gloss desktop, she squinted to follow his walk. The nails needed polish.

As she studied the young man rubbing her foot, the SCL wondered if he had a line. Could she push him to it? What would he do if she asked him to do something that crossed it? The diligence with which he worked his thumbs under her arches gave her the answer. She had thought it an embellishment when she said she owned him, but the truth in her words shone clearly in the boy's focused brow. She wondered how young he was.

The knock on the door disturbed the blissful euphoria of the foot massage, and she drained the last of the whiskey from the tumbler. Vescovi doddered in, devoid of the glimpse of vigor he showed the day before. He looked old again, especially as a background to the cute young man working the ball of her foot with both hands.

"Peter, that will be all." On Walter's words, *John* raised his eyes to Roberta's. She smiled at the thought of how quickly he had learned.

"Keep at it, John, you're doing great. Walter, speak freely. This kid knows everything going on here already."

"Roberta, they're calling for a vote of no confidence. In both of us."

41 | Idyllium Mission: Day 4

Belinda closed the video chat in disbelief about what she had discussed. Rarely had she received a call from the prime minister. She had interviewed him twice and found him to be a gentleman and competent leader, though a true politician—a rare combination in her experience. But this? She struggled to fit it into the sense her brain had of the world.

With her forehead in her palm, Belinda Mayers dug her fingers through the blond bangs to relax her troubled scalp. She'd have to clear her schedule to meet with an assassin, a fugitive on the run. Thinking of how long it had been since she had such exciting fieldwork energized her like her afternoon coffee fix. But that charming general from the conference dinner... came from another world? From a planet like hers, called "Earth."

He was into me. Cute too. We could have happened that night if he hadn't gone all ninja assassin on the PM.

She needed to focus.

"Sheila," she shouted to the frosted glass door that isolated her from her staff. Her personal assistant penetrated that barrier and asked what Miss Mayers needed. "Clear my schedule for the rest of the day, please. And hold all calls."

"Sure. Got a scoop or something? Anything new on the PM or the financial crisis?"

"Maybe something huge, but I can't talk about it." As she spoke, Belinda exchanged her skirt for a pair of jeans and tucked in her sky-blue blouse. "Taking the bike. It's one of *those* appointments."

Could the helmet's visor have skewed her vision? Looking at the Easy Stay Motel, Belinda hoped there wouldn't be a police raid with her there, afraid she'd be carted off as one of the discount prostitutes. A thought of this being where the fake general got his companion in that dress drew a smile over her lips.

She switched off the black electric motorcycle, lifted her leg over the seat, and considered the drab cinderblock motel. The general's escort didn't appear the sort to *work* in a place like this. Belinda figured she must have come from a high-class agency, and an evening with her likely cost an average person's monthly salary.

At room 204, she tapped her knuckles on a door the years neglected, letting the sun evaporate most of its dull green color. A short redhead opened it and glared up at her then peeked her head out to look left and right with squinted eyes.

"I think I've got the wrong room. I'm Bel—"

"I know. Get in here." The yank on her arm tripped the reporter into the dimly lit room to either get the story of her career or be raped and killed. Either possibility seemed likely to her at the time. Her pupils adjusted to bring another woman into focus. *The gorgeous escort does work here*.

"Hello, Belinda. Thank you for coming." A male voice. Either the would-be assassin turned ally or the man who'd toss her on the bed in a vicious assault.

"As we're on a first-name basis already, are you Marc?"

Desperate for answers, she focused on the silhouetted figure materializing into a man, the one from another world, as he stepped from the vanity light pushing off the mirror. The scent in her nostrils led her mind to expect a child who'd been outside playing, and she figured it was the room's natural fragrance. Marc was no child.

"Yes. Captain Marc Sanders. Nice to see you again."

"So, captain? Not a general. And according to Alistair Burgess, not an assassin."

"You're two for two." Looking at his raised hand with two fingers up, he raised a third. "Or was that three? Anyway, let me introduce you to the team. The feisty little redhead is Sharon, and, oh, I guess you met Kateryna."

"The team from another world. Okay, I'm going on faith here that the PM isn't insane or still in shock or something. He told me of the parallel world, called it Earth, and said you've been sent here to kill him then to take down our security grid. I'm interested in why you've flipped. Why help us stop your people when your world is about to die?"

"Can we sit?" Marc motioned to one of two chairs and took the other. The women each sat on the end of a bed and Belinda let go of a bit of apprehension and sat. Marc explained the situation and how he hoped to bring his family over shortly, then the human population of the tainted Earth. Belinda listened attentively, taking mental notes as her memory had never failed her, while Marc explained their desire to find a way to work together without destroying what he called the "utopia of this side." Mayers never considered her world that, but compared to Marc's Earth, it fit.

The brunette from the gala spoke with such passion for their altered mission and her reason for joining the team and crossing over. Sharon offered wholehearted agreement and added her absolute trust in her captain. Other than interjecting a question for clarification here or there, Belinda took it all in through active listening, building a mental image to see the situation as a complete picture. Not all the pieces fit.

"Excuse me, Katrina. You said you're friends with the one running the operation against us. And we're supposed to believe you're on our side now?"

"It's Kateryna. And yes, we've been friends for years. Roberta Hillthorpe is as power-hungry as she is ruthless about it. I think she desperately wants to save our world and sees this as the only way. As I understand it, we tried for a peaceful solution first, but your PM shot it down."

"Deputy PM, actually. Unfortunately, he's useless. Power-hungry, like yours, but short-sighted and not much for strategy. The few projects Alistair had entrusted to him blew up in his face. And today, the PM told me he hadn't been made aware of the initial contact by your people and failed peace agreement until months after. He's good. Balanced and reasonable. He'd have worked to help your people."

"Like if we sent ambassadors or... missionaries... over instead of spies and now soldiers?" The redhead hid something deeply personal in her lowered eyebrows. Belinda couldn't guess it beyond the wonder and speculation in her brilliant green irises.

"And now you all think we can get back to that? You propose a peaceful integration of your people in our world, and I'm supposed to help with that somehow?"

Marc stood, towering over her, so she hopped up to her feet. "Belinda, first, we need you to help us stop this. We're not the only ones from Earth here..."

Moments from going live, Belinda sat at her studio desk with a flutter that hadn't visited her stomach since her rookie days doing *filler* reports on local channel 11 in Sandy Plains. With next to no experience then, she had been made to show more skin. Her dues, they called it, to get her career started. Now, she felt respected and never got flustered before a broadcast. Of course, never had she reported anything like this.

After a finger countdown, the producer mouthed, "On the air."

"Good evening. I'm Belinda Mayers, and this evening, we're jumping right into the main story. I can think of nothing to prepare you for what I am about to report, so hold on and stay with me. You know, amid our economic crisis, there was an attempt on our PM's life. What I have learned is who is responsible and why. And, hard to believe as this will be for you, you'll want to listen carefully. A team of covert operatives from another—" With a thunderous thud, the near-blinding studio lights switched off, replaced by standard lighting. "—world are here... What happened? Why am I off the air? Get me back on. Get me back on *now!*"

The show's producer sprinted over to the news desk, a mess of perspiration-wrangled hair in strands over his forehead. "Belinda, we've been shut down. Order came from the deputy PM's office, and there's a bunch of soldiers here."

"Get me back on, *now*. I need to report this."

"Report what? You went way off script."

"Just get us up and live. *Now,* Burt."

"We can't. Soldiers. I said *soldiers* are here. They cut studio power."

"You've got to sneak me out of here. *Now.*"

Without a question, Belinda's manager ran them to the back staircase. A flight and a half into their escape, she heard the stairwell door slam open. "Go. Go. Go," someone yelled. The clatter of thick boots pounding the cement stairs echoed in her ears like the Grim Reaper's inescapable approach. She clenched

Burt's hand and drew her shoulders in. The escapees stopped on the half level, frozen and silent.

As Burt had surmised, the soldiers ran down at full speed, leaving him and his star reporter a flight and a half up from the studio level.

"Now what?" she whispered in his ear. "Down is the way out. Got any more brilliant ideas?"

"I do. Where's your bike? The alleyway, right? Where I always tell you *not* to park it." She nodded sheepishly. He had warned her repeatedly of his fear of her going into that dark alley late in the evenings alone after a broadcast. She never listened. "I'll get you there."

He led her up to the next floor and ran her across the sea of empty cubicles. The research staff had long since gone home. Belinda followed but worried about his plan, as she knew of no stairs on that side of the building. He ran into the restroom at the far end and straight into the back wall with the pop of a double palm-slap to stop his momentum. He opened the frosted window, which tilted out a few inches at the top.

"We're five flights up. And I can't squeeze through that. What's the plan here?"

Without answering, the man, as Belinda had never seen him before, frantically turned something at the hinge points at the bottom of the window. When he pulled the top, the window frame tilted down, opening the wall to a two-foot-high-by-three-foot-wide hole. *Big enough to climb through and then fall to my death*, she considered.

"Fire exit. No one ever reads the evacuation sign." Burt flashed a goofy but confident grin and motioned to the opening. "Look."

"I see the alley. But I'm not crazy about this ladder." A six-foot catwalk under the window joined a ladder with a rusted safety cage that ran the height of the building's twelve floors.

"This way or the soldiers get you. I have no idea what this is about, but I trust you. If you need to go, this is your way out. Go."

A peck on his cheek led to a hug full of gratitude for the unexpected bravado and assistance. The moment ended with the disruption of the elevator's ding and someone saying, "You go this way. I'll check there." A floor-by-floor search, no doubt.

"Hurry, Belinda. And get that story out, whatever it is. Four twenty-one Union Road. Remember that. Go there and get the story out. Now go."

Gingerly, she straddled the sill and climbed through the fifth-floor window and touched the toe of her shoe to the metal-grated walkway. Her turn almost toppled her to its floor when the tip of her heel pushed through the mesh, so she removed her shoes. She loved those shoes, expensive too. She took to the ladder, grateful for the safety cage, though it made her think of a distraught bird yearning for freedom.

Her descent carried the weight of worry for Burt in the restroom. What would happen to him when the soldiers found him? A glance up to check on him, to see what she knew she couldn't see, showed her the closed window. She knew him to be smart and kind, but she never would have guessed this level of bravery and ingenuity.

The end of the ladder came well above the ground, explaining why she'd never noticed it all those times she parked her bike so close to it. With numbing hands, she refused to loosen the tight grip she squeezed. Her head jerked side to side, up and down—she had to find it. There had to be a way to lower the second set of rungs she saw. A lightning storm's thunderclap fell on her ears before the pebbles of glass rained down. A soldier leaned out the window, and their eyes met.

With no high heels to slow him on the catwalk, he entered the birdcage in a second. Frantically, she groped up and down the side rails until she found it. The click released a howl of metal on metal as the oil-thirsty inner rungs dropped to make her way to the ground, where her bike waited to carry her to safety. She had to hurry. The distance of five floors shortened as the man raced down the rungs.

The bike switched to *active* by thumbprint, silent and ready to leap with full torque. Gripping the handle with her left hand, Belinda turned her head to see the nearness of the soldier in gray. He reached for her but grabbed more fabric than flesh and tore the right sleeve off her blouse when she twisted the accelerator.

With wind-pulled hair fluttering behind her head like a golden pirate flag, she darted toward the street when two soldiers stepped out to block the alleyway's exit. She didn't remember stopping the motorcycle. From behind, one man ran to catch her, a patch of white silk flapping in his clenched fist. The other two closed the path in front. Belinda wondered what they had done to poor Burt.

No helmet, no shoes, nothing but skin below her pulled-up skirt, and one bare arm. She twisted the throttle and shot at the wall of men like a bullet. In a blur of confusion, they drew handguns or tasers.

In a quick turn and lean while squeezing the brake—just as her riding instructor had told her never to do or she'd fall—she slid the bike's rear tire into a set of trash bins. Her bare foot hit the pavement in a desperate attempt to keep her balance. With a skinned knee, the reporter-turned-stunt driver pushed her foot into the ground to get the bike closer to level and twisted the accelerator again.

The bins cleared a hole down the center like a seven-ten split, and she rolled between the soldiers like a bowling ball clumsily missing its pins. Belinda raced off with nowhere to go until clarity popped into her mind. She knew exactly where to go.

42 | Earth: 3 Days After Crossover

THE AGE OF TECHNOLOGY dawned long before Henry O'Brien entered the world. He never cared for it. One of the few "people of the land" left on Earth, his dear Katheryn Marie used to say. Unimaginable technology now taunted him as the instrument of his daughter's exile to another world. What had become of his darling Shay?

As Henry kept the contact number of that stranger, the man with such sympathetic eyes had kept his word. Not that the updates came frequently or with any predictable regularity. Miles better than nothing, Henry followed the progress of Sharon's mission. She promised she'd not be the evil militaristic conqueror he feared the UGA to become. Henry found a basis to fuel his enduring fatherly pride in knowing how she'd successfully thwarted an assassination attempt on the prime minister of the dominant government of Idyllium.

On the corner of the bed in a decently acceptable Utah motel room, he waited. With no idea when the next connection request would come, waiting had been an all-too-familiar pastime of his of late. He turned his eyes to the wall behind the headboard, wondering if the girl had the stamina to endure the ordeal. The connection request alert interrupted the words of a silent prayer.

"*Peter.*" His voice's tremble wasn't from his advanced years. "How's my Sharon?"

"Hello, Mister O'Brien."

Henry's desperation manifested as impatience with the pockmark-faced young man. "Shay? How is she? What's going on over there, son?"

"It seems she's fine, sir. She and others on the team have had some scrapes and bruises, but nothing serious."

"Hurt? Are you telling me my daughter's been injured?"

"Sir, everyone is fine. The team has been working to thwart our operation over there. The UGA considers them traitors, guilty of treason, and possibly of sentencing the population of Earth to death."

"Oh no, son. We've done that very well ourselves, we have. All you've told me thus far is how Shay helped Captain Sanders stop that assassination of the prime minister over there. What's happened since? Where is she?"

"The team is working with a notable Idyllium reporter to broadcast a message to the whole world exposing our plan, and they hope to out many of our agents."

"But that PM and this message... that's a wee bit too much of nothin' to have any hope of halting the invasion. What of the soldiers, tanks, nuclear bombs? How does a reporter and a not-dead prime minister stop that, eh?"

"Our data is limited. Since Kateryna—she's the team's comms expert—stopped sending the official updates, and one not so official, we're only getting brief text updates from our man over there."

"What man? What do you mean, 'our man'? Is someone working against me Shay? Is she in danger?"

"Of course she's in danger. They all are. They're a rogue group invading from another world, so they are enemies of Idyllium. And they're viewed as deserters and traitors to

Earth—well, to the UGA. And Hillthorpe's got people in place, contingencies, she calls them."

"Another team?"

"Far as I know, no other team's been sent since your daughter's went. They initiated a full system diagnostic when Lieutenant Holland died in the chamber."

"That poor boy. I pray for his soul... So, you think this Hillthorpe has someone on Shay's team working for her?"

"Most definitely." The certainty on the boy's face troubled Henry.

After a contemplative pause, he said, "Now what?"

"Now is the defensive grid protecting Idyllium. The team's next objective was to take it offline, allowing the troops and weapons to cross over undetected and take out four cities."

"*My* Shay will have no part of that, I assure you." A hurried rise to his feet punctuated Henry's adamance with a bold exclamation point.

"As we suspect, as well. Under Captain Sanders, the team is clearly working against its mission objectives. The contingency should take out that grid soon. The team will try to prevent this."

Doing his best to wear out the carpet, Henry O'Brien paced the room. "And they will. I have no doubt me daughter will succeed. I'm praying the same, and it's the righteous thing to do."

"Sure." The helpful informant didn't look at all convinced. "Get ready. If we've got a shot, I think we need to move tomorrow."

"Okay. I'll ge—"

"John! Get back in here." The jarring voice, though distant, held within it the shrillness of approaching death.

"Sorry, sir. Gotta go."

The connection terminated, collapsing the hologram of the boy's head into the handheld.

We need to move tomorrow, the boy said. Henry's thought encouraged his feet to carry him to the wall separating the rooms. *Tomorrow.* He drummed his fist three times in rapid succession on the pale white surface above the bed.

43 | Idyllium Mission: Day 4

"What in the name of Pete just happened?" Sharon couldn't believe her eyes when they read, "Technical difficulties. Please stand by," on the motel room television. Belinda Mayers disappeared in mid-sentence to static, then a black screen with the worrying message. Whatever happened, Sharon knew it couldn't be good.

Marc jumped to his feet. "I'd better go check on her. Frank, stay here and stay sharp."

"Aye, Cap."

"Go where, Marc?" Kat pulled herself from the soft mattress and lumpy pillows she shared with Sharon.

"The studio. Belinda may be in trouble."

"Maybe you shouldn't go alone, Captain. Me or Frank can go with you."

Kat said, "I think you shouldn't go at all. We have no idea what's happened, but my guess is they shut her down. If so, that studio will be crawling with cops."

"We call them soldiers. And I dragged her into this. We brought all this mess to Idyllium. If she's in trouble, I need to go."

"Marc, you can't be the knight in shining armor for every damsel in distress."

Sharon nodded agreement. "Maybe she's right, Captain."

"If you go, take Sharon. She's trained, and we can't leave the civvy unprotected."

"Nice one, Frank. I agree with Kateryna, Captain. We all stay here."

"When this becomes a democracy, we'll take a vote. You three stay here. That's an order. I'll take the transport and check it out. If it's unsafe, I'll see how best to plan a way to get her back."

Marc slipped into his boots, grabbed a vest full of weapons and tools, and headed out. Sharon ran after him, trying to talk sense into her irrational captain, and found no way to diffuse his headstrong determination. He sped off in the conspicuous hotel transport.

When Sharon returned, she found her remaining teammates sitting in silence, Kat on one of the two chairs and Frank on the bed the guys shared.

"What'd I miss?"

"Nothing." Frank pouted childishly.

"Kateryna? Looks like something." Kat shook it off. "Frank, what'd you do?"

"Just tried to talk, is all. She's all worried again for Cap, so I tried to console her... Not used to having *civvies* on a mission."

When Kat went to use the restroom, Sharon learned how, despite her clear warning and sage counsel, the hopeless romantic put his arm around their civilian teammate. Her lecture neared its conclusion when Kat's return interrupted it.

The room's air thickened around them until hurried raps on the door popped the silence like an overinflated balloon, startling Sharon. Frank opened it to a one-sleeved reporter standing barefoot and disheveled, out of breath. Sharon waved her in.

The frantic woman settled herself with deep breaths enough to talk. With all eyes on her, Belinda reported her studio invasion and harrowing escape. Then she asked about Marc.

"Don't worry about the captain. He'll be back soon. Stay here with us." Noting the reporter's look over the two beds, Sharon clarified. "The guys can take the floor."

When Marc finally arrived, he expressed relief at seeing Belinda's motorcycle and finding her safe with his team. The beautiful reporter running into Marc's arms pursed Sharon's lips.

Belinda had a plan—or an idea that needed one. Her manager had given her the address of an old television studio scheduled to be repurposed. He believed it was in good working order, and she could broadcast from there if she had a decent technician.

After Marc praised Kat's comm skills, he smiled at the room. "Still on plan, then. See? Nothing to worry about."

"Sure, Captain. Still not convinced *this* isn't the mission."

Belinda looked puzzled by Sharon's comment. "Isn't the mission?"

"Isn't the mission where the captain's crazy plans blow up in our faces."

"*Oh.*"

"Let the civvy take the lead for a moment." Kat winked at Marc, and Sharon wondered if she and Belinda were engaging in that animalistic competition for her captain's attention. "I help Belinda get this message out, informing people about the parallel world and the invasion plans. We out all the agents we have working on Idyllium. We still must stop that other team from taking down the security grid tomorrow, and we're five people; two proper soldiers—no offense, Sharon—a scientist, and two civilians."

"Sounds like the perfect team to me."

"*Marc.* I'm being serious."

"So am I. This is an amazing team. And there's more to my brilliant plan. Sharon, tell them what you found out."

"Okay. So, one thing we didn't know was how to stop them sending nukes and armies here, right? We can't stop that, even from Earth, so how can we stop it from here?" A satisfying smirk curled Sharon's lip. "This is why you always bring a scientist. Planets all have what's known as a *natural frequency*. The Earth's natural frequency is called the *Schumann Resonance*, which pulsates at a rate of 7.83 hertz..."

At times, she felt she lost most of them, but the concentrated looks they wore said they tried to keep up. Under the captain's orders, Sharon had a series of scans running during their jump across the void. She hoped to confirm a hypothesis and gather as much data as possible—and she found it.

"... and the first scanners they sent had burned up in the transfer chamber without dematerializing. Others vanished but sent no data. We lost several agents, too. Eventually, they found a way to identify locations on Idyllium with virtually identical frequencies to Earth and with low lightning and storm activity. See, that can shift the resonance, and even a wee alteration could have devastating results."

Comparing that history with her data led Sharon to a highly plausible theory. "We can prevent anyone on Earth from crossing the void by causing acoustical interference in the sonic frequency at the destination. The landing points on Idyllium. If the transverse generators failed to synchronize the frequencies by even a wee margin, they'd not be able to make a successful jump."

"Hold on, Sharon." Kat looked at the ceiling with a face full of deep thought. "For the small generator we know of back on Earth, the one we used, we have one location here to block, the park where we landed. But Roberta told me she had two hundred massive ones built to send troops and artillery over. How can we block all those potential landing spots?"

"Kateryna, my mission sister, you are here for more than sending simple messages back. The captain chose you for this mission because you are the best communication specialist in the world—maybe in both worlds. You'll help me configure the global defensive grid to broadcast the interference signal."

"I see."

"Our mission is more than not to let that grid get destroyed. We need to use it." Marc looked at Belinda then back to Kat. "But first, we need your expertise to help Belinda make her broadcast. And maybe... lend her a shirt with *two* sleeves."

44 | Earth: 4 Days After Crossover

She didn't know which infuriated her more, the ridiculous call for a vote of no confidence or the time it took her away from the critical mission. Roberta Hillthorpe had been the one ruling the world for a decade and a half. She would have preferred a simple *thank you* and to be left alone to get on with her work of saving it.

What entered her mind next took all the pent-up rage and aimed it at a new target. Herself. Evidently, she had missed something in her restructuring when she became the Strategic Counsel Leader and Walter gave her free rein to empower herself and cement her position. To secure her authority, she included removing the limit of twelve consecutive years in office for both the chairperson and SCL. Contemplation of how on earth she could have missed something this big, allowing this farce, reddened her face as she entered the Chamber of Justice before the judge and a panel of the highest-ranking executives of the UGA. Her subordinates.

Roberta had expected her first time back in Chicago to be to revel in the success of Needle Prick and to finalize the details of Oncoming Storm. She'd already selected the intern she'd have join her in celebration. To be brought into this overly bright, white-walled room rubbed her every kind of wrong way. Worse, the person seated behind the elevated wood-paneled desk wasn't her, putting her in a meeting without running it. It meant she had to be creative.

She sat beside a primly dressed Walter in a booth alongside the judge, putting them on display to those there to strip them of office. A futile endeavor, she concluded, though she had worked out how to use it to her advantage.

After the judge spewed on about the purpose of the hearing and assured everyone they would proceed by the law to a just outcome, he invited *know-it-all* Nicholson to present an opening statement and provide reasons for the petition of a vote of no confidence. It took the man ten minutes to say what could have been summarized in two. Accusations of lies and conspiracies flew. The last one Roberta had to force herself not to smirk at: warmongering.

"... and the conniving mastermind behind it all is the SCL, Roberta Hillthorpe. We call for a vote of no confidence not only in her but also in Chairperson Walter Vescovi for empowering Miss Hillthorpe and allowing her free rein of UGA resources and agencies."

Several witnesses were called to testify before Walter or Roberta were given the chance to defend themselves. Amanda Blackshaw spoke openly of her disapproval of the whole operation but especially of the planned nuclear action and forced occupation. Roberta hoisted her eyebrows high on her forehead and left them there the entire time Lindsey McLaughlin spoke, never having heard more than two words from the young woman she considered barely more than a child. Cindy Peterson said little but agreed with the vote of no confidence for both.

Time came for Walter to make a statement in his defense. As Roberta expected, he had little to say. He expressed the confidence he had had in her as justification for handing her "the keys to the kingdom," as he said, and admitted he hadn't watched over her activities as closely as he should have. To her, he signed his own death warrant, exactly as she had hoped.

He sat, and her time to speak raised her to her feet. Hillthorpe adjusted the royal-blue business suit jacket she disdained but wore to bring an air of professionalism she normally had no use carrying. If fierce glares could have burned the eyes out of Amanda, Nicholson, and Lindsey, hers would have. She cleared her throat.

"My colleagues and friends, I am simply a public servant…"

Listening to the garbage regurgitating from her own mouth almost amused her as she recounted all the good she had accomplished in her years as SCL. She leaned heavily into the development and funding of the Global Health for All initiative and recounted some highlights of its success. To drive the point home, she emphasized how it had reduced the radiation sickness of everyone in the room, extending their life-expectancy. She doubted her monologue changed the minds of her staunch opposers, but she didn't need those.

The judge tapped a gavel to reclaim the room from the small crowd's murmurings. "We all acknowledge your record, the good and bad. But we are here, Miss SCL, Mister Chairperson, sir, to discuss your handling of our sister world. And I must say, especially to Miss Hillthorpe," with an accusatory finger point, he singled her out. "You have treated her worse than Cinderella's wicked stepsisters. I have only now learned of that Earth's existence and our activities over there thus far. From undermining their political and financial systems alone, I would support a vote of no confidence."

The clearly agitated man paused for a head wag.

"On top of that, an assassination order and planned nuclear annihilation of four of their cities. Look what the incidents did to our world. If we hope to migrate there, contaminating that pristine planet as we did our own may be grounds for a plea of insanity. So far, I see no justification for your actions in this matter."

"Your honor, sir, we have with us one of the most respected members of the chairperson's cabinet, who herself once held my office. I invite her to speak to that."

"Very well, Miss Hillthorpe, as is your right."

The white-haired lady stood with a stoney but wrinkled face in her gray business suit.

"Josephine Garret, you have the floor."

After thanking the judge, she spoke to her agreement of Roberta's actions and her plan to settle in the new world without destroying those cities if possible. Of course, both women knew it would likely come to that. Then the piece Roberta had counted on coming out, and not from herself, presented itself to the room.

"We have reached this unfortunate situation because our initial efforts to engage the PM of Greater Britannia, the ruling empire on that side, led us not to a peaceful agreement. The chairperson failed to negotiate with their deputy PM, and we learned we would not be welcome there. I warned Walter then, nearly four years ago, we should not detail how we ruined our own planet with thoughtless ambition, lack of foresight, and with weapons we created being ultimately used against ourselves."

Amanda rose without being given the floor. "But the SCL was involved in those negotiations. You can't put that on Walter. We all know he lets Roberta do everything."

"Settle down." Sharp bangs of the gavel filled all ears in the room. "And I remind everyone to raise their hand and speak only when invited to. Miss Garret, would you please clarify the SCL's involvement in those initial negotiations."

"Your honor, it's no secret I am no friend of Roberta Hillthorpe. We all know her reputation and have a reasonable assumption of how she got her power and my job. I was consulted on those negotiations and made my recommendations directly to the chairperson, and Walter dismissed them, saying we needed to make our plight known and call on their humanitarianism to come to our aid. Frankly, sir, and I love Walter dearly, but I believe we're in this predicament because of him."

Roberta couldn't have been happier, hidden under a somber countenance as if she felt bad for Walter. He had been useful, allowed her to get where she wanted to be and handed her the world, dying, but hers. And she always knew when to let him speak or act to cover her own backside. She had envisioned the time she would replace him as chairperson, and this only accelerated her timetable.

The SCL hadn't gotten out of the fire just yet.

A heated question-and-answer session began over her role since the failed negotiations. Roberta held the full attention of every ear when she outlined the operation from the initial scans to the first teams sent over. Her choice to send Marc's team and how she had contingencies on it raised some eyebrows. When she explained the collaboration with the deputy PM in all aspects of the mission, including the assassination and nuclear action, Roberta thought she had the majority leaning her way.

"There is one more thing." Nicholson. What Roberta wouldn't have done to have an aircar run through *his* home. "Secretary Solomon Michaels died under suspicious circumstance immediately after meeting with you and the chairperson. Can you explain that, Roberta?"

"I'm not an aircar mechanic, nor do I have any idea how our air guidance control system functions. I'd have thought what happened to be impossible. Maybe you should ask someone who'd know such things."

Mike Bradly followed instructions by raising his hand and waiting for the judge to invite his comment. "Someone like

Walter Vescovi. His company may specialize in climate control, but he's an accomplished engineer and knows about computer control systems not unlike our aircar guidance."

Debate ensued, and Roberta watched the points and counterpoints bounce back and forth like a tennis match where neither player missed a shot, an endless cycle of volley and return. The first vote of no confidence in the chairperson passed by an overwhelming majority. Roberta's would be close, and the time it took for the secret ballot moistened her lower back. Of course, she had a contingency, but it would be an ugly one.

The judge announced Roberta Hillthorpe would keep her position, by a narrow margin. With the chairperson deposed, she would ascend to the position, presenting another problem. Too much authority rested in the office of the SCL, whoever that would be without the secretary to succeed to the role. Roberta had a plan and a contingency for that and stood to give Plan A a shot.

"Your honor, esteemed colleagues. This may not be the forum, but everyone needed is here, and time is something we just don't have. Of course, Sol's unfortunate passing leaves the office of the SCL vacant. It's been my job for fifteen years, and as we have discussed in this hearing, we all know dear Walter did little in his position. Some details of the mission came to light recently, which all the cabinet members have learned directly from the team over there..."

Hillthorpe recounted the first objective failure and the report of the teams' doubles stopping them. When she revealed the report confirming no doppelgängers existed on the other world, some gasped. Marc and most of his team had gone rogue. The SCL, now chairperson, had an ace up her sleeve in Saul Mullins. He stayed on mission and would complete the next objective, allowing the start of Oncoming Storm. Of course, even her contingency had a contingency.

"With so much at stake, I propose a merger of the two offices. Acting as chairperson and strategic counsel leader, I can manage the remote teams and complete this operation. I remind you it is our last chance, our Plan B. If it fails, we're all gone in ten years."

A din floated over the room as some talked among themselves while others shouted their disapproval of the proposal at the judge, who had no role in this since the no-confidence votes had concluded. To Roberta's surprise, one voice bellowed above the rest. Lindsey McLaughlin.

"We can't hand her unlimited power."

Nicholson barked, "Like she didn't already have it."

Roberta shoved her pinkies into the corners of her mouth. Her deafening whistle cut through the room like a katana's blade, dealing a death stroke to the rumbling voices.

"If we fail, it won't matter. *All dead*, remember? And if we succeed, which I will, it still won't matter. We'll be migrating to another world, leaving the UGA behind."

45 | Idyllium Mission: Day 5

They brought her on the mission for this. Kateryna had sent her messages and worked the comms gear. When Marc insisted she be the distraction, she slinked around in that black dress, thinking Marc may have chosen her specifically for *that* job. She now understood why a civilian with her expertise tagged along on such an important military operation.

Belinda Mayers wore Kat's cream-colored cotton blouse well under her yellow hair. Frank stowed his tongue with the gear he inventoried and packed into cases and backpacks. While she and Sharon checked and packed their equipment cases, Kat kept the corner of her eye on Marc and Belinda chatting over the little round table. Idyllium's morning sun had slipped through the vertical slit in the thick brown curtain—what little could penetrate the grime-covered window behind it. Dust motes became sparkles dancing and twinkling like glitter in its golden beam.

An unfamiliar beep from the equipment Kat knew so well stopped her activity. She laid the silver case and the battery she was about to put into it on the bed beside her and raised the comms LCD screen. A local emergency alert flashed in red letters over a white background. When they first arrived, which felt like a year ago, she had set the unit to monitor all local emergency frequencies. This was broadcast everywhere, to every device on the data-net.

"Marc? Guys? They're evacuating New London Town. Some kind of citywide gas leak."

The reporter reached for something and donned a look of fright when she didn't find it. "I must have left my mobile at the station."

Marc touched her hand to stop her riffling through the pile of sheets on the floor. "Yeah, I looked for it while you showered last night. I would've broken it and tossed it if you had it. I guess they're as traceable as the devices we use on our world."

"Am I the only one who heard Kat?" Sharon got up off the floor, leaving her pile of equipment. "Why are they evacuating the city? A gas leak? Captain, is this us?"

"I'd assume so. When we balked at the nukes option and insisted it be a last resort, the SCL said they would coordinate an evacuation of all four cities to minimize casualties."

"Marc, that means Roberta's ready to go. She'll send those nukes and soldiers today."

"That was always the plan." Frank found his tongue and the nerve to use it. "With the PM still in office, the chairperson and SCL can't present their plan to help this side recover from financial and political collapses. The *new* PM was going to accept that and present it to the people." He pointed a judgmental finger and steel face at his captain. "You stopping that assassination pushed them to this."

"I disagree." Kat stood to address the room. "Roberta was always going to do this. She had two hundred transfer stations built. If she played the *Good Samaritan* card, she'd have no power over here. We'd have to come under the rule of Greater Britannia and under its new PM. And from what I've heard about Oliver Nelson, he's no world leader."

"No, you're right." Belinda turned to Marc. "She's right. I've interviewed the weasel, and he's no leader. No Alistair. But he's greedy and ambitious. He'd cut her out, probably have her arrested or killed along with your entire executive branch to ensure his place at the top."

"Team." Marc added power to his voice without yelling. "This was always the plan and why we're moving today to broadcast Belinda's report and get to that grid ahead of Saul and team two."

"Shouldn't we go there first, then? Skip the news report for now?"

"I think Sharon's right," Kat agreed.

"No. Timing is critical. If they take it down too early, it can be brought back online under secondary power reserves. The plan is to take it offline at exactly 18:15 in this time zone. The SCL wants the spectacle of the capital of GB being consumed in a brilliant flash of white light and a massive fireball under a mushroom cloud broadcast live, in time for citizens returning home for dinner to switch on the evening news."

"Goodness me." Belinda's face went white, eyes popped. "You people built something that can do *that?*"

"A lotta somethings, we did. A wee bit more than needed to incinerate our world... *oh*, fifteen to twenty times over."

"How pointless. And you want the people that would do that coming here to my world?"

"No, Belinda. Well, not mostly." Marc's hand on the blond bombshell reporter's arm raised Kat's eyebrow. "We've suppressed most of the governments that built them. I've been on countless missions to keep them out of the hands of those who'd use them, stop others from making them. We *will not* bring that here."

"Marc, those are words. Honestly, I can see why we refused your settling here. We've kept a pristine, peaceful world for over a millennium. I'd not be too quick to welcome your people."

"Fair point."

"But we're dying." Frank used a finger to wag his accusation in Belinda's face. "You'd let four and a half billion people die for your xenophobia and fear?"

"Settle down. That's an order. Belinda's right... but also wrong." Marc's contradiction laid a look of confusion on everyone's faces. "The PM didn't dismiss our plea. It was Deputy Nelson. Our chairperson and SCL met via video conference over a complex array of comms units in near-real-time chat across the void. On this side, it was only Nelson and his assistant."

"Susan Clayhill. I interviewed her once. She's almost as ambitious as Oliver."

"Yeah, I met her. Took the list you're going to read on TV from her."

"Marc?" Kat checked the time: 9:13. "Shouldn't we get going?"

Kat drove the hotel cart with Sharon and Frank and all the gear. She rolled her eyes when Marc said he would go with Belinda on her motorcycle in case they got separated. As Kat had to follow that bike, she didn't buy the reasoning. They rode along a bicycle path beside a main road flooded with transports and larger people movers. Like a wide river, both carriageways flowed in one direction—away from the city center. It seemed everyone heeded the call to get away from New London Town while Kat followed Belinda deeper inside it.

The pair on two wheels led them to a faded yellow office park sign. The rear-most building's exterior boasted more glass than any Earth structure. It looked better maintained than most in-use office complexes Kat had seen on that tainted planet—her windowless world.

After they parked around back, Frank broke the emergency exit door hinges with a sonic destabilizer. He and Marc wore thick black vests Kat imagined were full of weapons. Belinda snaked them through dim hallways and through a sea of lifeless cubicles. They reached a control room saturated in darkness. Emergency lights noticed their arrival and dripped a ghostly green glow over the cobweb-infested space. For Kat to work her magic, Marc and Sharon needed to get the solar power grid online.

"Everything's ready to go live. I just need to direct the signal output to the global emergency channel. Every television, computer screen, and mobile device in the world will switch on and see our report."

"Impressive, Kateryna. I'm not sure my producer could do that. I hope he's okay. He helped me escape and stall the soldiers."

With nothing to say to reassure the woman, Kat kept working. The blip on the screen came with the pleasant beep of a successful connection alert. When lights as bright as Idyllium's sun whitened the room, Sharon operated the camera with a crash course from Kat. Belinda stood with the weather reporter's green screen at her back. An outline around a lighter shade of white flooring was all that remained of the anchor desk. After sending Frank to guard the hallway, Marc stood beside Kat.

Leaning over the control console, Kat raised three fingers toward Belinda, folded one, then another. The last one lowered to point at the reporter, and she mouthed, *On the air*.

Belinda summed up the existence of a parallel planet and the spies, agents, and soldiers who had infiltrated their world. After expounding on the plan to destroy the four cities, she urged everyone in them to take the evacuation order seriously. (While it looked like *everyone* had taken to the road, the local resident among them said it was a fraction of the city's population. Government evacuation plans allowed a minimum of two days for a ninety-percent survival rate, and this wouldn't come close.)

Next, the reporter explained how the deputy PM had collaborated with an enemy in the plot to assassinate the PM. That enemy, she elucidated, was a *handful* of government officials from a planet called "Earth."

Marc stepped beside the reporter, flustering her. He introduced himself and his assignment on their world and explained how he'd been working against his own government. Raising his wrist, he said he had a recording from the PM. The holographic emitter on his bio-pad created a six-inch image of Alister Burgess's face.

"People of Greater Britannia, I am alive today thanks to this man, Marc Sanders. A deserter from the other world who accepted a mission to prepare for his people to conquer us. He has come here to actively work against that same initiative. His team is helping to stop an imminent invasion. Be cautious, but do not fear. The empire will prevail."

Audio fizzled, and the hologram flickered. Marc's frantic taps on his wrist pad did little. With a frustrated palm slap, the image stabilized.

"We believe the orchestrators of this plot against us are a small faction in collaboration with our own deputy PM. Once we resolve this and all parties face justice, we will discuss a peaceful means of assisting our neighbors on our sister planet. Belinda Mayers will read a list of all those from the other world working in ours in corporate and government positions. I authorize all law enforcement and military agencies to arrest these—"

Booming pops of gunfire roiled in from the corridor. Marc disappeared. Belinda began reading the names of the foreign agents along with their locations and positions. Kat instinctively lowered her head over the console before she noticed Sharon lying at the base of the camera pedestal. Marc hunched over her, yelled Kat's name, and took off running toward the echoing of bullets ripping the air.

Abandoning her station, Kat leapt up and ran to Sharon, Belinda now hurriedly reading through the list, raising her voice. A growing puddle of blood wet the floor around the wounded scientist and soaked her pant leg at the thigh. Kat pulled her *mission sister* along the floor away from the line of sight of the corridor. She frantically yanked a first aid kit out of the backpack and tied the leg above the wound and cut away the material below it, exposing the mangled flesh. When Kat poured sterilizing fluid on the wound, Sharon pinched her green eyes shut, scrunching her freckled face.

"It's in me. You gotta get it out before the glue."

Using a bullet extractor—which reminded her of a pepper grinder George loved—Kat yanked the projectile from the fleshy mess of sinew strands and pulses of blood. The focus almost removed the sounds of violence behind her. Although the ghostly green glimmer revisited the room, Belinda continued reading. The control board had darkened, the power cut. They couldn't know how much of that list got out.

Marc came running back in. "She okay?" Kat nodded. "Let's go. We handled them, but I'd guess more are on the way."

With the ease of lifting a sack of feathers, Marc hoisted Sharon from the floor and ran with her in his arms as Kat and Belinda followed. Frank sat in the driver's seat of the transport and Marc hopped on, still cradling Sharon like a baby in his thick arms.

"Kat, ride with Belinda."

"Where to?"

The cart jolted forward and sped off. Belinda told Kat to hold on and gave chase.

46 | Earth: 4 Days After Crossover

Something about her office in the Utah complex appealed to her. The openness of the space left her boundless. Mostly empty and unfurnished, it spoke to her of the lust, greed, and waste of the super wealthy and powerful that squandered their planet. It served as a reminder of what made her different. Lustful, sure, on several levels, and she never tried to hide any of them. But for Roberta Hillthorpe, chairperson *and* strategic counsel leader of the UGA, ruler of all the Earth, the goal made all the difference.

Those who had come and gone before her had fulfilled their longings with selfish pursuits while all others, even their planet, be damned. Not that she considered herself unselfish. She had certainly fulfilled her lustful desires in numerous ways no one could have called selfless. Leaving her past where it belonged, Roberta glanced around the enormous room. She considered herself the right person for the job of saving the four and a half billion people in her care.

Nothing in the scent brought the right tingle to her nose hairs when she took a deep breath and craved fresh tea and something else... Would she have had greater or less indignation toward Marc for going rogue if he had accepted her sendoff offer? Rejection never sat right with her, and it rarely visited.

John entered when summoned with a pot of steeping tea leaves.

"I feel like celebrating this afternoon. Do you know why?"

"You won the vote of no confidence. Congratulations, SCL."

"And you're my new assistant."

"Um, am I not still the *chairperson's* assistant?"

"His vote didn't go so well. Now, I get both offices. And you're not just answering phones and making tea. You are my *personal* assistant in *everything*. At my side at all times."

A smile came to her lips as she watched the young man's eyes walking over her as she stood. That she had such an effect on someone close to half her age invigorated her and she hit the Do Not Disturb button on her desk's holographic display.

After a late lunch, John sat across from her in the chair he had pulled in from his tiny desk in the waiting area and watched Roberta make phone calls and demand updates from several generals around the world. The young man had little to do, but for a reason she'd never admit, she wanted him involved. He prepared a spicy chai, but inhaling its warm scent was all the enjoyment she took from it. When a new message soured her expression, John's face paled.

"I knew Marc would be a problem."

"Do you mean Captain Sanders?"

"Look, John, your new role will have you in my face a lot, but you need to learn, *now*, not to speak unless I tell you to." He nodded. "Marc's gone rogue, and not only did he not kill the *bleeding* GB prime minister, but he also stopped my man from doing it. And he's got the list of our agents on that world and even tried to go public with it. The deputy PM there has himself a *you*. Well, she's a she, but a good assistant. They stopped a reporter Marc schmoozed into spilling the entire story before she could. Can you believe that?"

Sheepishly lifting his eyes in his lowered head, the young man chanced a look. She nodded.

"No, SCL. I thought he was a loyal soldier."

"And one of my closest friends is helping him. But I always have contingencies for my contingencies. We will have their defensive grid offline this evening. We'll send the nukes to make our point... then the soldiers. I've been preparing for this for a decade. Those mindless puppets thought they could take me down with a vote of no confidence. And on the eve of Operation Oncoming Storm. Wait until they see the oncoming storm I have for them."

Roberta had her new assistant connect her to each of the nuclear transverse sites. A status update verified the nukes were prepared and ready for deployment. Carefully preselected landing sites had been meticulously calibrated to drop just above ground level. No one wanted the bombs to detonate immediately, taking her soldiers out with them. Idyllium's four major cities, including New London Town, would be obliterated.

When the commander at the Wales launch site questioned the order, she yelled for two minutes. Like the flip of a switch, she calmed and flatly told him how the deputy PM had issued phony warnings to evacuate those cities. While true, Roberta knew they'd not get everyone out, and a no-death-toll action would lack the needed impact for peaceful surrender and occupation.

Consulting her only remaining trusted advisor, she twirled the glass. *A justification*, she considered. Disturbed by the notion, the ice cubes plinked the walls of their crystal cage. *To kill so many under the guise of saving more... was that hubris?* The new chairperson ignored the thought as she often did.

With the last swig of Jack Daniels warming her throat, Roberta had John connect all two hundred mass transversal generator sites. One million troops, every soldier from every UGA and government military force, including those drafted and trained for this mission, stood at attention. Time for a stirring pep talk.

The newly sworn-in chairperson spoke of the sins of the past leading them to the brink of extermination and how they had found their second chance. Most of those soldiers and new inductees did not know where they would be later that day. The scope of the project was unimaginable. They knew nothing beyond their five-thousand-person force and how they needed to stop those who threatened their future.

"...We call on you for unequivocal resolve and devotion to the preservation of our world and its billions of inhabitants. Soon, you will see the situation as it truly is and how we will make a future for ourselves."

Rousing the troops and envisioning the glorious success of her operation, making her the savior of the world, swirled inside her as a powerful high. She looked at John's pockmarked face. "How did you like that speech?"

"Very moving, SCL. May I ask...? You seem so confident, yet we have a rogue team working against us. And they're some of our best. You're not worried about them?"

"What did I say about contingencies? I have someone loyal to me on that team."

47 | Idyllium Mission: Day 5

To anyone unaware of its significance, the building could have been any number of things, from a warehouse to a small office complex. Looking at it on approach, Marc would have passed it by, assuming it was the headquarters of a moderately successful corporation. With knowledge of the economics of Idyllium comprising less than a basic understanding, he assumed a similar structure to the corporate entities of Earth, albeit with tighter government controls and regulations.

"Are we sure about the location?"

Marc had the correct information. Expressing doubt vocally helped him wrestle ideas of their intel being a misdirect. After all, the people who passed the data along did so to allow an invasion of their world. An idea so foreign to Marc, he maintained a healthy suspicion of their true motives.

"Yes, Cap." Frank shoved the drive control into the off position and rested both hands on the steering wheel. "The intel is solid."

The blur in Marc's periphery solidified into Belinda and Kat, the latter with a twisted bird's nest climbing from her head in all directions. Somehow, Belinda's wind-tossed blond hair settled back into position like soldiers shifting from an at-ease posture to attention in their captain's presence.

"How's Sharon?" Kat asked as the motorcycle jerked to a stop.

"I'm good." Sharon hopped from the cart, leaning heavily on her good leg.

With skeptical eyes, Marc scanned the building made entirely of glass panels outlined in thin black metal frames. "It's smart. The building doesn't scream military installation and no idiot posted an enormous sign saying *Defense Grid Control Center of Idyllium*. UGA hubris would have and may as well have painted a massive target on it."

Belinda swung her leg over the bike once Kat had dismounted. "He's right. We've enjoyed peace for centuries, and such cautions are among the reasons GB has been unthreatened for a millennium."

"Your people pompously claim its benevolence and indiscrimination keep the peace. But you're saying it's because of GB's impenetrable might?" Frank pulled his disdainful look from Belinda to roll his eyes at Marc as he yanked some gear from the back of the transport.

"Marc..." Kat composed herself from being obviously disoriented from the motorcycle ride and pulled Sharon's arm over her shoulder to help her walk. "Regardless of outward appearances, this building must be highly secured. How do we get inside?"

"While we had a back way in from plans provided by the deputy PM's assistant, now, we've been granted entrance by the PM. Of course, we'll be under guard. His trust in me has its limitations."

Belinda grabbed his shoulder as Marc hoisted Kat's gear from the cart. "Alister is granting you, agents from the world trying to conquer us, access to the most important facility of our planetary defense grid?"

"Saving someone's life goes a long way on the trust meter."

The main entrance appeared less protected than any office building on Earth, with no soldiers or guards standing watch.

No security checkpoints were visible. Marc figured it added to the camouflage effect, as he would have ignored the building completely. Even with their intel, each footfall toward the double glass doors as he ascended the steps sent tingles of doubts climbing into him from the ground.

"Frank, you stand guard here. We assume Saul is coming and have no idea if Hillthorpe has anyone else in her contingency. Maintain comms and alert us at the first sign of anyone approaching."

"Aye, Cap. But you mean Saul, or anyone from Earth, right?"

"I mean *anyone*, Corporal. Anyone coming here is either helping us or here to take down the grid. The city is being evacuated, and that requires military coordination. So I'm certain, other than any soldiers in this building under orders from the PM, no one's coming to help us."

While the experience of being transported across a void of who-knew-what and dropped on a new and alien version of their own planet would likely never be matched in anyone's lifetime, for Marc, this came in at a close second. Stepping through those frosted glass doors, they left the dull could-be-any-building vibe outside and found themselves in a high-security military compound. A dozen soldiers stood as a wall behind a security screen of body scanners, x-ray machines, an array of cameras, and targeting lasers on every corner of the walls.

A synthesized human-sounding voice announced, "Marc Sanders. Access granted."

The wall of soldiers lost trace amounts of its firmness as one of the large men stepped toward Marc. "Captain Sanders, I'm Colonel Thompson. We have the building secured." Glancing at the torn pant leg and messy patch-up job on Sharon's thigh, he added, "Does she need medical attention?"

"I'm fine," she replied as she freed herself from Kat's support and limped forward.

The intimidating human barrier dissolved into men and women ignoring the blips and beeps of a security system protesting the entry of an armed and equipped group of unknowns as the team followed Marc through the scanners.

"I have a man outside these doors." The stern nod said the colonel had seen Frank there. "Make sure no one gets in here. We must defend this grid, and I have no idea how many are coming to take it down. At least one may have a weapon of incredible power, enough to immobilize your platoon here in a single shot." If his look contained surprise at Marc's revelation, Thompson hid it well under an intensely focused brow. "My team must use the grid to send an interrupt signal to prevent our people from crossing over."

Colonel Thompson brought his chin over his shoulder to address the soldier behind him. "Sullivan, escort Captain Sanders and his team to the primary control room."

In the control room, an open space twice as large as Marc's entire home and crowded with computer terminals and large display screens, Kat hurried to the comms station. Sharon hobbled after her with a clenched jaw, sucking in a suppression of the pain of her abused leg. From personal experience, Marc knew the spit-laden inhalation well.

Deafening echoes of an onslaught of gunfire raced in from the corridor, unhindered by the closed reenforced door.

"Sharon, you and Kat stay on this. We need that disruption signal active in," he checked his wrist, "fifteen minutes, or they'll lock on and send the nukes. Belinda, secure this door behind us."

Racing down the hallway with Sullivan toward the source of the commotion, Marc fondled his weapon with well-trained fingertips to verify the readiness of the semiautomatic assault rifle. The short barrel swung from the run, and he tried to steady it for quick aim.

The corridor overflowed with the ominous quiet before battle.

Broken by a thud, no, a succession of rapid thuds, the silence fell, replaced by the sound of distant bodies collapsing like lifeless sacks onto the cement floor.

The Hertzog, Marc reasonably concluded. *Saul must have taken it and is pushing ahead with the original mission objectives.* Knowing Saul, Marc expected no less. *Clever, that Roberta Hillthorpe.* Pieces came together in his mind. *Making us think Mal was the only one DNA-matched to the thing so we'd not suspect her contingency plan. No wonder Saul left no trace of his assassination attempt. He must have used a holographic bullet—they only materialize in flesh and bone.*

The rifle in Marc's unyielding grip would be no match for the Hertzog weapon. Neither would the secure door to the control center. He had precious few moments to act. After a wide-burst stun shot, the implement of horrific technology in Saul's hand had to reset and build a charge to fire again.

Slightly hunched with head lowered and eyes raised, Marc charged ahead, rounding a corner to put himself in the line of fire, Sullivan trailing close behind him. A massive open floorspace held a plethora of furniture and walls for cover across from their defenseless position. He hoped surprise might have given them an edge, the only chance to stop Saul.

A familiar and terrifying buzz grazed Marc's ear and exploded on the wall behind him. The trained and experienced soldier knew the solidity of the bullet before it showered him with bits of plaster. Either Saul was faster on the draw than Marc suspected, switched from the Hertzog in a single blink to take aim, or he'd been targeted by a second shooter.

He fired back blindly as he retreated. The GB soldier stood his ground, spraying bullets at the unseen shooter not to leave Marc without cover.

Pivoting into a turn, Marc slammed into a wall—no, into Sharon, knocking her to the floor. Marc fumbled over her collapsing body and tumbled onto the inhospitable cement, rolling past her with a momentum he failed to stifle. Sullivan took cover in the opposite corridor.

By the time he focused his eyes and found her, Sharon had a finger locked in a firm squeeze on the trigger of her semiautomatic, sending a barrage of bullets into a cloud of concrete powder and dust hiding their enemy combatants. A scientist, not a soldier, she'd rolled into the posture as well as Marc could have done it. It impressed her captain, who quickly returned to fearing for Sharon's life.

A vision of Tim Mullins—Uncle Tim to Jewel—manifested before him within the smoke of gunfire and motes of the bullet-riddled wall swirling around him—a ghost enveloped by a tornado of chaos.

"I've got this, sir. Marc! Get the team out of here," the young man had said. Months ago, those were the last words Marc heard from the guy who had transcended friendship to become family. They echoed in his mind now, those same words he should have objected to then. Marc pinched the braided keychain in his pants pocket through the thick fabric.

When Tim turned to run headlong, a one-man assault on the army pinning down his team, the cloud of gunsmoke and debris cleared to reveal Sharon lying on the floor. The shooting had stopped, and silence crawled over Marc's skin, unsettling him more than the roaring outburst of the gunfire exchange had. Why did it stop? Was someone killed?

No, I won't lose another soldier. Marc couldn't be sure if the words stayed in his determined mind or escaped his lips. Crawling like a centipede, he reached for Sharon and grabbed the shoulder straps of her vest. With a firm yank, he heaved her toward him, which signaled the aggressors they needed to finish the job with a fresh volley of bullets.

After a hurried fumble over his vest pockets, Marc found the silver orb his hand sought and dropped it between Sharon's limp body and the shooters. Although the bullets relentlessly did their best to find him and Sharon, the smoke made hitting their targets more of a challenge. Marc couldn't see Sullivan and the muzzle flashes from his side of the corridor had stopped.

Safely around the corner, Marc examined Sharon's face, hoping it held onto life. Three silver craters dotted the black vest over her chest. Desperately he searched every part of her not covered in microshield protective gear and saw no blood.

"Sharon. *Sharon*."

Nothing.

Did she send the disruption signal?

"Saul," Marc barked at full volume around the corner and down the hall. "We need to stop this."

"Why, Marc? Did you sacrifice another soldier to save your sorry skin?"

"*What?* No."

"In a few minutes, none of us will matter, Marc. Nukes and platoons of soldiers will arrive. This defensive grid's just a warning system. It won't stop that."

"We can stop it. Sharon can. Look, we're on the same side here."

Saul's pauses could be as deadly as his sarcasm. "Not sure I see it that way, *Captain*."

48 | Earth: 4 Days After Crossover

AFTER THAT ONE TIME, Peter had stopped bothering to correct her. To the SCL, now also the chairperson, he answered to "John." At least until Miss Hillthorpe decided differently. The change came unexpectedly, when she had informed him of his new job description as her personal assistant. It entailed many things serving Walter Vescovi never required—thankfully. Not all were bad. Peter enjoyed fulfilling some of her demands.

His planet had little left to give its inhabitants. To him, Earth reacted to the infestation of humankind as a body does to any parasite or virus. These were people, and he vacillated now over his choices, the side he had taken. Peter served at the pleasure of the orchestrator of Operation Oncoming Storm, the most powerful person on the planet. The one who sent infiltrators, had enacted espionage, and worked to corrupt the stability of each of Idyllium's core institutions. In her eyes—he assumed—she saw a lackey, a minion, someone to bounce ideas off without wanting a reply. An outlet for her pent-up frustrations.

Henry O'Brien. Peter didn't know what to make of his request at first. Concern for his daughter had been evident. The physical location of his post exposed Peter to secrets that towered above his pay grade, not meant for his young and unimportant ears. He knew of the parallel world and plans to migrate to it by forced occupation. In honesty, he had to admit he never gave it a second thought until speaking with Mister O'Brien.

That haunting voice bellowed through the open door, not over the intercom. "*John.* Get your scrawny self in here and give me the bleeding report."

For the first time, relief spilled into him for not being called in to serve as her physical release. In a way that confounded him, that old Irishman's words robbed Peter's boss of *some* of her appeal.

"Yes, SCL. I mean, Chairperson. I just received the update as you called me."

She stood and hunched over the desk like a bird of prey, eyes squinted to focus on her next meal. "I thought I told you to sit in here. I need these updates instantly. This ridiculous office is too big for me to wait as you shlep yourself across the floor."

While true, her commands often contradicted themselves. Peter thought it best not to remind her she had asked him to prepare a pot of tea. He discreetly placed the porcelain carafe on the desk with one teacup.

"Well...? Are you going to read me the report, or am I supposed to read your mind?"

Hillthorpe sat and crossed her legs. She hadn't lost *all* her appeal to Peter's carnal gaze. He blinked to clear his head.

"Your man is reporting Marc and the team did indeed try to stop them shutting down Idyllium's defense grid. Saul attacked, but the grid is still online. Something about a standoff, but it's not clear."

"What do you mean, not clear? What's *happening* over there?"

"Well..." Peter's shoulders tensed at the deadly tone of the powerful woman's voice. "We get a few words of text since the team stopped sending reports from their full comms kit.

I'm trying to decipher abbreviations and some military... shorthand, I guess it is."

"Do I have to go over there myself to get this done? Do I have to rule two worlds at once, or can I please get some *competent* help around here?" Peter shrugged. "Pour me a whisky, John. I'm feeling too tense. I need to think straight."

Peter knew where the whisky often led, and he strangely had lost the urge to meet her there. "I prepared some tea. That calms you more than the whisky."

Her grimace could have meant a scathing retort where she'd unleash every bit of wrath she held for the mission, the team's betrayal, and the possibility of failure he knew she could not consider. When her face softened, he poured the tea, and she sipped liberally.

Peter said, "There's more."

One eyebrow rose over the tea's steam and Hillthorpe pressed her lips into a straight, thin line.

"It just came in now." Lifting his tablet, Peter gulped, knowing the messenger would receive the wrath summoned by the message. "All transfer stations are reporting loss of target lock. They have no primer, no coordinates for a jump."

Spattered drops of hot liquid pricked his neck like fiery needles and doused his shoulder as something whizzed by his ear. Only the shattering of the porcelain teacup crashing onto the marble tile behind him told his brain what had happened.

She stood, shoulders rising and falling with each seething breath. Peter trembled in his shoes.

"*And*—I don't have to ask, surrounded by such incompetence—do any of these brilliant minds at even one of my *bleeding* transfer stations have *any* clue... *why?*"

"Um..." Peter's gulp likely echoed in the corridor. "No. Only that something seems to be interfering, blocking them from locking on."

"*Kateryna*. My good friend is a traitor. I never trusted cats. They lie in wait for their master to die. Did you know they'll eat their owner's dead body? And when Marc asked for her, I thought it was because, well, he likes... No matter. Or *Sharon*. I wondered why we needed to send her, in particular. Her history with Marc. No, that scoundrel. He planned this from the start. He knew the two he'd need to block the invasion. Somehow... they figured out how to do it."

"What do we do now?"

"We, John? *We?* Me. I take control of this mess Marc's made. Connect me to General Whiting. *Now*."

The volume of the last word sent trepidatious energy through Peter's fingers. He had the connection open in an instant. Hillthorpe ripped the tablet from his hands.

"Yes, Madam Chairperson."

Like an open book, Peter read the loathing on her face for the use of "Madam." A mistake he never repeated.

With a white-knuckle grip Peter thought could shatter the rigid glass, the rapacious woman shook the tablet as if she could physically assault the man on the other end.

"Send all teams now."

"Send where? We cannot get a lock on any location."

"Then send them anywhere on Idyllium. Just send my *bleeding* troops."

"No." The general's reply stiffened Hillthorpe. Peter imagined steam rising from her head. "I mean, that's just it. We cannot hit a landing anywhere on the planet. If we send troops or weapons across without a synchronous landing point, they'll be lost in the void between."

"Send a small team, then, with comms gear. You see, I just don't trust your judgment, Whiting. After a decade of sending small teams over there, we're still speculating on the science behind it. Prep a team. Tell them to report back when they get there. And prep all teams at all stations. Tell them they go in one hour."

"You mean if we confirm the first team's successful arrival on Idyllium?"

"Never presume to tell me what I mean. The teams are going *regardless*."

The clatter of glass on tile rattled the air in the perceived diminished space. Peter fetched the device, which looked remarkably unbothered by being thrown across the room. The general's face upon it appeared to have taken more damage than the tablet's screen. Peter closed the connection.

49 | Idyllium Mission: Day 5

Saul always completed the mission, and this would be no exception. Not only for the four and a half billion on Earth counting on him—even if none of them had a clue—but also because Saul was Saul. The soldier. The "mission is everything" mentality wouldn't let him fail.

What did Marc mean, he "could stop it"?

All he had to do was flick the setting gear and blow away what his former captain considered cover. A wall of plaster and beams his weapon would melt away like butter on a hot day. He didn't even consider Sharon. She had his permission to live, to be tried for treason in the aftermath. Once the two faced him with nothing left to hide behind, a holographic bullet would be a fitting end to Marc Sanders.

Justice for Bubba.

Yet he ignored the click of a fully charged and ready Hertzog 550.

The second shooter's identity didn't concern Saul. All that mattered was he shot at Marc. They stood, without words or oath, on the same side. For some unknowable reason, his ally also stopped shooting.

"Saul? You still there, buddy?"

Marc calling him *buddy* gave Saul reason enough to shoot.

"What's on your mind, *Captain?*" He spat the word with as much contempt as he could pile onto it.

"I'm just thinking we don't need to do this. We both want what's best for the people we love. For everyone back on Earth."

"You sure about that?" Saul baited.

"I never liked your methods, and we may never be friends, but I never doubted your *loyalty*. Saul, let's lay down the weapons and talk this over."

The word "loyalty" ruminated around Saul's brain as he stared into the hazy corridor that hurled it at him. "See, Marc, that's where we differ, you and me. I always doubted your loyalty. Not to yourself, maybe even your family. But to the mission? To the UGA and the people of Earth? No. Just as you put your life ahead of Bubba's, like a piss-poor captain, I never considered you a loyal soldier."

Scuffling sounds pulled Saul's attention from the conversation impeding his next action. The rumble of hand-to-hand combat, Saul assumed, came from his stealthy ally being confronted by the Idyllium soldier.

"I may never be able to explain that situation to you. You weren't there. But I live with that every day of my life. What we do here, now... this will stay with us. Saul, we're not only talking about the people on Earth. We're holding the lives of more than twelve billion, on two worlds, in our hands. We're playing gods when we're nothing more than soldiers."

That *soldiers* bit hit a raw nerve, pulling Saul's thumb over the settings gear. Thoughtlessly, he scrolled as the clicks of the selector focused his mind. "Soldiers expected to follow orders."

"Some orders must be questioned. I know you agree. Sharon outranks you, and you asserted yourself over my team. You're in violation of direct orders now."

"That's some twisted reasoning you've got there, Marc. Not only should that scientist never outrank me, but her orders directly contradict those from the SCL herself. The thing about the chain of command you don't seem to get, *soldier*, is you can't pick which link to start from."

Saul considered Marc's pause a ploy. His flirtatious nature did not only flatter and woo women. He also had an ability to persuade his way through some of the toughest-skinned people.

"Is that why you tried to kill me?"

That made Saul's head shake. "If I *tried* to kill you, Marc, we'd not be able to have this here conversation, would we?"

"Even you miss, Saul. You missed the PM, and you missed me when they busted me out of the police van."

"First, I didn't miss. You tackled the PM... against our mission objectives." Red-faced and ready to explode, he felt the heat boiling inside him. A breath calmed Saul enough to speak. "And I got no idea what van and what shot you think I took when your misguided friends—yes, they're friends because they sure don't act like mission soldiers—freed you. I'd've let you rot."

"What? Frank saw you... Look, we need to put personal issues aside, just for now. You can kill me later. *Fine*. For now, we need to do what's *right*... for both worlds."

"*Isn't* anything personal, *yet*, Captain, but right now you're the guy trying to stop the only plan for our survival. If I get to take you out while completing the mission, we'll call that a bonus."

"Yet we're still talking. I know you've got the Hertzog and that it's been ready for another shot for some time now. You've got doubts. Not about me, about the morality of what we've been asked to do by a ruthlessly ambitious, conniving, power-hungry politician." Marc paused, and Saul said nothing. "We accomplish this mission, we obliterate four cities, killing millions, and we introduce the same cycle that destroyed our planet."

All these words meant little to Saul, who never considered he had much use for them. A man of action, he'd say. It made building a life with Alyssa more than difficult. The only one to ever break through the barrier, she found the man behind the persona—a wall the death of their child reassembled. Marc used his selfish tongue masterfully, and Saul wasn't about to allow himself to be duped.

"Saul...? You thinking it over? You know we can't do this. This will not give our people the secure future we both want. You know that. If we do this, we'll ruin this world, same as ours. Can you justify these means to reach *that* end? It won't be the happy ending they told us." Another silent pause elicited no reply from Saul. "The PM never rejected us like Hillthorpe said. It was his deputy. Burgess is willing to help our people, there's another way, a better way. Can we call a ceasefire and talk?"

A shot ripped the air.

Confusion filled him as Saul glanced to confirm his assault rifle hung from its shoulder strap and his finger rested safely off the Hertzog's trigger. *Marc?* No, the pop of a bullet discharging from its barrel came from the other side of the open space. The second shooter must have freed himself from his combatants, tired of the conversation, and fired at Marc. Thoughts of Marc being at best a mediocre captain without Bubba tweaking his plans wrestled the idea in his mind that Marc may have been right—in this instance.

There was no doubt in Saul's mind Roberta Hillthorpe couldn't be trusted and manipulated everyone who knew about Idyllium from Vescovi to Marc's entire team... maybe even *him*. Had Saul been suckered in by his patriotism and loyalty and fallen victim to that woman's devious machinations?

For the first time in his career, Commander Saul Mullins thought beyond the mission's parameters. He raised his rifle and shot toward whoever hadn't bought into Marc's plea. Running ahead while maintaining cover fire, Saul dove around the corner and rolled into a one-kneed pose between Marc and Sharon. Without looking, he tossed a smoke grenade down the hall.

"She dead?"

"The vest took it all."

Sounds of thick boots falling to the ground in a military charge filled the corridor, and Saul knew the second shooter would soon be taken out of play. Together, he and Marc dragged their teammate's debilitated body to the control room and secured the door. Saul looked over Kat and Belinda and scanned the room and asked if they blocked the crossover, not knowing how they would do that.

"I did what Sharon said, and my broadcast is good, but..." Kat slammed two fists on the communications console. "It's *not* working!"

Marc jammed a small syringe into Sharon's neck, and Saul helped him get her to her feet. Groggy and in obvious pain, she leaned over the console, pushing Kat out of the way.

"It needs another minor modulation adjustment." She coughed. "I based my calculations on Earth, but Idyllium's frequency is a little different..."

Marc yelled, "Two minutes! Come on, Sharon."

Saul checked his wrist, and looked around the room. "Where's Frank?"

50 | Earth:
4 Days After Crossover

Evening's twilight contemplated pushing away the hazy blue of day, and Roberta reduced the filter on her picture window. She'd come out of the shower and dressed as if a new day had just begun. What sky her operatives on Idyllium saw filled her mind with images she had seen under a canopy that blanketed her memories from old films she hadn't watched in years.

Was it raining on Idyllium as the first trickles snaked down her window?

Even with her "Master of All the Earth" new status, her window answered to a higher power. It resumed its job of protecting her from the dangers lurking on the other side of the glass, despite her orders to the contrary.

A meditative stroll carried her more slowly than her usual stride back to her desk, where she found John hard at work doing something or other. She didn't remember her last orders and didn't care, except that he remained there, not to leave her alone in the empty space of her massive office. Looking at the thin boy with the unfortunate facial skin, she wondered why his company brought such calm.

"Miss Hillthorpe." John appeared startled by her presence.

With a hand upon his arm, she smiled. It put a blank look of confusion on his face, and Roberta realized she had scarcely smiled in recent days. Her plan fell apart, and someone she considered her best friend had betrayed her. No fuming, no rage, no pent-up frustration. She'd given those to John but noticed his acceptance lacked the enthusiasm it had days prior.

She sank into her chair across from her youthful assistant. "Anything yet?"

"Yes." He hesitated, and Roberta noticed him take a discrete half step back. "General Whiting reports his team hasn't checked in, and it's been over one hour. He says they must be lost in the void, which he says means dead, crushed out of existence."

"Crushed out of existence? Now he knows the chasm between worlds is a black hole? When did the good general become an astrophysicist or an expert in quantum mechanics?"

"I... don't know."

In their time together, John still hadn't learned when she didn't want an answer. This time, it didn't bother her.

"Get him on for me. Tell him to send the troops."

"Um, you want *me* to tell him?"

With a calmness that surprised her, Roberta replied, "That is what I said."

Within seconds, the tablet lit up with the general's face.

"Peter. Did you tell the SCL our test failed?"

John looked at her seated in the chair with a stone expression on her face. "Yes, General. The SCL, chairperson, says to launch as planned. Send all troops across."

"Is she out of her mind?"

Pale as a ghost, John looked at her. She offered no typical reaction at first, merely extending her arm to request the tablet. The general's face retracted like a child's when caught sneaking sweets before dinner.

"General."

"Um, sorry, SCL. I didn't realize—"

"I prefer honesty, Steve. I also demand obedience. Our team over there is royally hosing things up, and we need to take control of the situation. We've run out of time here; we're gagging on our fumes and facing our extinction. If we don't send the troops for fear they may not make it, they'll die with the rest of us sooner rather than later, anyway."

"I'd rather send them to be with their families for the last years we've got than sentence them to an immediate death on a suicide mission."

The calmness retreated. "Did I ask for your opinion, *General?* You're there to obey orders. Go do what I told you to *bleeding* do."

"No, Roberta. I will not needlessly send these soldiers to their deaths."

Boiling rage quickly claimed the space vacated by the unusual calm—a better fit on her. As she settled back into herself, Roberta saw his use of her first name as an obvious attempt to assert himself, to defy her position and authority. The ruler of the world readied herself to unleash hell's fury on the distinguished older general when the connection closed, her mouth left open. She stared back at herself from the darkened display with eyes brimming with fury.

"No he *did not,*" she bellowed as the tablet flew across the office, bounced off the tile floor, and slid out the door and under John's desk. "Get him back, or get someone who'll obey orders. Find out who's next in succession under him as I order his termination."

The assistant ran out and crawled under his desk to retrieve the offending device and remained outside her office to carry out Roberta's orders. Just as well, as she figured she would heap unmerited abuse upon him, and somewhere over their days working closely together, she'd developed a soft spot for the boy.

Sitting with her bare feet over her wide desk, Roberta rubbed her fingers over her temples. When her assistant stood across the desktop's smooth, reflective surface, the SCL wondered if his tongue held back the words it knew she'd not want to hear. A likely possibility, she had concluded the outcome of his diligent efforts to climb down the chain of command, link by link, to find someone who'd carry out her order.

The stern, demanding, and forceful woman sought to balance her robust character with reason and wisdom. It was why she figured she'd been so successful, rising from being the hidden leader of the world to take the role of uncontested ruler of Earth. Or most of it, at least. No, she realized no one would carry out her order to wipe out all the UGA's military in a single last-ditch and futile effort to complete Operation Oncoming Storm. They'd also likely not relish the idea of needlessly sending those people—Roberta knew fully well her army consisted of people with families and lives—to an unknown blackness of nothing.

"There may be another way."

She'd almost forgotten about John until he spoke. Had he finally understood the point of her having multiple contingencies?

"Yes, I always prepare multiple options."

"No, Miss Hillthorpe. I'm not talking about Saul Mullins."

"Don't worry about it. I have another agent in play."

"Oh." The surprisingly energetic assistant went blank-faced until his eyes rounded. "No. I think *I have* another option."

"You, John? *You* have a contingency?"

"I've been talking to Henry O'Brien."

51 | Idyllium Mission: Day 5

Belinda Mayers tugged the bottom of her blazer for the fifth time as she fidgeted in her seat. It felt like forever and a day, as she'd say, since she sat here. Looking over the cables covering the floor between herself and the cameras, a smile filled her with warmth as she caught Burt's gaze. A wave of relief had swept through her when she learned he evaded arrest and injury helping her escape this very room.

Never had she felt a twinge of nervousness interviewing Alister Burgess, yet it fluttered in her stomach now. Earlier today, he had told Idyllium of the parallel world and their plan to invade. He'd touted Marc Sanders as a hero, working against the plans of Earth while hoping for a peaceful unification of the peoples of the two worlds. How many had seen that broadcast? No recording had been made, and the four major cities of Greater Britannia were in the throes of evacuation at that time for reasons then unknown to them.

Word had spread in under twenty-four hours—it always did. Now, close to midnight, using Kat's modifications to push this broadcast to all televisions and devices in GB, the reporter began her special news bulletin. The people of Idyllium would have questions, and Belinda would be the one to ask them on their behalf.

After experiencing what felt like lurking in the shadows, a fugitive from her own beloved government, the heat and op-pressive light of the studio welcomed her back to normality. The world, her world, would never be "normal" again.

With a voice as shaky as in her earliest broadcasts, the seasoned reporter introduced herself and the topic front and center on everyone's minds. When the camera panned out, the audience saw the prime minister seated beside her. After a brief introduction, which seemed hardly necessary, as the whole of Idyllium knew the man, she led them into the question-and-answer session. Belinda began with a wide-ended request.

"Tell us about our sister planet, Earth."

The PM confirmed its existence and quelled the rumors of Idyllium citizens having crossed over. People of Earth had discovered Idyllium and learned to traverse the void between them years before he or anyone in GB knew of the parallel world. He expounded on the plan of the leadership of Earth to crumble the foundations of their society and addressed the financial crises as the most impactful result of those efforts.

He paused, perhaps looking to Belinda for a question. She obliged.

"We are already seeing the first signs of recovery, and several corporations are being assisted by government agencies to reopen in coming weeks. You mentioned agents from Earth in some of these companies. Are you confident we have identified and arrested them all?"

"Oh, no, Belinda. We do have a list we believe to be up to date. My deputy had been collaborating with the other side for some time, and Captain Marc Sanders retrieved the list from his assistant. We have begun the process of identifying and hunting these down, as some have gone into hiding. That list will be made public after this broadcast."

"That is good news, Mister Prime Minister. I think we need to discuss this harrowing day we all experienced. We saw mass panic as our four major cities, including here in New London

Town, were issued evacuation orders. Gas leaks affecting an entire city is an unbelievable enough excuse, but four cities on the same day? These must be connected to the invasion plan."

"Quite right, Belinda. And let me add that my office did not issue the evacuation order. You see, *some* in the upper management of Earth, as with some of our own, were perfectly willing to occupy our world by force, destroying four cities and killing millions in the process. This is a small minority. Others from Earth, good people, ordered the evacuations."

"Of course, we mustn't allow this to foster any prejudice or ill will toward the mostly peaceful people of Earth."

"Indeed. If we did, we would have to do the same for ourselves. Remember, we had collaborators high in our own government. If we are to judge the people of Earth, let us put ourselves on the same scale."

"Well said. In fact, the actions of Marc Sanders and his team from Earth speak to the honorable intentions and good nature of their people."

As the interview continued, they dispensed details about the plan to disable the defensive grid to the world—a world no doubt trying to absorb these unbelievable revelations. How the team from Earth prevented the grid from being taken offline and created an interference signal to impede the forces of Earth from crossing over came next.

"Fascinating. I'm sure there are many watching that find this all too fantastical, too hard to believe. In time, they will see evidence of Earth's existence in the form of people from there walking among us." The PM nodded but didn't interrupt. "And let me assure you, as one who spent some time with Marc Sanders and his team, they are as human as we are. Contrary to some popular multiverse fiction, there are no doppelgängers, no duplicates of us on Earth."

"Correct, Belinda. But there are over four billion humans on our sister planet in desperate need of our assistance..."

PM Burgess continued to outline his plan to initiate talks with members of the leadership of Earth. To clarify, he explained he would work with the ones *not* responsible for the invasion plan. Together, they would discuss options for a peaceful migration to Idyllium. He mentioned the ten to twelve years of the projected livability of Earth's environment and pledged to complete the transfer of their neighbors within eight.

52 | Earth: 5 Days After Crossover

Forty-eight hours since they left home, it was the longest time Jewel had been without her nurse in months. Casey did her best, administering the medicines. She moved her daughter to prevent bedsores, kept her eating, and helped her to the bathroom. Jewel lacked the strength to shower, and they couldn't take along her bathing kit, so a washcloth had to do. The graying complexion overtaking her little girl's withdrawn cheeks kept Casey up at night.

The motel bed didn't appear to bother Jewel. At least, she told her mother as much. That she slept almost constantly since they arrived meant little. She had been sleeping twenty hours a day since Marc left for his mission. Casey could read the ache in Jewel's eyes for her father's absence. The concern for his safety in the unknown other world ran deep, and Casey still couldn't fully conceptualize its reality. Henry O'Brien gave a convincing recounting of the transfer he had witnessed. It seemed so unbelievable to her.

As part of her role as the soldier's spouse, she lived in constant expectation of that unwelcome visit. A knock on the door would reveal some high-ranking officer in their ceremonial dress uniform. Always expecting it, she could never be ready for the pomp and circumstance of a funeral with full honors. Who would have the misfortune to be the one to regret to inform her…?

Yet here she sat on the edge of Jewel's bed somewhere in Utah, of all places. If word didn't come soon, she would have to take Jewel to a hospital and return home to have her in a nurse's care for the rest of her days.

All the love in her heart wouldn't be enough to care for her darling Jewel.

Three knocks on the wall meant Henry O'Brien telling her to get ready to go.

It took all her might, added to the older gentleman's diminished strength, to get Jewel from the bed to the rental car. That effort consumed all the allotted outdoor exposure time for the day, being on the low end, as many more days had been in recent weeks. Casey sat in the back seat with Jewel's head laid gently on her lap as the vehicle floated over the roadway.

Their first test of the credentials in which Mister O'Brien claimed absolute certainty came at the gate. The complex appeared as a small brown lump in the far distance. To Casey, his eyes betrayed doubt. Him having the guest pass which had allowed him to view the team's departure was "miracle enough for one Old Irish Catholic's life," as the Irish Catholic himself had said. That it hadn't been cancelled by now pushed Casey's faith in the system.

"Welcome, Mister O'Brien. Straight ahead. Stay on the road."

As they sped along the dirt path, a cloud of orange dust trailing them, Casey asked about her and Jewel being allowed through. The pass specifically stated Henry O'Brien's name alone. Her speculation that the family of Captain Marc Sanders may have been granted entry fell flat as Henry explained his connection to the young man in the chairperson's office.

Here they were, outside the building where her husband had vanished from the face of the Earth. Could he have been walking on another world? Would this be the salvation he hoped for their precious Jewel? They were about to find out.

A young man with disheveled hair and clothes that appeared to have finished with him days ago greeted them at the entrance. Solid doors with no glass opened into an uninviting dirt-colored building as industrial-looking as it was military. Fortunately, the car reached within a few feet of the entrance. With the boy's help, they got Jewel into a waiting wheelchair and out of the deadly exposure.

As they hurried down the corridor, Casey pushing the wheelchair at the slow pace of the older man's stride, the boy spoke over his shoulder, almost bumping a wall at one point. He explained the latest update from Hillthorpe's man on Idyllium and how the transverse stations couldn't lock onto any coordinates on the other side. Marc and Sharon had, at least for the time being, stopped the invasion. Pride glowing on Mister O'Brien's face could have lit the hallway, brighter than the fatal sunlight.

"Wait." While Casey couldn't hope to understand the process, she found a hole in their plan. "If the machines to send people to Idyllium can't lock onto a location, how do we get across?"

"Ma'am, I'm Peter. I work for the chairperson and SCL. There is one traverse chamber in the world that already has locked coordinates. We can send you to the exact location where your husband landed."

"Is it ready yet?" The older man's question puzzled Casey. The machine had sent her husband, his team, countless teams before them. Why wouldn't it be ready?

"It came online this morning. They did a full shutdown and diagnostic after Lieutenant Holland's unfortunate accident. A few more control tests, and it will be fully operational, sir."

"Wait, what accident? What happened to Mal?"

"Oh, my dear Casey. Goodness me, I forgot you knew Malcom. I saw the poor lad fall down dead during the transfer."

"You mean it's dangerous? There's a chance we could be killed trying to cross?"

"Anything is risky. You could have been in a car wreck driving here." The young man stood straight with an air of self-confidence in his pulled back shoulders. "But he was the only casualty we had after they got it working right years ago. And it was only because of a prior health issue."

"Health issue? Do you see my daughter?" Casey waved her arm emphatically over the frail girl slouching in the wheelchair. "Is this thing going to kill her?"

"I'm sorry, ma'am. I should have worded that better. It was an experimental drug treatment that caused complications for Lieutenant Holland. I took the liberty of accessing your daughter's medical file and shared this with the technicians that operate the chamber. They feel confident she won't have the same problem."

"They *feel* confident? I don't know about this."

"Casey, dear. What choice do you have? Even if your little girl could make it to the start of planned migration, if the politicians ever work that out, she'd have to cross in the same way. And by then, she'll be worse for wear at that."

"I'm not ready for this. I had no idea…"

"Mom." Jewel whimpered out a cough with the word. "I want to try. I want to be with Daddy."

Decision made; they entered the chamber. Their helpful guide would not be joining them, as he said he needed to operate the controls. When Casey questioned this, having been told of the chamber operators, the young man explained his conversation with them had been hypothetical. This would be an unauthorized crossing without the technical crew's knowledge.

While that unsettled her, they had passed the turning point. Seated in the chamber chair, Casey checked the grip Jewel had on the armrests. Peter cautioned them not to hold on to anything but their own chair as smoke filled the chamber and Casey's eyes lost their fix on Jewel.

The shaking became violent, and Casey thought she might vomit. She couldn't see her baby girl. The worried mom strained her ears but heard nothing over the deafening groaning of the machine.

As the gray cloud consuming her appeared to solidify, the sound of a new commotion pierced the noise saturation. A shrill voice yelling at someone called John.

The world disappeared.

53 | Idyllium Mission: Terminated

LESS THAN TWENTY-FOUR HOURS had passed since Sharon had gone GI Jane saving him and then sent the disruption signal. Thanks to his team, talks would soon start between worlds. Marc's gamble had paid off, and a migration—the salvation of the people of Earth—would begin without forced occupation and the needless slaughter of millions.

Now his mind filled with one thought: his girls crossing the void. That led to a second contemplation he couldn't dismiss. Did his ways to get his family here justify the means, even if the migration of the four and a half billion on his planet didn't happen?

The commotion lit the small tree-lined area like a daytime lightning flash powerful enough to outshine the sun. Not knowing exactly where the travelers would land, Marc, Kat, and Sharon had taken diverse positions in the park. The waiting proved more difficult than the mission, than tackling the PM, getting shot at, and facing Saul. Frenetically, Marc scoured the park until he found his little angel cradled in the arms of Henry O'Brien. The elderly man had scrapes and bruises on his elbows, and the rough scratches on his pants told of similar damage to his knees.

Marc held Jewel so gingerly, desperate to squeeze her tight but afraid to break her. He'd never seen her so pale gray. Now she breathed the clean air of Idyllium, and she'd get better, he was sure.

Brushing back the hair, Marc laid a series of overdue kisses on Jewel's forehead. She had landed on soft grass not far from the concrete patch onto which Henry fumbled from the crossing's fall. Jewel's dull eyes sparkled to life on seeing her dad. Raising her hand, she extended an unsteady finger to lift a tear from Marc's cheek, but her arm lost the fight with gravity. He pulled the purple-and-white braided keychain from his pocket and held it toward her. Her smile made everything he had done worthwhile.

"Mom?" she faintly whispered.

"She probably arrived on the other side of the park. It's how my team landed too. I've got Sharon and Kat looking. They'll find her. Can you stand so I can help Mister O'Brien up?"

Jewel stood, wobbly, supporting herself on a tree trunk. Marc hoisted Henry to his feet. Aged bones tried to steady him, and Marc helped stabilize him on the same tree before letting go.

"So this was your plan, Cap? Why you betrayed us."

The familiar voice snuck up from behind. Marc stood a statue, no longer a soldier but a father frightened of what would come next. He hadn't thought to carry a firearm to meet his family. Carefully, hands ascending in slow motion so as not to alarm Frank, he turned.

"You're Hillthorpe's other contingency. You shot at us in the defense grid center."

"You're a real master of the obvious, Cap."

"Wait, you said you saw Saul shoot at me when you broke me out of jail, but it wasn't him. You were with me, so who took the shot?"

While Marc genuinely wanted to know, the stall tactic gave him time to think of a way out of this. Frank pointed a handgun at him and had the semiautomatic's holster strap over his shoulder. Unarmed, Marc stood between him and a frail little girl and weak older man with no way to protect them.

"Wasn't too hard finding someone willing to take out the man who tried to kill their PM. If you'd only been able to keep your head up, we'd not be here now, and my shoulder wouldn't be sore."

"What's the endgame here, Corporal?" Marc moved a half step, trying to keep his body between Frank and the two civilians—a human shield to protect Jewel.

"Endgame? Corporal? You talk like there's still a mission. You ruined everything, *Cap*. And now, more than four billion people will pay for your selfishness. These people should have welcomed us as their saviors—*today*. Our people would have known what we did for them, and we'd be the heroes of Earth."

Marc's next step brought him inches closer to the man holding his life in his hands. "*That's* what this is about, Frank? You wanted to play the savior... but at what cost? You'd kill millions of people here, bring nuclear weapons to this world, just so you could be some big hero?"

"You're the one with the savior complex, Cap. Not for the world. You couldn't care about anyone else, not even a planet full of people. You wanted to save your daughter. *Why?* Not for her. No, Marc, you did that for *yourself*. You condemned four and a half billion people to death so you could save *one*, really, to save yourself from grief."

"No, Frank. Let's talk this out. We can—"

"Everyone's on to you, Cap. The way you sweet-talk the ladies, talk yourself out of a jam with your men. Saul told me, you know... How you got his kid brother to go in your place, sacrificed him to save your platoon—*no, to save you*."

Frank's ramblings allowed Marc another step closer. Eight feet—more or less. At six, Marc thought he'd have a chance at jumping him before he could fire. He'd not get that chance.

"I think it's time you knew what that feels like, Marc. To lose what you love most."

When the gun lost interest in him, panic stiffened Marc. The bullet with his name on it now sought Jewel, slouched against the tree. The shot's boom assaulted Marc's heart through his ears. Time raced forward, stealing the second needed to block the deadly projectile. Powerless, he failed to protect his baby girl, after all he'd done to save her. He turned his dread-soaked eyes to face the horror, sure they'd find a bloody mess, an image that would haunt him the rest of his days. He needed to see her.

His gaze fell upon Henry draped over his little girl, even smaller under his bulk. The red disk spread over his back as it saturated his shirt. *How did he move so quickly?* Marc stammered in a haze of confusion so thick he lost sight of what to do next. Standing over Henry's body, he looked for signs of life in the little girl crushed underneath it.

"Guess you'll have to do. Goodbye, Cap, you pathetic trait—"

The pop stiffened Marc, and his chest superheated as if he'd been speared with a fiery blade. The sensation of a bullet piercing his flesh, muscle, and bone, as he'd felt too many times before. This one had killed him.

The stinging heat dissipated. No, it had never come. No exit wound, no blood, no pain; he hadn't been shot. In disbelief, Marc spun on his heels to find Frank's lifeless body on the ground, his near-afro cropped hair a mess of red goo and bits of bone and flesh. He saw a smoking gun, a small golden barrel on a dainty ivory handle in the hand of... *Roberta Hillthorpe?*

"Marc." She nodded and lowered the gun. That young man with the acne-scarred face ran up behind her, and Marc's brain searched for words to add sense to the scene.

"SCL? What? How?"

"I'd think the how is obvious, Marc. We crossed right after your family. Frank was my contingency for the defense grid, but he failed me. This? Coming after your family. That crosses the line, even for me. Now... shouldn't you check on your daughter?"

Surprised someone needed to tell him to do it, Marc pulled Jewel from under the body of the man who saved her life. Fright and relief appeared to wage a war over what to display on Jewel's face until her eyes met her dad's. She wrapped her weak arms around his thick neck.

"*Marc.*" Casey's melodious voice caressed his ears.

She ran into him, and they shared a family embrace Marc wished to lose himself in for the rest of time. He'd gotten his family to Idyllium, even if he'd gone by way of Avernus.

The situation's tragedy sapped the moment's euphoria. Sharon ran up, screaming out to her father in a voice drenched in sorrow, and fell over his body and rolled him onto his back. The bullet hadn't pierced his front; his shirt held no evidence of his heroic deed's consequence. His daughter lay over him, clutching him and sobbing openly.

"He saved her." Marc laid a hand on the weeping woman's shoulder. "Frank shot at Jewel to punish me, and your father leapt in front to take the bullet."

Looking upon the lifeless body of the man who had helped her get Jewel to Idyllium, Casey's eyes glossed over with a thankful sadness. Marc shared her immeasurable gratitude for Henry saving his daughter twice.

54 | Idyllium: Day 1

Kateryna arrived last to a scene she couldn't assemble in her mind. Frank lay dead on the ground, and Sharon had folded herself over her father, a mess of tears and heart-crushing sobs that matured into a bellowing gasp. Roberta was there, holding a gun at her hip. Marc held Casey in one arm, the other wrapped around his daughter. Kat didn't recognize the young man beside Roberta.

"Kateryna," Marc said softly. "I'm sorry. I know you and Frank had—"

"No, Marc, we didn't. And, well, what happened to him? And goodness me, Mister O'Brien. Is he...?"

"Frank turned on us, was the one who fired on us at the grid complex. He tried to kill Jewel, but Henry saved her."

Moving toward Sharon, Kat extended her hand and squeezed her shoulder, feeling her own grief for George in her friend's weeping. The touch lifted Sharon to her feet, and she fell into Kat's arms, whimpering into her sympathetic embrace.

Over the red curls, Kat looked at Roberta, trying to piece her into this puzzle. "Roberta, you're on Idyllium?"

"Things fell apart with the operation, so I had to come salvage what I could."

The young man with Roberta handed Sharon some tissues and said, "Your father was incredibly proud of you."

Sharon thanked the boy with a brief smile and composed herself before making the sign of the cross over her father's body. "You finally did it, you stubborn old coot," she said through sniffles.

"Did what?" Kat asked.

"He restored my faith. Been trying since my mum died. That's when I lost it, you know? I just couldn't see God in that, in allowing that. That whole 'God took her' nonsense they said."

"And now you see God in your father's death? How does that make any sense?" Roberta squinted with her question, and Kat read genuine inquiry, not her typical sarcasm.

After blowing her nose, Sharon replied, "Because God had nothing to do with it..., yet He had everything to do with it."

Kat said, "Now I'm lost."

"My father did what was right because it was the righteous thing to do. He lived by his faith and died in his faith." She wiped her nose with the wad of crumpled tissues. "God didn't take Pops. And neither did Frank, for that matter. *He gave* his life and, in doing that, proved that we have the capacity for self-sacrifice because there is... there is something... more."

"That's a beautiful way to look at it." Kat took Sharon's hand and smiled warmly. "I think, maybe it gives me some faith too. Faith in humanity, at least. If that's from God, I'm not qualified to say, but who can say it isn't."

Sliding her wedding ring off her finger, Kat placed it in Sharon's hand.

"What's this for?"

"I'd like to bury it with your dad. A symbol of life and faith reborn. I think it's time I started to live my life again, here on Idyllium. It's what George would want for me."

Sharon put the ring in her pocket and knelt beside her father.

Marc smirked at Kat. "You mean a new life with Alistair Burgess?"

Kat shrugged.

"Good, very good." Roberta handed her little gun to her aide and put a hand on Kat's shoulder. "Take me to meet this Alistair Burgess. I'm sure he and I have a lot to discuss about the future of our people back on Earth."

Marc raised his hand in protest. "Um, SCL, that's not such a great idea. The PM said he's willing to work with our leaders who *weren't* involved in plotting to overthrow their government and slaughter his people to forcibly occupy this planet."

"My dear Marc. Casey, you're one lucky woman." Roberta's lustful glare tightened Casey's grip on Marc's arm. "Much has happened at UGA since you left. Walter Vescovi was voted out of office for his involvement in this whole messy business with Idyllium. I inherited his job and retained the office of SCL, as my assistant John can attest."

"My name's Peter."

Roberta ignored the young man's correction. "So you see, that's why I'm here. To clean up his mess and move forward toward peaceful unification and migration. As my dear friend Kateryna is in good with the PM," she turned a devious smirk to Kat, "you will introduce me as the one who issued the evacuation notice. Let's go."

"Roberta, you're incorrigible." Kat turned to Marc. "What about Saul?"

"Who knows? Maybe he'll find a quiet place to settle down in the countryside."

"You think he's forgiven you?"

"I highly doubt that. And I'm not sure I deserve it. It was a life-or-death call, and I may have..." He cleared his throat. "I should have gone when I let Tim go in my place. As captain, it was *my job* to protect the platoon and get them out safely. But I... Jewel needed me... and I... I let Tim go instead."

"Marc." Casey grabbed him in a hug. "Don't think that way. Tim would have given his life for you any day of the week, anytime. To see us together, here, is exactly what he'd have wanted."

"I don't think Saul would ever see it that way. But I think, even if he can't forgive me, he's finally able to let it go, to get on with his life."

"Always think you got all the answers, eh, Marc?"

Surprised by his presence, Kat wondered how long Saul had been there.

"Saul?" Marc turned almost white and stepped in front of Jewel. "What are you doing here? How'd you find us?"

"I've been tracking your bio-pads. Instead of that country life you said, I think I'll escort the SCL here to meet the PM and join her in managing the migration."

"I do need a loyal soldier, strong and fit, to keep order and make sure this goes smoothly. We have little time."

"Indeed, Miss Hillthorpe." The assistant spoke with a surprisingly commanding voice. "We should get underway."

"Saul." Marc stepped before the tall, bald soldier and extended a hand. "You saved my life. I know I don't deserve it, but... thank you."

Saul looked at Marc's hand. "You're right about one thing: I can never forgive you. Good hearing you face the truth of what happened... I'll move on in my own way. Have a nice life, Marc."

Little arms wrapped around Saul's waist, bringing his eyes down to find Jewel holding him tight. "You're Uncle Tim's brother. Thanks for saving my daddy."

Kat swore she saw a tear trying to form in the steel man's eyes. She turned to Marc as Jewel returned to her father's arms.

"What's next for you? After what you've done for Idyllium and Earth, the PM will give you any position you wanted."

"I'm done with all this. Now that she's here, I think my little girl is gonna be all right. It's time for me to be with my family. Maybe you could put in a word for me with your new friend, Alistair? A simple job and modest home, healthcare for Jewel."

Kat nodded then said softly, "Marc... mission accomplished."

Epilogue

Fingers pressed against his nostrils, he inhaled another long, satisfying sniff. A strange new habit he developed in the weeks since the crossover. The only stress he needed to relieve now was his own. Right place, right time, he figured. Still, one must use that combination wisely—a skill he learned from his former boss. Recently, she had been consulting her friend Jack with greater frequency. She said it tasted better on this side, though it took more of the amber liquid's sage counsel for her to get her job done now.

Counsel, he considered.
Information.
That's where the genuine power always lay.

Misinformation led good people, soldiers, into a cold war steeped in espionage and the covert sabotage of an entire planet. Well-timed and carefully placed information helped set the needed players on the right course, exposing the lies and cunning of the UGA as if under a blacklight. Vital bits were sent to Marc before he knew he needed them: the messaging address of the cabinet members; the true motivations of Idyllium's deputy PM and Earth's SCL.

After reports of the decommissioning of all nuclear warheads on Earth, the migration forecasts filled his holographic screen. Once he approved them, he pushed the display into the glass surface with a flattened palm. His desk didn't need to fill the width of an absurdly large office's cold, hard tile flooring. Freed toes wiggled to savor the plush carpet gently caressing his bare feet. They yearned to feel the soothing pressure of his assistant's thumbs and indulged themselves often.

Working under his newfound authority, a handful of Earthers had crossed over to begin strategic planning. Filling an already well-populated world with an additional four and a half billion people required endless waves of logistical forethought.

Sharon O'Brien had joined GB's science ministry and closely monitored the environment for impact of opening conduits across the void. Today's report showed no harmful effects, but they took nothing for granted.

While all message request notifications reached his ears with the same chime, he didn't have to guess whose face would appear on his desk when he pressed the glowing holographic *Accept* button projected over the thick glass desktop. A ball of bluish flickering pixels rose from its glossy surface and assembled themselves into the face of his assistant.

"Oh, yes. Um... I received your latest migration forecast."

"Very good. Please start coordinating with the housing commission for the first batch of migrants."

"Yes, Deputy PM. I wanted to confirm you were ready for me to begin."

"Please do. And Roberta, I've told you. You may call me Peter."

Thank You!

My reward as an author is having people read and enjoy my stories, engage with the characters, and empathize with the themes. I truly appreciate you as a science fiction fan and reader and thank you for following Marc and the others on their journey to find Idyllium without losing their humanity. Hopefully we will all learn to unmask that basic premise of 'the end justifying the means' and live in a world where horrific things are never again enacted in the name of the greater good.

Independent authors are supported by word-of-mouth and reviews. Please share this book with someone who may enjoy it. If you have a few seconds, a review will help other readers find Idyllium.

Also by

Overlap: The Lives of a Former Time Jumper

Overlap is a story about a love unbound by time, but not without consequence. Marcus is forced to consider the choices he made and their repercussions. A former time traveler is "stuck in the past" letting one moment define his life. Can he finally move on? Is redemption possible? Be a fly on the wall as Marcus Hollister, the inventor of the time travel *chamber,* reveals its dark secrets for the first time.

The New Europa trilogy

A story of life's challenges in a small Mars colony after two centuries. Conspiracy theories spread, and the seeds of social unrest are actively fertilized and watered by disgruntled individuals and small groups determined to 'get the truth out there.'

In *Colony's Dawn*, our protagonist, Gift Ojo, struggles to overcome her initial dismissal of any issues, desperately clinging to her belief that life is fine, and everyone works for the good of the colony. When suspicions cement and acts of sabotage ensue, she must become something more, an unwitting hero to rally her friends and save her colony.

In *Colony's Fall,* our characters' world expands into something they never could have imagined. Along with the marvels and wonder come new and horrific tests of their humanity, threatening their existence.

In *Colony's End*, we follow Gift on her journey to grow into her own person to face all-out war. Will she have what it takes to stand against her people and find her choice, a solution to stop the endless cycle of humanity fighting and killing each other?

neweuropatrilogy.com

About the author
N Joseph Glass

Reading is a passion; writing is an obsession.

And *IT consulting is a job*. While N Joseph Glass enjoys the challenges of managing a virtual infrastructure, backups, email systems, and cloud environments, crafting stories is his cherished second job.

Born and raised in Brooklyn, NY, Glass lives and writes in Milan, Italy. A fan of science fiction and other genres, he loves to expound stories that are driven by relatable characters on meaningful journeys.

Drawing from personal experiences enriches the writing process and leaves readers feeling like they know the characters they spend time with in a story. That human connection between his characters, readers, and himself, fuels his drive as an author.

Optimistic views of the future through art always interest him, as Glass believes ours will be bright.

www.glassauthor.com